T0137628

——————————— *Other Books by Frank O'Rourke* ———————————

VIOLENCE AT SUNDOWN	BATTLE ROYAL
INSTANT GOLD	BLACKWATER
GUN HAND	DAKOTA RIFLE
SEGUNDO	A MULE FOR MARQUESA
LATIGO	(THE PROFESSIONALS)
THE FOOTBALL GRAVY TRAIN	WARBONNET LAW
BADGER	BANDOLEER CROSSING
THUNDER ON BUCKHORN	GUNSMOKE OVER BIG MUDDY
THE BRAVADOS	AMBUSCADE
THE SHOTGUN MAN	VIOLENT COUNTRY
GOLD UNDER SKULL PEAK	THE BIG FIFTY
HIGH VENGEANCE	LEGEND IN THE DUST
THE HEAVENLY WORLD SERIES	THUNDER IN THE SUN
THE LAST CAHNCE	THE BRIDE STEALER
A TEXAN CAME RIDING	

THE
DIAMOND
HITCH

Published by William Morrow and Company 1956

Library of Congress Cataloging-in-Publication Data is available.
ISBN 978-1-94043-628-9

Cover and interior design by Faceout Studio

Printed in the United States of America

Counterpoint
2560 Ninth Street, Suite 318
Berkeley, CA 94710

www.counterpointpress.com

SELECTED AND INTRODUCED BY
MOLLY GLOSS

THE DIAMOND HITCH

by

FRANK O'ROURKE

COUNTERPOINT

BERKELEY, CALIFORNIA

INTRODUCTION BY
MOLLY GLOSS

I must have been around twelve years old when I fell in love with the books my dad was reading, the cowboy novels of Zane Grey, Max Brand, Luke Short. I had a child's view of the world then, and the adventure, the clean violence and simple morality of my dad's white-hatted cowboy heroes suited me just fine. And it would have been a few years later, after I'd reached a more complicated understanding of the world, that I first stumbled on Frank O'Rourke's novel *The Diamond Hitch*, not shelved with Max Brand and his cohorts but residing (as I thought of it) on the *real* shelves with the *real* books.

I read it two or three times in my teens. I understood, even then, that if it was not quite a book for the Literary Canon it was more authentic in feeling, in landscape, in the depth of its perceptions, more accurate in its details and in the complexity of the lives of its characters than the traditional western fiction I'd grown up loving. It was my first encounter with a writer nudging the mythology of the cowboy away from blood and bravery toward a darker, more complex truth.

When Dewey Jones steps off the train in Holbrook, Arizona, he's flat broke after a summer following the rodeo circuit. He lands work as a cook and horse breaker for a winter roundup, and this first long part of the novel follows Dewey and the rest of the roundup crew through days and weeks of hard, hot, exhausting, dusty, dangerous work. There is little that might be called "adventure." There are two Apaches working the roundup, though none of the other men remark on this in any particular way. There is no gunplay—Dewey has a gun in his bedroll but he never brings it out. And when he returns to the rodeo that summer it's to a nervous, bright, seductive world with its own dangers—his dreams of big wins perennially wrecked by late nights and too much bootleg liquor. There is no straight-up villain, just an overweening rival for the affections of Mary Ashford. And this is not a West frozen in the amber of the 1880s, but the real and changing West of Model T Fords and moving pictures and Prohibition.

When I began to write about the West myself, it was O'Rourke's novel more than any other that I sometimes consciously and more often unconsciously took as a model. I didn't have Dewey Jones in mind, for instance, when I wrote *The Jump-Off Creek*, but Tim Whiteaker is a cowhand who bakes pies for his neighbors and takes off-season work as a cook for a logging crew; in this, and in many other small details of western life and work as I've written of it, I know that I owe a debt to *The Diamond Hitch*. And I also know, in a larger sense, that O'Rourke's novel is one of the main reasons I have spent my writing life trying to reimagine the cowboy hero—steering clear, as he did, of gunslingers and savages, looking always for stories grounded in the heroism of ordinary lives.

In the traditional western novel, violence is the easy and only answer to every problem, an answer without honest pain or consequence; and it seems to me that the shadow of that violence, the shadow of the cowboy hero, has darkened our American politics, our national identity, our values and beliefs. But I feel strongly that storytelling can not only help us witness ourselves as we are in the world, but also think in fresh ways about ourselves as we might become. In *The Diamond Hitch*, Frank O'Rourke was working in a smaller, quieter corner of the West, a place where the heroism and the violence were downplayed, half-concealed in the mundane details of a hard life, a life in which the best values of the western myth—the courage, the self-reliance, the toughness—were always mindfully upheld.

And there is one more very particular and very personal reason I hold *The Diamond Hitch* in high regard.

When my husband died in February of 2000 I was about 20 pages and a few research notes into a new novel, my fourth. But I was not the same writer I'd been before Ed's death; grief and loss were now the lens through which I viewed the world. And although I had always avoided any conscious use of my own life in my fiction, I now found that I couldn't go on writing without acknowledging my experience of Ed's death. The story I had started, the story I had thought I wanted to write, was no longer one I was interested in. Whatever I wrote would have to have a place in it for Ed, and for the new reality of my life.

I read and reread all the notes I'd kept over the years, wisps of ideas for possible novels, but for a long while I wrote nothing; I filled my time with what I now think of as "comfort reading"—seeking out and rereading novels I remembered loving when I was younger. I took Jane Austen for a good long spin, and I reread *Black Beauty* and *The Black Stallion*, all of Tolkien and *The Once and Future King*. I don't remember what brought O'Rourke's novel into my mind but I think it must have been a yearning for the simplicity of those cowboy westerns of my youth. I had only the barest memory of the story in *The Diamond Hitch* by then, but I remembered it as a western without gunplay, several notches above the two-gun novels of Max Brand. The library no longer kept a copy, so I hunted one up from an on-line used-book store and began a slow reread; and I was struck anew by the quiet telling, the honest plotting—a story about real men inhabiting real lives.

The greater part of the novel deals with rodeo, and the roundup, but there's a last section in which Dewey takes winter work "breaking broncs on a circle job" for several ranchers and farmers. When I came to that part of the story I remembered, among my notes for possible novels, one about a young woman horse-breaker in the 1910s. There had been no place for Ed in that girl bronco-buster's story, I had thought. But reading—rereading—*The Diamond Hitch* I realized that if that young woman was breaking horses on a circle ride I'd have the beginnings of a novel not only about her but about all the people on her circle. There would be room for the dark complexity of real death. Room for Ed.

Every writer begins to be a writer by first being a reader. In rereading *The Diamond Hitch* for this introduction, I am struck yet again by how Story ties everything together. How, as artists, everything we've experienced becomes an opportunity to meaningfully integrate our lives with our art. There are a great many reasons to celebrate the reissue of O'Rourke's novel—to celebrate the quiet reshaping of western myth and the western hero. For me, there's also this: I know unequivocally, *The Hearts of Horses* would not have been written if I hadn't found my way back to *The Diamond Hitch*—found ways to talk about grief and love in a genre that once had shown me only simple adventure and unambiguous heroism.

— MOLLY GLOSS

THE
DIAMOND
HITCH

CONTENTS

PART ONE
THE DIAMOND HITCH. 1

PART TWO
RODEO 97

PART THREE
THE RED DRESS 177

to my friend

DOUGHBELLY PRICE

who lived this book

PART ONE:

THE DIAMOND HITCH

CHAPTER ONE

HE WAS NOT an old man but he had lived a good many hard years in his time. He got down from the morning passenger in the clear, sweet air speckled with engine soot and carried his gear through the depot waiting room into the street. He had sat up overnight on the smoking car, rolling Bull Durham, wondering if the job was still open.

He was thin and gaunted out, his face was deeply wrinkled and those lines crossed his sharp jawbone corners into the corded muscles of his neck. Weather had burned itself into the saddle-brownness of his cheeks and down the reddened, open V of his pull-over wool shirt. His hands showed the callused, thick-healed burn scars that came from the rope and the reins, his fingers were bent and three, once broken, had set crookedly. He walked deliberately on worn boot heels and, from behind, he had the stoop of an old man; but his eyes were a happy gray flecked with hazel and had not yet turned as old as an old man's treasured memories.

He crossed the street to the Chink restaurant and dropped his gear beside the first stool. When a man was broke he was always hungry, even if he was sick he was still hungry. Dewey Jones ordered ham and eggs and ate slowly, thinking back over the reasons that brought him here.

At the start of the Fort Worth Fat Stock Show he had gotten in a fight with a big army sergeant. After that, old John Henry led him around two days with his eyes full of hamburger meat. That ruined his chances for the money until the final night when he picked up twenty-five dollars riding Ross Jackson's Seven G horse in the exhibition show, and grabbed another twenty-five bulldogging a steer. He bought a ticket to Trinidad, rode over the pass to Raton, and ran into Mike Cunico. Mike showed him a letter from the Flying A outfit in Arizona, wanting a cook and horse breaker right away. Dewey Jones bought his ticket to Holbrook and now, eating breakfast, owned a dollar and eighty cents to his name. Breakfast was taking a seventy-cent bite from that thin roll, and he wasn't even certain of the job.

He looked down on his gear, saddle and chaps and spurs, bedroll holding his quilt and two blankets wrapped in the paraffin-treated tarpaulin. He scratched a match on his worn Levis that betrayed the threadbareness of the young-old man who had sat too many broncs and had flown off before the final whistle.

He smoked over black coffee, the man who had known too many jobs, ridden too many miles, and owned to his name the gear beside the counter stool and the clothes on his back. Dewey Jones paid the check and carried his gear back around the depot where he heard cattle bawling in the stock-pens. He walked on down toward the first chute and watched a crew loading on steers in the choky brown dust and rising day heat.

Dewey Jones counted thirty-some pens facing the alleys, with gates spaced regular so a crew could cut out small bunches and fill up a car. He admired the way the crew worked their job on horseback, driving the cattle up the alley. He saw one man outside the alley fence, prodding stubborn cows with a stick, and awhile later that tall, gangling man peered at him through the dust and yelled a surprised greeting.

"Dewey Jones—what you doin' way out here?"

Dewey Jones said, "Howdy, Raymond," and watched the tall man prod a last cow and then come around from the alley fence.

Raymond Holly was a comical cuss who was once kicked in the jaw by a horse. The jaw healed crooked and the teeth laid down so Raymond chewed on their sides. When Raymond talked he jabbed a finger into a man's chest and slobbered all over him, talking through those flat teeth. Raymond shook hands and started jabbing and talking as if they had parted only yesterday. It was all of four years, Dewey Jones recalled, since he last saw Raymond at the Las Vegas show.

"How far to Flying A headquarters?" Dewey Jones finally asked.

"Twelve miles," Raymond said. "These here are Flying A cattle, Dewey. That's the general manager right over there."

Dewey Jones turned and saw a wiry man of about fifty coming down the chute platform from the last car. He said, "Reckon he still needs that cook and horse breaker?"

"He sure does," Raymond said. "His name's Hank Cochrane. Go over and jump him."

Dewey Jones said, "Thanks, Raymond," and went over to the chute and introduced himself, showed the letter Mike Cunico had received in Raton, and popped the big question; and right off, studying Cochrane, did not find any particular admiration for the man. Cochrane rubbed the letter between his thumb and forefinger before he said cautiously, "I need both. Can you handle it?"

"I don't know how different it is here," Dewey Jones said honestly.

"You savvy a pack outfit," Cochrane said. "You know a diamond hitch?"

"Yes," Dewey Jones said.

"The ranch is all pack," Cochrane said. "Ain't been a wagon on it in fifteen years. Pay is eighty-five."

"That's okay," Dewey Jones said quickly.

He decided that Cochrane was more man than he'd figured on first size-up. Cochrane had judged him and figured he'd do, at least on the surface, and besides Cochrane was in a tearing hurry to ship his cattle out. Cochrane said, "We got a horse you can ride back. Tomorrow morning you pick up the chuck-wagon teams and come back to town and get your bill of groceries for ninety days." Then Cochrane gave him another, sharper stare and added, "You want anything else, smoking tobacco, clothes, you get it with the groceries and charge it to the ranch."

"Thanks," Dewey Jones said.

"All right, go meet the boys."

Raymond Holly was waiting down the fence. Dewey Jones followed him to the back pen and shook out his hair blanket while Raymond brought up the extra horse, an old cutting sorrel about fifteen years old who grazed along with the herd coming in. Dewey Jones slapped the old sorrel and spoke a few words, saddled up, and rode out with Raymond to join the crew.

He met Jim Thornhill and Driver Gobet and George Spradley. They didn't say much, just smoked and sized Dewey Jones up and reserved judgment. They stood in the depot shade while Cochrane made out the papers for shipping the thirty-one cars of cattle to the Flying A grazing land in California. Then Cochrane came around the depot and said, "Let's pull stakes," and led them out of Holbrook on a dirt road that ran south across the level plateau country.

The road wound through arroyos and over level flats toward Snowflake and Show Low. They rode a bare land sprinkled with sage and chamiso, with a few stunted cedars growing in the shade of arroyo banks and along the slopes where topsoil was thicker. Cochrane took the lead, the others strung out, and Raymond Holly brought up the rear with Dewey Jones.

Raymond hadn't changed a bit. He was always eager for talk, he fairly begged Dewey Jones to start asking questions like any new hand was bound to. Dewey Jones let him slobber a reasonable time before he said, "Raymond, what kind of an outfit is this?"

Raymond sighed with relief, coming unstoppered like a bottle of home brew. "Greasy sack, Dewey."

"They got a pretty good string of horses?"

"Fair," Raymond said. "But they ain't broke out no young stuff the last two years. The horses is gettin' run down. Boss bought thirty head from the Bar R, that's what you'll be aworkin' when you get time off from cookin'."

Dewey Jones wondered how much time he'd have off from cooking on a pack outfit. He said, "How's the watering places on the ranch, Raymond?"

"Pretty good in some spots, not so good in others."

"They got decent corrals?" Dewey asked. "Good bronc pen?"

"Yup."

"These bronc pens," Dewey said. "They round corrals with a snubbin' post in the middle?"

Raymond squinted a moment in thought. "Well, they's a good one at Cherry Creek made outa aspen poles with wire wove in between. That's our headquarters for the long stay, and our first move."

"Where's the next move?" Dewey asked.

"Hole-In-The-Ground."

"Where's that?"

"Way to hell and gone from headquarters," Raymond said. "We go to workin' from there on back."

Dewey Jones frowned. He had to build camp on water and when he had to shoe a bronc or work around, away from the cooking, he'd have little time to haul water up from any far place. He said, "How far these corrals from water?"

"On Cherry Creek," Raymond said, "you're right on water, just out of dust range. But that Hole-In-The-Ground country, well, you got to pack it about a hundred yards up the hill. Use the burros, put a ten-gallon keg on one burro, two keg'll last the day. The wrangler'll handle that and the wood."

"I know," Dewey Jones said shortly. "What about this string of broncs. They pretty big stuff, any well-bred, or just common mountain ponies?"

"Just common," Raymond said. "They won't give you much trouble, Dewey, not the way you can ride."

Dewey Jones accepted Raymond's compliment and rode in silence, thinking he wasn't much shucks as a bronc rider considering his present condition. A dollar-ten in his pockets and the clothes on his back. Then he straightened and glanced at the country and drummed up a dust-caked grin for Raymond.

If he could stick for three months, he'd come back to town with a decent grubstake and, this time, he'd get on the train and head for Las Vegas and the big Fourth of July show. No drunk this time, he promised himself, no throwing it away. Then he remembered all the times in the past, all the drunks and the bad mornings and the washed-out feeling, and hunched over in his saddle and rode in silence through the rising dust.

A man made himself big promises and, like the wind, they kept on blowing ever hopeful until life was gone. But there had to come a time; there must be a time in every man's life when he corked the last bottle and took the train.

Cochrane led them down a long grassy slope into ranch headquarters at suppertime. Dewey Jones unsaddled and turned the old cutting sorrel into the big corral and followed Raymond around the blacksmith shop to the ranch house. They washed at the wooden stand outside the kitchen door and faced the soft night wind, rolling a smoke, waiting for supper. Dewey Jones looked the home ranch over critically and liked what he saw; and just then the cowboss rode in from the south and shook hands and Dewey Jones knew that here was the real boss of the Flying A.

Hank Marlowe was a little bitty dried up fellow with a thin leathery face, the kind of man who didn't know buying or selling cattle, but sure knew them on the range, where to catch, how to handle, where to run. Cochrane was the storekeeper who ran up the figure columns, but

Dewey Jones had more respect for the Hank Marlowes. He knew what they could do. Hank gave him an easy first look and headed inside, the cook yelled, "Come get it before I throw it away," and Dewey Jones followed the crew into the kitchen for supper.

He kept his mouth shut and listened, and thought over everything he'd noticed about the home ranch. The ranch house was L-shaped, built of reddish-brown sandstone mortared with adobe mud and flat-roofed with big viga pines that came, Raymond told him, from near the ranger station at the foot of the Mogollons up Hebron way. The west end was private quarters for Cochrane's family, the kitchen occupied the middle, and the lower leg of the L facing south was the big bunk room.

Down by the corrals Dewey had noticed the old up-and-down bellows in the blacksmith shop, with plenty of ought and double-ought shoes for the small mountain horses. The big corral had long feed troughs for cotton-seed cake. The crew brought cattle down from the hills, fed cake and gentled them to the sight of humans before making the final drive to the train. The home ranch was about two thousand acres fenced into two big pastures with fine grass, and everything was in first-class condition.

"Comin'?" Raymond said.

"I'll hang around," Dewey Jones said.

The crew went into the bunk room and Dewey grabbed a dish towel and began helping the cook clean up. Bob Buford was about sixty-five, bald-headed and stumpy, a typical Irishman who threw his brogue around reckless and, like most cooks, started right in giving Dewey the low-down on the ranch. Buford was an old railroader who'd lost one hand on the Denver & Rio Grande long ago at Durango, and what with telling Dewey all that personal history, old Buford filled him in on the crew. It was funny how those men, ridden with and seen less than a day, had already taken certain shape in Dewey's mind. Old Buford elaborated on each one, and Dewey Jones felt pretty good inside because his own first judgments were borne out.

George Spradley was forty, one of those real quiet, good cowboys who came from Young, Arizona, and had a wife and two kids. He was five-eight and weighed around one-fifty and sported a big handle-bar moustache. His riding partner was Driver Gobet, old Buford explained, and Driver was a good man, taller than Spradley, slender and well built, with a hatchet face spilling down sharply behind a long nose. There was Jim Thornhill, called Thistlepatch, who was an easy six-two and weighed over two hundred pounds. He had sandy hair and red whiskers, he talked in a slow drawl and didn't say too much. Old Buford explained that Thistlepatch was now twenty-five, a Montana boy who'd left home at thirteen and worked down into Arizona and been riding ever since on different cow outfits, the Cherrycows, the R4, at times for the government on the reservation keeping outfits off the Indian grass, and finally for the Flying A.

Buford began talking about Raymond Holly, but Dewey cut him off because he knew Raymond from way back. That brought them to Hank Marlowe and old Buford spared no praise regarding the cowboss. Buford maintained that Hank was the best roper Buford knew, one of those men who could walk out in the morning and say, "What do you want?" and take another man's rope and ketch, either hand, in nothing flat. Hank had grown up around Winslow and spent his childhood roping wild burros, and now he was rated the best cowboss in the country.

"Bob," Dewey Jones finally said. "What kind of a bird is this Cochrane? How is he on feeding the boys?"

"Damned penny pincher," Buford said. "Saves pennies on the groceries."

"How long you been here?" Dewey asked.

"About eighteen years," Buford said. "Cochrane's the first bastard I've worked for, but his wife's a fine woman and they got a good kid."

Dewey Jones said meaningly, "I'm getting groceries tomorrow—"

"Buy what you want," Buford said flatly. "Hank's the cowboss, he feeds his men. Cochrane won't know what you buy because the bill goes to the Los Angeles office."

Old Buford didn't tell Dewey Jones what to buy, but he did guess that Dewey might be a greenhorn on pack outfits, and so began giving the low-down on that subject. "Pard," old Buford said passionately, "you sure got to watch them goddamned ornery burros. Them sonsabitches'll rifle camp every time you get ten feet away from 'em."

Dewey said, "Which ones are bad?"

"Them kitchen burros," old Buford said. "Tom, Jerry, Jim Toddy, and Benstega. Them four with their black hearts!"

"You must know 'em," Dewey Jones said.

"Know 'em! Lemme tell you!"

Old Buford began working up a big head of steam, but Dewey Jones waved and escaped into the bunk room, found an empty bunk and unrolled his bed. He lay back and smoked and listened to the boys talk, because you could learn more just listening, getting the real feel of an outfit. He felt their respect for the cowboss, but any time Cochrane's name was mentioned it came offhand and gave him the feeling none of the boys thought too much of the G.M.

He smoked a final cigaret and closed his eyes when Thornhill snuffed out the lamp. Nobody had asked him any questions. They were all reserving judgment until he proved up. Raymond turned in the next bunk and said, " 'Night, Dewey," and Dewey Jones mumbled, " 'Night, Raymond," and let sleep take him down the long, soft trail with the sore-muscled dreams of gone shows and bad rides and carnivals, of women he'd known and drunks he'd been on, of twenty-eight years spent and gone. He didn't move until five o'clock when Raymond shook him awake and old Buford yelled stridently.

"Come and get it!"

Cochrane showed up to give the day's order at breakfast. Cochrane told Dewey Jones to get the chuck-wagon team, drive to town, and get a bill of groceries to last ninety days. Raymond went out and had the four chuck-wagon mules ready when Dewey came down from the house. Raymond showed him the harness in the tackroom, wished him luck, and hurried off to saddle up and join the crew. Hank Marlowe said, "See you tonight, Dewey," and led them off about the day's business. Dewey Jones harnessed the mules and headed for town, making notes all the way, studying out his order for Babbitt Brothers Mercantile Company in Holbrook, letting the mules follow the road, paying no attention to the country as he licked his pencil stub and made out his order. When he hit town and entered the store, he had the bill nearly ready for the clerk.

And right off the bat his first item made the clerk laugh. The clerk said, "What in hell are you doing with fifty pounds of corn meal on a cow outfit?"

"Listen," Dewey Jones said stiffly. "Onions and corn meal and sage make a good dressing for roast beef where I come from. You got any objections?"

"No," the clerk said.

"All right," Dewey Jones said. "Let's get to popping."

The clerk grinned and began filling the boxes. Twenty-five pounds each of onions and pinto beans, hundred and fifty pounds of Hill Brothers Blue Box Coffee, the one-pound square boxes only because Dewey Jones used a pound and a half for breakfast, and the other pound and a half for supper; then twenty-five pound boxes of dried apricots, prunes, and peaches; four hundred pounds of flour, ten pounds of Arm & Hammer soda, ten pounds of salt, four pounds of pepper, sage for the dressing, two hundred pounds of sugar. With these staples, Dewey Jones ordered five dozen eggs and forty pounds of bacon and fifty pounds of potatoes. He pulled down fifteen pounds of P&G yellow soap for the hard water country they were going into; twenty-five pounds of lard in a big pail, and six cases of Pet milk in twenty-four can boxes.

He grinned a little then, thinking how he had a dollar-ten in his pocket and yesterday he was just hoping for luck; and here he stood buying groceries and spending money like a drunk Swede in a parlor house. He added three cases each of tomatoes and corn, six gallons of molasses, and baking powder. Then he gave the clerk his own personal order and asked for a separate bill. The clerk got him two pairs of Levis, two shirts, one Levi jumper, half a dozen pairs of socks, two suits of light underwear, three cartons of Bull Durham, and an extra carton of papers.

"That does it in here," Dewey Jones said. "I'll swing around back."

He drove the chuck wagon behind to the loading dock and helped the clerk carry out the order. They topped off the load with sacks of clean oats and cotton-seed cake, Dewey signed the bills, and crossed over to the Chink's for his meal. He ate with a fine appetite and rolled a cigaret on the sidewalk, staring sideways at the saloon doors ten steps on his right. He was heading out for three months, a long, rocky road before he'd get another drink. He ought to have a couple just for the road and then head for the ranch.

Dewey Jones started toward the saloon, sniffing the malt odor that drifted through the swinging doors; and then he stopped and walked across the street and down the alley toward the loading dock. If he couldn't trust himself yet, he had no business trying two drinks and maybe signing away his unearned pay and ending with twenty. He climbed aboard, shook out the lines, and spoke gently to the mules.

"Good luck," the clerk called.

"Thanks," Dewey Jones said. "See you in July."

CHAPTER TWO

DEWEY JONES DROVE into headquarters just ahead of supper call. He located the big canvas tarp in the tackroom and snugged it over the chuck wagon, fed the mules, and went to supper. Later on he smoked in his bunk and listened to the talk. Jim Thornhill said softly, "Sure don't look forward to that Black Brush," and the others began talking about the Salt River country, building up a vague word-picture in Dewey's mind. Finally the lamp was snuffed and five o'clock came all too soon, with old Buford's stentorian yell jerking them upright.

After breakfast Dewey Jones harnessed his mules while the boys saddled their number one horses and rounded up fifteen extra. Bedrolls were lashed atop the chuck wagon and Cochrane gave them some parting words which consisted of wishing them good luck and reminding Hank Marlowe that the front office expected a damned good gather. Hank said, "Do our best," and Dewey knew the boys didn't particularly take to Cochrane's way of talk.

Heading south, Dewey set the pace because their speed had to match the mule gait. They made twenty-three miles that day and camped just outside Snowflake on the irrigation ditch under big, old cottonwood trees. Throwing horses and mules into the pasture, Raymond explained that the Mormons kept the little twenty-five acre pasture for the convenience of travelers.

"Good folks," Dewey said.

"Sure," Raymond said. "I was born here. You and me'll go to the dance tonight."

Snowflake had about three hundred people and you couldn't buy coffee, smoking tobacco, or cigars because of the Mormon religion. Raymond knew everybody in town and was treated kindly, but he'd backslid and was called a jack Mormon. The other boys turned down Raymond's invitation and hit the sack early, and Raymond took Dewey into town for the dance.

"Just mind your p's and q's," Raymond said. "Don't start no trouble."

The dance was opened with prayer and a song; then Raymond introduced Dewey to a cousin and she took him around the hall and made him acquainted with everyone. He danced with the girls and liked one pretty little thing who was all blue eyes and yellow hair and kept smiling at him as they whirled around in waltzes and two-steps. Dewey worked up a sharp appetite for the midnight supper, just peeking over at the long table loaded down with fried chicken and ham and cake and pie. He got to bed at one and was up at five, feeling fresh despite the short rest. They ate breakfast at the local cafe and Hank signed the tab which went to Cochrane, and thanked the lady for rising so early to cook just for them; and then they wasted no time lining out south on the Show Low road.

They got into piñons and junipers and cedars that day, and the first high stands of ponderosa pine, with mountains looming up jagged dark to the south and west. Making a twenty-eight mile drive, they hit Show Low at sundown, coming through a shallow valley into the town that sprawled on a slope with trees standing up black and thick to the west. Show Low had gotten its name from a game of Seven Up played on this spot in the early days. There was a big hand with a seven-thousand-acre ranch at stake and the first bidder begged on five and the other fellow gave him one and then said, "Show low, and take it," and the man showed it and won the ranch, and the name stuck until it became official.

They camped out that night and Dewey cooked a good breakfast of bacon and eggs and fried potatoes. They drove to Cibecue, camped out, and the following morning went seven miles to the rock storehouse where groceries and supplies were kept for outlying ranch work. The storehouse had no windows and just one door lined with flat iron slabs. The next morning Hank, who had gone on ahead during the night, returned with an Apache Indian boy and the string of pack burros.

Dewey studied those burros while he cooked breakfast. He didn't know much about burros and his first thought was, if that was his kitchen transportation, and he had to pack and unpack those little demons, he wondered who was going to keep them close at hand and how many days it would be before the boys quit because the meals weren't put out on time.

Hank opened the storehouse and everybody got busy, splitting up all supplies for storage or packing. The storehouse sat in the northeast corner of a big pasture about three sections square, with a little stream running through the middle. The pasture was barbwire fenced, five strands high on cedar posts, and used mainly as a holding pasture. It was one day's ride from the main ranch and the boys usually rested cattle here before driving on to the railroad. "In a couple of weeks," Hank Marlowe said, "Cochrane and old Bob'll come down, pick up the chuck wagon and mules, and take 'em back to headquarters. Now we got to pack and get started. Squab, cut out the kitchen canaries!"

The Apache boy drove the four kitchen burros over and gave Dewey his first close look. He could tell the leader right off, that was Benstega, who weighed around four hundred and seventy-five pounds. Benstega was brown with a white face that boasted a brown streak down the middle.

"Jim Toddy," Squab said, pointing to the other brown burro.

Jim Toddy was smaller than Benstega. Tom was mouse-colored and a little bigger than Jim Toddy. "This one," Squab said, slapping the last burro, "Jerry."

Jerry weighed around four hundred and was sort of grayish-white, more from age than anything else. Dewey looked them over while they eyed him in burro fashion, and Hank Marlowe swallowed a grin. Dewey Jones might not understand burros now, but a month from today he'd know too damned much and wish he never learned.

Hank laid out blankets and hair pads for each burro, put good blankets over the hair pads, with pack covers all ready. Dewey sorted out his kitchen equipment while Squab led the other ten pack burros up and saddled them. Dewey got everything in neat stacks, dried fruit, flour, sugar, Dutch ovens and pots and pans, cutlery and tin cups and plates. He'd never packed burros before but he could load a mule, and this couldn't be too different. Hank had brought a quarter of fresh beef from the home ranch, and this was on a piece of canvas, waiting to be packed.

Hank said then, "You ever pack burros?"

"No," Dewey said honestly, "but I can learn."

Hank slapped the kyack boxes and pointed to a canvas bag hanging on Tom's saddle. "Each one can handle a hundred and fifty pounds, so we split up the loads equal as possible. Put your odds and ends in that bag, stuff like baking powder and bacon and tin cups. We'll load today, you watch how it's done."

Benstega got the flour and one box of fruit. Jim Toddy got three boxes of fruit and three cases of Pet milk. Tom got his kyack boxes filled with pots and pans, and the odds and ends in the canvas bag, Dutch ovens and the quarter of beef on top. Jerry got the sugar, a sack on each side and one on top. "Now," Hank said, "the rest goes on the other burros."

They packed the cotton-seed cake, the other three cases of Pet milk, the oats, the tomatoes and corn and bedrolls on the ten pack burros. Dewey was rusty at the job and the burros were different from mules, but he gradually got the hang of things. He had trouble with his diamond hitches; his fingers were all thumbs, he felt like a rank amateur because Squab and Hank tied down so fast. But finally the burros were packed, the few extra supplies locked in the storehouse. The other boys had left, driving the spare saddle horses, leaving Dewey with Hank and Squab. The Indian boy lined the burros up and took his place at the lead, the burros fiddling around a little while before following him up the trail nose-to-tail.

"We got twelve miles to go," Hank said. "Can't hurry burros, so enjoy yourself."

They rode in the rising sunlight that filtered down through the trees, on a winding trail that bore steadily south and east into wild country. The Indian boy slouched lazily in his saddle, paying no mind to the trail, letting horse and burros follow a path they knew from long experience. Hank rolled a smoke and then said casually, "You ever worked in rough country before, Dewey?"

"Not this kind," Dewey said, "but I worked for the Adams Cattle Company back in New Mexico, that's the old A6. I sure can see the difference in the way you do things."

"Rougher country," Hank said. "I reckon you used wagons back there."

"Yes," Dewey said. "We had line camps at the Adams and you could get over near all of it in a wagon so we never knowed what a pack horse was except for carrying beds. There was line camps with good ranges, and the wagons carried bedrolls and groceries from one camp to another. We'd start roundup at Red River Camp."

Hank pushed his old black Stetson back and nodded in understanding. Like all cowmen, Hank was interested in other parts of a common land and trade, in a big country where methods might differ but down-to-earth working and living were always the same. Then too, Hank had stayed back today to ride with Dewey Jones and find out some more about the new cook.

"I been through that country," Hank said. "Just where is that camp?"

"On the east end," Dewey said, "near the old town of Catskill. The

Adams was fenced in pastures and we'd round up a pasture and throw it into the corrals at Red River Camp. Next day them cattle was transferred on up to the Carrizo Camp, and from there to Castle Rock Camp close to Vermejo Park, and then to Penaflor Camp where they done all the earmarking and branding. Then the cattle was turned loose and went on up into the Costilla country on summer range. Them old cows, when they was turned loose, would mother right up to their calves and hit a shuck for that summer range. The Penaflor Camp was on the old U. S. trail going up into the Costilla."

"Sounds like a pretty good outfit," Hank said.

"It was," Dewey said. "The ranch was twenty-eight by seventy-one miles. There was streams in every valley, and springs come out of most hills. Plenty of grass when it showed from under the snow. But hell, Hank, it gets cold in that country. Nothin' uncommon to get ten, fifteen below zero."

Hank looked around them at the rocky slopes and the cloudless sky that forewarned of blistering summer days. Hank said wistfully, "We could stand some of that cold, running water here."

"Say," Dewey said, "about this horse-breaking. How many you got to break, are they all raw broncs, how does the horse-breaking fit in with cooking on this outfit?"

"You ever done both before?"

"In New Mexico," Dewey said. "You know, when I'm in camp and cooking don't take full time, I like to use that spare time breaking a few broncs. But very seldom out of the breaking pen back in New Mexico because if a man has stuff acookin' and turns his bronc out, he's apt to stampede and you might not get back till everything is burnt up. What do you think about me asking how much extra some bronc breaking would be worth?"

Hank said, "What's Cochrane payin' you for cooking?"

"Eighty-five a month."

"What do you think about forty a month for whatever bronc breaking you can do?" Hank said. "But understand, I don't want you to neglect the cooking job. Cooking and keeping these cowboys fed is worth a lot more than the bronc breaking."

"Fair enough," Dewey said. "My breaking'll be in the corrals, hackamore breaking them because I understand these broncs has got to be turned out every night to feed."

"That's right."

"Well," Dewey said, "I cain't have drag ropes on over two or three at a time, so when that Indian boy wrangles the horses he can pick up the drag ropes on a couple of broncs and tie them to a post and then, as I get time, I can tie up a foot on those broncs and saddle and unsaddle 'em and as they go along I can ride them quite a bit in the corrals and have them pretty well on the way to be broken by the time roundup is over."

"That's fine," Hank said. "So the price is agreed on?"

"Suits me fine," Dewey said. "I sure don't like laying around camp. Once I get things lined up, I can turn out the meals pronto. I got fifty pounds of corn-meal and onions and sage, and I think a good roast beef will produce just as good corn-meal dressing as turkey or chicken, and it sure breaks the monotony of these sourdough catheads."

"Sounds good to me," Hank said, "but I never heard of that corn-meal dressing before."

"Hell," Dewey said, "you never get too old to learn, Hank."

Hank Marlowe laughed softly. "You New Mexico punchers might not be worth a damn in Arizona, but your cooking routine sounds fine to me. . . . Squab, keep them burros moving!"

Hank was evidently satisfied with their talk because he rode out on the flanks through the remainder of the day, scouting the country as they moved along. They hit the main ranch at five o'clock, unpacked the burros, and carried the groceries into the kitchen and the big storeroom at the other end of the ranch house. The boys had arrived earlier but nobody had started a fire in the kitchen, so Dewey built a blaze in the double-oven Majestic Range and began throwing a fast meal together. Squab carried in plenty of dry piñon wood and hung around close, watching Dewey with sharp black eyes in a dark face that never moved with outward emotion. Dewey cooked a feed of baking powder biscuits, cream gravy, beef, and stewed apples for dessert. After supper Squab helped him clean up the kitchen and once everybody had spread their bedrolls on the grass outside, Dewey got right to work on his sourdough.

He boiled two medium-sized potatoes until they began falling apart. He strained them through a cloth that took the juice off, poured that juice into the five-gallon wooden keg that originally held kraut. He added a cup of sugar and then flour until he had a thin batter. He set the keg on the hot water reservoir and clamped the wooden lid down tight. The lid had two cleats on top and side handles, so when packing it, the pack cover fitted down over the keg and the diamond hitch held it snug all the way.

Dewey had to keep the keg warm all night. He got up at two and made sure the sourdough was warm. Whenever it started working— some folks called it rotting—it was on the road and would be ready for making biscuits in another twenty-four to thirty-six hours, depending on weather conditions. If the weather was rainy and damp, it took sourdough twelve to twenty-four hours longer to work than in bright, warm times.

Next morning the boys brought in sixty head of burros from surrounding hills and canyons. Dewey wondered what in hell they wanted with so many burros, but the best way to learn was keep his mouth shut and listen. He watched the boys feed each burro a quart of oats and half a pound of cotton-seed cake; next morning those burros were right in camp, johnny-on-the-spot, braying and bawling for more. Then Raymond told Dewey that after being fed that way three or four days, the burros would always come back here.

That night Dewey made sourdough biscuits along with a big beef roast. The boys ate everything and yelled for more. They were talking easy with him by then, for they knew he could handle the cooking job, and he was on time with meals when they rode in tired and hungry. Driver Gobet said, "Dewey, where'd you learn to cook?"

"All over," Dewey said. "When I was a kid in Texas, then on shows and around cow outfits."

"Raymond was sayin' you rode and bulldogged," Jim Thornhill said. "You ever stick a bronc till the last whistle?"

Dewey grinned and took a seat on the doorstep facing the others who were sprawled out on the grass with their coffee cups and after-supper smokes. "I stuck a few," he said, "but I sure been in plenty of balloon ascensions."

"Was you ever at Prescott?" George Spradley said. "I was there four years back."

"Not that year," Dewey said. "But I hit the show two years ago."

"When'd you start bronc ridin' and bulldogging like that?" Driver Gobet asked.

"I was thirteen," Dewey Jones said. "My older brother was on a show; I run off and joined him."

"It sure always sounded to me like a good life," Spradley said. "That big prize money and all that travel."

Dewey Jones looked at them, and through them, down the lost years at all the shows and the money that came and went so fast, at the broken bones and the broke spells when a man tightened his belt and hoped for luck in the next town. They saw that life with the eyes of anyone who did not know, and he saw it as he had lived it, and he could not lie to them.

"No," Dewey Jones said gently. "It ain't a good life, George. I been at it, off and on, for sixteen years, an' I got off the train in Holbrook with a dollar and eighty cents to my name. There's a few boys can make it pay, but most of us have got to work half the year to make enough money to catch the next big show and do some more hoping again. If I had any sense I'd quit."

"You goin' back?" Raymond asked.

"I figure," Dewey Jones said, "on hittin' the Las Vegas, New Mexico show right off this job. I'll give it a good try. If I don' finish in the money I ought to be old enough to get some of that sense."

"I rode at Prescott," George Spradley said. "Four summers ago. I figured I knew one end of a bronc from the other, Dewey. I sure found out different. Them boys are really good."

"You get that way," Dewey Jones said. "For whatever it means or what it's worth."

Hank wandered off to the storeroom and came back with a thirty-foot length of new lariat rope cut from the big coil. He sat down beside Dewey and began working the rope, kneading out the bigger kinks. All day long the boys had been shoeing horses and greasing chaps and repairing saddles, cutting off fresh ropes, getting them stretched between trees to remove the kinks. Hank started making the honda in his new rope and Driver Gobet worked on the turkhead knot in the end that was tied to the saddle horn. They hadn't shaved in a week; they were paring down to hard working weight, getting browner from sun and wind, rubbing the new blue off their Levi jumpers and pants. And with that, they had accepted Dewey as one of the outfit. Just talking tonight, he knew, kidding him about bronc riding and asking questions, showed how they felt. It was funny how a man could work anywhere in the West and feel right at home. "Them was good biscuits," Hank said, fingers working on his honda. "What's your recipe, Dewey?"

" 'bout like anybody's," Dewey said. "You want to know?"

"Sure," Jim Thornhill said. "I got just one belly. Sometimes I wonder what I'm shoveling into it."

Dewey Jones smiled into his chest and started talking, "Well, whenever I get my sourdough to working into a reasonable thick batter and it smells a lot like it's already been eat, I take out whatever I want and of course put back the same amount of flour into the keg, and pour some lukewarm water into the keg, then a spoonful of sugar, stir it good, and keep it in the sunshine. Then I take soda and salt and put that in some flour, and mix it good so the soda don't cake and make brown spots in my baked biscuits. I take my hand and run out a hole in the bowlful, make a bird-nest, pour the sourdough in there, work it into the dry flour until it gets hard enough to handle without sticking, then lay it on the board and work hell out of it with my hands, maybe work in a little more dry flour, choke the biscuits out from the doughstack and jam 'em in the oven pretty close together. Then I dip my hand in grease and pat the tops, and let them raise about thirty to forty minutes, get about three to three and a half inches thick. Then I've kept my Dutch oven on the fire all this time to get hot, and I put the lid back with some live coals on top. I found out that whenever you set the oven onto live coals, be sure and bank up around it or air'll make the coals flare up and burn two or three biscuits and the others don't seem to get more than just done on the bottom. When the biscuits are done—that oughta take about thirty minutes over a slow fire—I take my ganch hook and raise the lid, and if they ain't brown on top, put on a shovelful of coals and let them go a few minutes more. Then raise the lid and yell for them ignorant cowboys to come and get it."

"And that's all?" Jim Thornhill said innocently.

"Sure," Dewey said. "Nothin' to it."

"You do the cooking," Thornhill said. "I'll just stick to the simple work."

Everybody laughed and got ready for bed. Dewey went into the kitchen and felt pretty good inside and out. Sometimes a man never got close to a new outfit, and other times he was made to feel at home within a few days. He was still the tenderfoot on this outfit, but the boys liked his cooking and had no complaints about his behavior. That was enough to sleep solid on, and work through the next day while the boys finished shoeing and repairing equipment. After supper that night

Hank came to the kitchen for a cup of coffee and sat on the woodbox awhile before unloading his mind to Dewey.

"Well," Hank said. "We go south and east in the morning, into the Black Brush country. We'll be gone eight days, but somebody'll be here every day and can bring you anything you might forget."

"Any corrals out there for bronc breaking?" Dewey asked.

"No," Hank said. "So just as well leave your equipment here. We'll be back for another round of provisions before we take off for Cherry Creek, that's our first stop on the general roundup. Now we're leaving early with seventy head of burros. You and Squab pack up and follow along. You better take two horses, Dewey."

"I'll take the old sorrel," Dewey said. "An' that old bone-spavined dun."

"Fine," Hank said. "Well, see you tomorrow, Dewey."

" 'Night, Hank," Dewey said.

He heard the boys settling down for the night, rolling over in their blankets on the grass, working the stones and twigs from under their shoulders and hips. Squab came in the back door with an armload of piñon wood, silent as always, making no sound on his moccasins.

"Goin' in the morning," Dewey said. "Better sort out eight days provisions now, Squab."

"Good," Squab said. "What you need, Dewey?"

Dewey rattled off his list and Squab helped him stack up the groceries beside the table, ready for packing after breakfast. Dewey checked his sourdough keg and made sure he had plenty of salt and pepper. Then he heated some water and propped up the mirror on the stove back and shaved off his week's beard. He changed into new Levis and shirt and jumper, and lay down on his blankets long after the other boys were asleep. He heard Squab rolling up nearby, fitting his skinny frame to the ground.

"Rough country tomorrow?" Dewey asked sleepily.

Squab said, "Jesus!" and began snoring.

CHAPTER THREE

NEXT MORNING the boys put on thick leather jackets and batwing chaps, and flat little hats with floppy brims and throat latches that snugged firm under their jaws. They shoved piggin strings under right chap legs, and nobody bothered toting a gun. Ropes were wound in tight coils on the saddle fork and were shielded by the right knee. Saddling up, every man laced heavy leather tapaderos over his stirrups to protect his feet. During breakfast Hank gave Dewey a quick run-down on the nature of the work ahead.

"These cattle are renegades," Hank explained. "Been out here since the year one, a lot of 'em. It ain't an easy job and it goes like this. . . ."

Jumping a steer, Hank explained, they whipped the little loop out about eighteen inches and laid it right back over the right shoulder. When old bossy hit an open space it was just one quick swing to open a reasonable loop, then squeeze it down as it left the hand. If they caught, fine; if not they'd take off again, winding up rope on the run. The brush was a kind of blackjack oak with little limbs that grew out and then curled inward, so hard you could scarce cut it with a sharp knife. When one of those limbs hooked a boot or shirt, it tore deep. "It's rough work," Hank said, "an' the boys come in hungry, Dewey. Don't ever just cook enough. Cook more."

Hank and the boys left after breakfast, driving seventy head of burros and the extra saddle horses. Dewey had an idea and rummaged through the storeroom, found a little sheep bell, and hung it around Benstega's neck. "Good," Squab said. "Others won't leave him, Dewey, this way we hear him easy all the time."

They packed supplies for eight days and took off, Squab leading and Jim Toddy ambling out first behind Squab's horse. But inside of twenty steps Jim Toddy stopped abruptly and old Benstega took the lead, the sheep bell tinkling under his neck. Not far down the trail Benstega bent his packbox around an outthrust limb and the other burros repeated that maneuver, stepping exactly in Benstega's tracks. Dewey realized that a man might be trailing burros and figure he was following maybe two, when there could be six or more. Riding that morning, he watched them closely and began what was to be a long, rewarding—and sometimes maddening—education.

They traveled a wild country where timber grew on the north slopes, piñon and cedar, and ponderosa that went up thirty feet but no more. When they topped out on Wild Horse Mesa the country changed abruptly and sheered off into brush, and Squab led them on a downward trail that headed straight for Jesus into the Black Brush country. Dewey saw the tiny limbs that hooked out and waited to rip holes in a man. It was rough, wild country but it was free and open and clean. No fences, no houses, no people. It made him feel free inside and hope that nothing ever happened to change the sweep of canyons and mountains and endless brush flats.

They hit the regular camp at two o'clock and found it a cleared space above a nice spring that ran off down a ravine and formed a tiny stream. The boys had already killed a beef and hung the four quarters on tree limbs; and far out in the surrounding brush, floating inward once in a while, came the sounds of Hank and the boys chasing cattle. Dewey unpacked the burros and watched them head for a sandy place and take their roll. They went down like a horse but turned over all the way like a cat, and once they were dusted good Benstega led them into the trees where they rubbed necks and backs against the trunks. They were still shedding winter coats and the warming weather probably made their hides itch under the thick hair.

Dewey set up his camp just as he'd done back in New Mexico. He placed two kyack boxes on the ground and put one on top. He stored his flour, suet, and extra pans and pots in the bottom boxes; he kept cold biscuits in the top box for any boy who might come in during working hours with a pulled shoe. A man was always hungry when he had a few minutes to breathe, and Dewey wanted meat and biscuits on tap every hour of the day. Squab gathered flat rocks for the cooking fireplace and from that job headed out to pick up dry wood. Just as Dewey turned to the fresh beef he saw the rider coming down the slope into camp. Squab said, "Indian Tom," and dropped an armload of wood beside the rocks.

Indian Tom was part of the crew but had just come up from the reservation. He looked Dewey over when Squab introduced them, accepted cold beef and biscuits, and wolfed the food down. He was almost six feet tall and weighed about a hundred and seventy, and he was as bald-headed as any Indian Dewey ever saw. His neck hair was plaited in thin pigtails and Tom wore the ends under his leather jacket and batwing chaps, with big tapaderos on his stirrups. Tom finished his beef, took a swig of water, and rode off without a word of good-by.

"No talker," Squab said. "Hard worker."

Dewey nodded and got to work on the beef. He lowered the four quarters and took them down to the spring and washed each one thoroughly, then got his four drawstring canvas sacks and shook them out clean. He didn't have time to cook a roast for supper, so he put a beef quarter in each bag, laid them on a blanket, and covered them over with spare blankets and pack covers. That kept the meat fairly cool during the day, and at night he would always hang them up in the trees.

Dewey got out the cold beef and biscuits for supper. He built up the fire and had coffee going strong just before the boys rode in from their first day's work. From today on Dewey would follow a regular cooking schedule. He'd cut meat in the morning, cook dinner and supper together. That way he would always have meat left over from dinner to warm for supper. They never moved meat from one camp to another in this country, so when that time came Dewey would take enough meat for one meal and leave the rest for animals.

When the boys rode in Dewey saw just how tough the job was—fresh rips in jackets and chaps, deep gouge marks on the rounded noses of the tapaderos. They ate and smoked and rolled up in their blankets, all of them dead-tired and half-morose in their weariness. Hank lingered over coffee and finally said, "Get your cuttin' horse in the morning, Dewey, come on out and see how the work's done."

"I'd like that," Dewey said.

"But you don' want no part of it," Hank said. "I'm just warning you."

Dewey grinned. "I'm the cook, Hank. I reckon that's true. I might go lally-gagging out there and bust a leg. Anyway, I'll have a nice roast day after tomorrow."

Next morning Dewey rode out and saw the renegade cattle tied up to trees. "We got a dozen," Hank said, "and plenty got away. Today we'll start things moving. You watch now, in case you ever need to help out."

Dewey watched, and solved the mystery of bringing so many burros along. The boys had twelve cattle, no young stuff, all old cows and bulls and steers. Driver Gobet and George Spradley came up driving twelve burros and held them on one side while Jim Thornhill and the others closed in on the first cow.

By the time a cow had fought the tree all night, its head was pretty sore and some of the fight was soothed down. Raymond sawed off an outside horn, leaving a little stump about four inches long. During this time Driver Gobet was putting a surcingle around a burro, with a breast strap in front and britching behind. There was a four-inch steel ring braided into the right side of the surcingle, halfway down the burro's side.

Then Thornhill rode up to the cow and dallied off, and Driver Gobet caught the free end of Thornhill's fifteen-foot rope and pulled it through the steel ring and led the burro up against the cow. Gobet grabbed a six-foot length of rope and tied one end to the ring and the other around the cow's horns, anchoring the cow about three feet from the burro. Thornhill took off the long rope, and they turned cow and burro loose.

Dewey saw that the only trouble the burro had was in the beginning minutes. If the cow tried to jab that horn nub into the burro, the burro just hauled off and kicked him in the belly about ten times, and that settled matters. The cow might fight two or three times, but no more, and then every time the burro took a step the cow went right along.

Dewey watched the first pair fight it out, then the burro lined straight for the the main ranch where he'd been fed all that good cotton-seed cake and oats. That was the simple reason for bringing the cake and oats, and feeding the burros so good before work started. Dewey went back to camp and started dinner, but he watched operations while he cooked. It didn't take the boys long to tie up twelve burros and cows, and after that they all disappeared into the deep brush to rope more cattle through the balance of the day.

Squab had fresh horses ready when the boys came in for dinner. They ate fast, changed mounts, and took off again. It was routine work settling into a rough and tough pattern, and Dewey realized that day how much difference there was in this country compared to New Mexico. And he woke to the fact that, compared to these men, he was about zero so far as being a real cowboy. It made him buckle down all the harder and do his best to carry his share of the load.

Right after breakfast Raymond and George Spradley took off for the main ranch to meet the burros coming in with their cows, where they'd turn the cows into the pasture, feed the burros good, and bring them right back to camp. That was how it worked, roping the cattle, tying them to burros, taking turns going back to the main ranch and meeting the burros. Dewey sent the boys off with a big breakfast and then got started on his roast.

He put a twelve pound rib roast on the fire and mixed his dressing. When the roast was done he poured the dressing all around and over the meat, and set the oven in the coals for thirty minutes of browning. No flavor got away and when the boys rode in at noon and began eating, their faces made Dewey grin with pleasure.

"By God," Thornhill said. "You *can* cook."

"I get by," Dewey said modestly.

"Got enough for supper?" Hank asked.

"It'll stretch," Dewey said. "You like that corn-bread dressing?"

"Fine," Hank said. "You New Mexico cowboys can do somethin' right."

The boys went out for the afternoon work and Dewey spent the rest of the day cleaning up camp, burying refuse and burning odds and ends. He watched the burros and felt he was getting on their good side. He was always kind to them, fed them cold biscuits and pieces of beef, but he knew he'd never get one to be real friendly. They were independent and their motto seemed to be: "You let me alone and I won't bother you." They were not like horses, but then, they were smarter in some respects. Damned smart, Dewey decided the next morning.

He rode out with Squab to help bring in the saddle horses for the noon change. When he got back, Benstega and the other three had ransacked camp. Old Benstega was standing out behind a tree, flour all over his face and ears, and the others were close by, giving Benstega wistful looks because he'd beaten them to the good pickings. And they had left their calling card—a pile of droppings—right beside Dewey's bedroll. Dewey knew he'd have to recook his bread, and was just lucky they hadn't bothered anything else because supper was on the fire and too hot to grab.

"You thieving bastards!" Dewey shouted. "I'll—"

Then he sat down on his bedroll and looked at Squab, and had to laugh. He'd been warned and plumb forgot to protect stuff, and old Benstega had offered him a sample of the life burros could lead an honest man. That night after supper he got Hank talking about burros, knowing that Hank knew more about the little devils than anybody else. They lay back on the blankets, drinking coffee, and Hank told about his growing up days around Winslow and how he roped wild burros for practice.

"There's always a leader," Hank said. "A lot like wild horses, Dewey. Out on guard on some high knoll, you can pop up over a hill right in his face and there's a good chance he'll give you a close inspection before he turns to lead his bunch away. At the same time he's looking you over, his bunch is moving off just like he gave them some signal you can never make out. And they never run and buck. Little burro colts won't do anything except stick their noses close to the ground, wring their tail, and run like hell."

"They sure will eat most anything," Dewey said.

Hank smiled. "Been feedin' them good?"

"Plenty," Dewey said disgustedly. "So they turn around and rifle camp."

"Hell, that's their nature," Hank said. "Every time you leave camp, they'll try to rob it. And they don' miss a thing. It's funny the way they seem to know. They can be way off grazing and maybe you sneak out to break broncs, and when you come back, there you'll find 'em with flour in their ears. And when you finish eating, they'll be around looking for that handout. Missed your dishrags yet?"

"Not yet," Dewey said.

"You will."

Dewey said, "The hell I will! Say, what size bunches do these wild burros run in?"

"Oh, eight to ten," Hank said. "They're like deer in many ways. When it comes time to have a colt the mare'll go off by herself but the bunch won't be too far away. Just as soon as she's had the colt and it can wobble along, she'll rejoin the bunch again. Dewey, you noticed how their ears stand up?"

"Sure," Dewey said. "It appears they got mighty keen hearing."

"You watch a burro's ears," Hank said. "He'll tell you if anything is happening or somebody's comin'. A burro can be standing out yonder asleep, let something happen way off on the hillside and he'll point an ear like he's looking that way, and it might be twenty seconds before he opens his eyes. I guess that's because his hearing is best and it has to come on down into his brain before his eyes get the signal to take a look. An' talking about dishrags, Dewey, you better watch everything. They don't stop at nothin' except anything rotten."

"Dried fruit," Thornhill said. "And grain. I remember one old burro on the Circle C that could open the granary door faster'n a man. They knew he was thirty-eight years old. He was out on pension, he just hung around, always in the way, sneaking grain."

"Benstega's pretty old," Dewey said.

"Could be thirty," Driver Gobet said. "I don' know for sure. You can't tell their age by their teeth. They got big teeth like a mule's, but different from a horse."

"Say, Hank," George Spradley said sleepily. "How about that big red steer today. He sure was salty."

"They're all salty," Hank said. "We just get luckier with some. That old black cow was a handful herself."

Dewey lay back and drank his coffee, and listened while they discussed the red steer and went on to talk of others met and roped, or missed, during the day's work. It went like that through the eight days of the Black Brush job, everybody talking slow and easy around the night fire, the burros in the trees nearby, horses outside the firelight circle in the grass, the raspy sounds from a tied cow rubbing against a tree deep in the brush. Indian Tom never talked. He'd come in for his food, go off by himself, and squat down like a coyote to eat. Hank very seldom gave Tom any orders. Tom savvied English and he'd catch the next day's orders from general conversation, and about the only orders Hank ever gave him was in case somebody changed partners. Then Hank might say, "Tom, you work with so-and-so tomorrow." But most of the time Tom worked by himself and got plenty done. He was all man, and Dewey liked and respected him. Near suppertime on the last day Dewey saw Tom come tearing through the brush, chasing a big brindle steer. Tom flipped that small loop and made the ketch and tied old bossy to a tree so fast it was like watching a speeded up moving picture scene of some joker riding a livery stable horse in a getaway.

That brindle steer was the last one roped during the eight days, and Hank told Dewey the tally at supper. They'd caught and sent in a hundred and twenty-one cattle, and Dewey didn't need to be told it was a mighty high count for such country. Next morning when they topped off on Wild Horse Mesa, heading for the main ranch, the boys were far out on both flanks scouting the country for steers and burros that might have gotten hung up enroute. And to rope any cow that came along, Dewey knew, to raise that hundred and twenty-one total if possible.

About eleven o'clock Dewey and Squab, driving the kitchen burros, come up on Indian Tom's horse where the trail wound near the edge of a big canyon.

"Hold up," Dewey called. "Something wrong."

Squab just pointed downward to a lower ledge. "Tom's all right, Dewey."

Dewey looked down and finally saw Tom standing on the ledge with a little square looking glass in one hand. Squab nudged Dewey and he looked on out across the country to the northwest and finally made out the rising dust.

"Indian roundup," Squab said.

Tom was down there working that glass against the sun, up and down and sideways, and for a minute Dewey figured Tom was off his nut. Dewey watched him fifteen minutes, until Tom turned and climbed up beside them and shoved the looking glass into a front pocket.

"Three Flying A cows," Tom said. "Two Flying A calves, Indian roundup." Tom held up his fingers to show the count.

"That's old R4," Squab said. "Big Indian cowman roundup."

Indian Tom grunted and rode away. Watching him go, Dewey began thinking about those looking glass signals that had come across ten or twelve miles of country to Tom, who must have signaled the roundup, asked a question, and got his answers the same way. Riding along, Dewey realized that those signals must have been learned during the days of Crook and Miles and Geronimo, when the army tried to catch the Apaches that way. Just a few years ago, Dewey thought, and now the Indians were like anybody else in this country, only it seemed they remembered everything they saw and got around to using it in one way or another. That was a pretty good way to judge the whole country, too, because men out here had a habit of using everything at hand. They had to, or they didn't stick around long.

CHAPTER FOUR

THREE DAYS were spent at the main ranch, shoeing horses and sewing up jackets and chaps—in fact, there was a sight more sewing done than in most any Ladies' Aid on a Tuesday afternoon. Dewey had no spare time either, cooking three meals a day and preparing for the Cherry Creek move.

"There's about ninety thousand acres on this ranch," Hank told him, "and Cherry Creek is the big job. It's a two-day drive straight east through Hole-In-The-Ground Camp, twenty-two miles as the crow flies, but we ain't flyin'. Make sure you get everything tied down tight, Dewey. She's a rough ride."

Hank didn't lie. They started next morning, driving burros and saddle horses, Dewey and Squab bringing up the rear as usual. They made Hole-In-The-Ground Camp the first night, riding all day through brush and trees into rough country cut all to pieces with arroyos and canyons and crazy-angled ravines. The Hole was six sections of rough country three to eight hundred feet lower than the surrounding land; it was literally a hole in the ground, cut off by sheer cliffs except for the one pass in and out. Cattle drifted in but they rarely got out.

While Dewey cooked supper, George Spradley and Thornhill scouted around through the maze of canyons and arroyos, trying to get a fair tally on the cows. They got back just in time for supper with a good report, and Hank decided on staying two days. During that time the boys rode out every canyon and ravine, doing no roping or driving, just making a close count of the cattle. On the third morning they climbed from the Hole and headed east for Cherry Creek. It was a rough trail, but Squab knew a few short cuts and led Dewey down a long approach in late afternoon, around a big sandstone bluff, into permanent camp.

Dewey saw a clear stream of water, good corrals on the far slope, and rising above the slope a sheer six-hundred-foot wall of brownish-gray sandstone rock. That high bluff was the result of God alone knew how many centuries of water rushing down the dry arroyo in yearly bursts, just wearing away the soft rock until the little stream now flowed innocently at the bottom.

Unpacked and camp set up, Dewey crossed the creek for a look at the corrals and the wall. Squab pointed to the Indian picture cut halfway up the wall. Dewey saw the crude outlines of an eagle and snake, carved taller than a man, and the eagle had a long arrow shot through its body.

"Indian letter," Squab said. "Means snake shot an arrow through eagle."

"Oh, sure," Dewey said.

He wondered what it really meant. He doubted that Squab knew. But most of all, he wondered how those ancient Indians ever got down the side of that sheer cliff some three hundred feet to carve the picture. That was the wonder in his mind; that was another mystery of the west.

"You don't think so?" Squab asked.

"I don't think what?"

"That snake shot eagle?"

Dewey grinned. "I guess it makes no difference. But I sure know what does . . . we better get to work."

Then Squab grinned. "Dewey shot arrow through Squab!"

"You damned right," Dewey said. "Let's get the firewood. I want dinner fixed so I can start on the broncs."

Just like Black Brush Camp, the boys had killed and dressed a beef before Dewey arrived. He threw together a fast dinner and, after the boys ate at noon and headed out again, got to work with the broncs.

But first he checked up on the kitchen burros. If old Benstega figured on rifling camp while he was out, well, that old demon had another guess coming.

"Squab," Dewey said. "We both keep an eye on 'em. If they come sneaking in, sing out."

"Maybe not today," Squab said. "Look—"

Benstega had led the others down the creek into the cottonwood and willow trees. They were chewing at the cottonwood bark and Jim Toddy reached around and took a bite off a willow tree. That willow bark was bitter and Dewey thought he finally knew why burros never seemed to get the scours. Their droppings were always well molded, as if they were constipated, but that wasn't true. Maybe it was because they ate such things as willow bark and dishrags.

"I still don't trust 'em," Dewey said. "Keep your eyes peeled."

Dewey crossed the creek and got to work. He roped and hackamored two broncs. He left twenty-foot drag ropes on them, and stretched a rope between two posts to tie them up so they wouldn't break their necks before next morning. Hank nodded approval at suppertime and said, "Before you start on 'em, ride out with us in the morning, see how it goes in case we need you."

"Different from the Black Brush?" Dewey asked.

"Some," Hank said. "But hell, nothin' ever turns out the same. We'll want breakfast at four-thirty."

That cut the night short. Dewey dished out breakfast on time, saddled the old sorrel, and rode out at five o'clock to watch the boys catch wild cattle on water. They took twenty burros, and the over-all plan was somewhat like the method used in the Black Brush.

They topped out on a mesa not far east of camp, where a known water hole stayed filled the year round. Hank deployed everybody around the hole, and the boys began working down from all sides. If they could hold any cattle thus found they would throw the burros right into the bunch. The burros were all surcingled before leaving camp, the cinches loose, of course, until they hung beef, but ready to go. So, if this trick worked, the boys just moved around the caught bunch a couple of hours, getting the wild cattle accustomed to men and horses and burros. Then Hank put two boys in the lead, two behind, and others on the flanks.

"We just ease 'em along," Hank said. "Let the burros lead out. Never rush these wild cattle. If one busts past a boy, then it's time to rope and either tie that cow to a burro or flail hell out of her. If the same cow busts loose a second time and we're lucky enough to ketch, then we damned sure tie her to a burro. Sometimes, if we have good luck on these morning water-hole hunts, we can bring the bunch into camp by ten o'clock."

But they had no such luck that morning. There was one old cow at the water hole, and Dewey had to make tracks back to camp and begin dinner. Squab had the saddle horses out grazing along the creek on fresh grass, and the four quarters of beef were all cleaned and covered well with blankets and packs. The fire was built and the burros hadn't sneaked into the flour. Dewey waved his thanks to Squab and got his beef on the fire, washed up the breakfast dishes, and began fixing a big pot of beans.

The biggest Dutch oven was fourteen inches deep. Dewey put beans and suet in the oven, clapped the lid down tight, and put a small fire underneath, live coals on top, and covered the oven over with hot ashes. No steam got away and he never added water because he covered the beans three inches deep at the start.

In about four hours he had tender beans, and then he tossed a few boiled potatoes into the pot. They never got mushy or came apart, probably because no fresh air reached them. Dewey didn't salt his beans until tender, and when he did salt that morning he knew the pot was coming out fine. But watching beans and cooking dinner left no time for bronc work that day. The boys came in, ate and changed horses, and hurried out for the afternoon. Dewey just got across the creek once that afternoon, then came back in a hurry when Benstega tried a raid on the biscuits and flour. Dewey said, "The hell with it," and let the broncs go.

"Getting started on 'em?" Hank asked him at supper.

"Tomorrow," Dewey said.

"Don't bust a leg," Hank said.

Dewey grinned. "Mine or the bronc's?"

"Well," Jim Thornhill said. "Them broncs is hard to find so draw your own conclusions."

Next morning, once the boys had saddled up, Squab took the two broncs to the rope stretched between the posts. Dewey got his dinner on, checked the burros, and went right to work.

He followed his old routine, same as back in New Mexico. The first morning he tied up a foot while the broncs were on the stretched rope. He put a rope around their necks, got behind them, and let them drag that rope until it came between their hind legs. He picked up the loose end and went for the left hind foot if possible, running to that side and putting the rope into the loop around the bronc's neck and pulling that left hind foot up snug against the belly.

Then Dewey got a pack saddle, cinched it up on the bronc, and started throwing a blanket over and under him. He got the bronc mad, made him rear and fight, and in doing so naturally got the bronc pretty well sweated down. Dewey rolled a smoke and went back to camp for a look at dinner, and then returned to the bronc who was standing there on three legs, eyeballs rolling white, sweat glistening on his shaggy coat. Dewey kept up the routine for two days, the broncs being turned out at night to get their feed, and on the third morning Dewey proceeded to the next lesson.

He saddled the broncs and turned them loose, let the left hind foot down, and allowed them to buck all they wanted while getting used to the saddle feel. That afternoon he tied the left hind foot up again, put a length of rope on the pack saddle to use as a rough stirrup, and began getting up and down on them. That was always a touchy moment, coming up close, feeling them tremble and bunch their muscles as they smelled him so nearby.

"All right," Dewey said. "You ain't goin' nowhere."

He patted them between the legs, under the belly, on the neck. He talked to them, soft and easy, then gruff and sharp, he did everything they were leery of. If they came along well he led one into another corral, got his saddle, and saddled up that bronc with a hackamore and two reins. Then Dewey got up and down on him until the bronc stood and took it. If that happened fairly quick, Dewey could let the hind foot down, cheek the bronc, step on him with the foot down and see if he'd stand.

Dewey never rushed the broncs. When he got into the saddle, he let the bronc stand a bit, but kept his legs firm against the body just to let the bronc know he was all set for any funny business. He had a broad piece of leather, eighteen inches long, with a hand hold trimmed down on the end. If the bronc stood, Dewey let him alone awhile, then began whacking him with that leather. That was the only way to find out just how he really stood with the bronc.

If the bronc blew the plug and started bucking, Dewey let him go, rode him out, then worked him easy for an hour or so around the corral, reining him, stepping down to smoke a cigaret, stepping up again. Then Dewey put the hackamore back on, with the drag rope, and got the other bronc and went through the same routine.

If the boys came in for dinner and rode out again by one, it gave Dewey four hours of afternoon time with the broncs. But any time a boy rode in, he had to leave off and hurry back to camp.

During those days Squab rode the pasture fence, repairing breaks and checking the posts. When the boys got lucky and brought cattle in by ten o'clock, Squab always spotted their dust and got back in time to have the extra saddle horses waiting for the change. Then it was eat on the run, change horses, and get going. And it appeared that Hank knew every old renegade steer in the country. He always knew where the boys could ride out and rope a few wild ones, tie them to trees, and bring out the burros. And while that tough work was going on endlessly, Squab sometimes helped Dewey work the broncs around in the corral. Plus riding fence and getting horse changes ready, Squab somehow found time to carry firewood, help get water, and even wash up a little bit around camp.

The boys followed the same routine every day, once they had cattle in the pasture. They cut out around twenty-five head of burros, rounded up the cattle, and shoved the burros into the bunch. If a cow broke away she was roped and brought back. Then the boys just rode around the bunch and moved them three or four hundred yards, stopped, worked around again, moved again, stopped again. That was to gaunt the cattle down, gentle them, get them used to the burros. The boys were averaging around twenty head roped and caught each day, and they had a hundred and sixty head at the end of eight days.

"We can't handle any more on the drive in," Hank said that night. "We'll start back in the morning, Dewey. Everybody has to turn out and help."

"But we ain't done here?" Dewey asked.

"No," Hank said. "We'll come right back, but cover another slice of ground."

"Does it get tougher?" Dewey said.

"It sure don't get no easier," Hank said. "Pass them beans."

Next morning everybody was on the job because, when they opened the holding pasture gate, that was the most likely place for a run. Hank cut out a good cow horse for Dewey, and Squab had the best horses ready for all the boys. First off, the boys tied twenty of the wildest cattle to twenty burros, and two boys—Spradley and Raymond—pushed them up close to the gate. Squab opened the gate on Hank's signal and jumped right back on his horse, and inside the holding pasture Spradley and Raymond eased those tied burros and cattle outside where all the boys held them in a kind of barricade.

Then the loose cattle and burros were pushed out and held up against and behind the leaders, and made to sit still an hour. Every boy was ready, loops spread to catch a breakaway. Finally Hank nodded and the boys started moving the entire herd up the canyon. Dewey and Squab helped for a mile, and then Hank said, "All right, Dewey. Better get back and pack up."

Dewey and Squab high-tailed back to camp, packed the kitchen burros, and followed along. Dewey cut off enough beef for two meals, and spread out the rest for the animals and birds. Ten days was about the limit for fresh beef in this country; after that it began to get sour and smell just a trifle high.

There was no dinner that day, and Dewey was lucky to manage supper. He and Squab had the kitchen burros and the horse remuda on their hands. Squab led out on a trail that took them pretty high, and never closer than a half mile to the moving herd. They worked along five miles and Squab cut out saddle horses and drove them down to the herd.

The boys came out one at a time to rope and change horses, and each time Squab leaped onto the gaunted horse and rode it back into the bunch, and finally drove all the work-out horses up the hill into the remuda where Dewey was holding horses and cussing burros at the same time.

They made Hole-In-The-Ground about five-thirty, threw the horses into the holding pasture, and got ready for the boys who had lagged behind today, easing those wild cattle along at a snail's pace.

Dewey built a fire and started cooking beefsteak, biscuits, and cream gravy. He threw some dried prunes into a potful of water and hoped they'd get soft in time, and warmed up his last pan of beans. Squab was across the creek cutting out another relay of horses. Dewey straightened up from the fire, his eyes burning from smoke, in time to see Squab head down the trail with the horses. He couldn't make out where Squab met the herd, but pretty soon the Indian boy rode in with the gaunted horses and turned them into the corral. And while he watched that, Benstega sneaked up and snaked a dishrag off the low branch of a tree.

"Hey!" Dewey yelled. "Get away from there!"

He threw a few stones at Benstega and the others, until they moved off a ways, and then he was busy as a one-armed paper hanger turning beefsteaks, watching his biscuits, and making gravy.

The boys pulled in at sunset, dust roiling up above the herd, turning orange and red in the slanting sunrays. They put the herd into the holding pasture, untied the burros from the wild cows, and came stiff-legged for camp. Then it was time to eat like hungry wolves, unroll the beds, and just plain fall down. Nobody lingered over coffee. They were bone-weary, caked with dust and dried sweat, and even Raymond was too tired to click his teeth and slobber. Hank lay on one elbow, unbuttoning his shirt, and nodded sleepily.

"We'll stay two days," Hank said. "Got to rest 'em up."

"Boys or cattle?" Dewey said.

Hank managed a wry grin. "A little of both, Dewey."

They camped two days before moving the herd on to the main ranch. Dewey left the pack outfit and burros in the Hole, hung everything high, and helped drive the herd back. It was a one-day trip to turn the cattle into the big main ranch pasture; and one night's rest was all Hank allowed.

Next morning Dewey packed provisions on a horse and rode straight to Hole-In-The-Ground. Dewey and Squab spent that afternoon working over the supplies, getting set for a morning move. He had no time until after supper and then it got dark before he did much more than putter with the two half-broke broncs. Raymond brought along the shoeing tools and sewing kit, and everybody worked before and after supper.

"It'll be the same routine," Hank said. "But we move over and sweep fresh ground."

"Same time?" Dewey asked.

"Eighty-nine days," Hank said. "With luck. But I wish we could handle more cattle. We just cain't drive a bigger bunch than the last. That's what takes the time."

"Can we finish up in ninety days?" Dewey said.

"Got to," Hank said. "Them's the orders . . . sure, we can do it."

Dewey said, "I ain't breaking many broncs, Hank."

"Never mind," Hank said. "Cooking comes first. Do what you can, Dewey. A man's only got two hands."

Dewey sat beside the fire and watched Hank fall asleep the moment his head hit the folded jacket. The other boys were already sleeping, Raymond snoring through his teeth, George Spradley curled up like a bear, Thornhill flat on his back, making no sound. Indian Tom was off somewhere alone, using that single blanket, apparently never bothered by stones or sticks.

Squab drifted in silently with an armload of wood, stacked it beside the fireplace, and sat down on his blankets. Squab pulled off his moccasins and rubbed his dirty feet, staring downward at the flattened toes, eyes reddish in the fireglow. The kitchen burros moved nearby and the horses stomped restlessly in the thin grass beside the water hole. Dewey poked the fire and then lay back and looked at the sky and the stars. He wondered if they could do the job in ninety days; it seemed like a lot of work for their number of boys.

"Squab," he said. "Can we get the job done on time?"

"Sure," Squab said, "if nobody gets hurt."

"We been lucky," Dewey said. "Mighty lucky."

He thought on ahead to the Las Vegas show. He was getting in great shape, not real hard yet, but working toward it. He began adding up the contestants who'd be at Las Vegas, all the top riders and bulldoggers, and for once he knew he would stand a good chance of pulling down first money. The McCarty string of bucking horses was scheduled for the show, and Dewey knew those horses, old Midnight and Overall Bill and Deertrail and all the rest. To go in there sober and hard, with no bruises or cracked ribs or other worries, was a chance he might never get again.

"You asleep?" Squab asked.

"Not yet," Dewey said. "Just thinkin'."

"What about?"

"Nothing much," Dewey said. "Good night, Squab."

" 'Night, Dewey."

Chapter Five

DEWEY RODE one of his hackamore-broke broncs back to the Hole next day, and rode the other on to Cherry Creek the second day. Hank and the boys fanned wide on both flanks, scouting for water holes and possible hide-outs of small bunches. The boys rode mountains and arroyos and canyons, finding cattle around far-off holes and deep in hidden canyons and once atop a dry, innocent mesa. Riding on the trail, Dewey saw the boys appear off-and-on, tiny black silhouettes against the sky as they topped ridgelines and tipped downward from view.

Back in Cherry Creek Camp the second night, Hank killed a fresh beef and Thornhill helped butcher, clean, and hang the quarters on the tree limbs. Dewey cooked supper and then caught out two new broncs and tied them to the rope stretched between the posts. Hank took a look at one, a nine-hundred-and-fifty pound buckskin, and rubbed his jaw thoughtfully.

"How's he look to you?" Hank asked.

"About the same," Dewey said.

"Maybe," Hank said. "I wouldn't read no book on his back."

After breakfast next morning Dewey sacked and bedded down the fresh meat, got dinner on, and crossed the creek. He roped the buckskin's neck and walked alongside, and nothing happened. That was funny, so Dewey dropped the long rope between the buckskin's legs and, funnier still, had no trouble at all tying up a left hind foot.

"Well, all right," Dewey said. "I'll just skip the kindergarten and put a hackamore on you."

He cinched on his saddle and hackamore, and got up and down a few times with the hind foot tied. The buckskin just stood and Dewey figured he surely had been ridden. But you never could tell. Dewey let the hind foot down, took a short hold on the left rein, stepped into the middle of the buckskin, and expected the balloon ascension.

The buckskin threw up a little back kink and sort of tiptoed off. "I'll be damned," Dewey said. "Don' you want no trouble at all?" Then, just to be sure, he plowed in with both spurs.

And then buckskin shot the curves to Dewey. He blew the cork and went high and wide and nasty. Dewey had always considered himself a good bronc rider, but that buckskin really worked him over. Dewey lost one hackamore rein, one stirrup, and was just leaving the saddle for the dirt when the buckskin quit and ambled around the corral in a quiet fashion.

"By God," Dewey said. "Let's take a close look at you, boy."

He got down and inspected the buckskin's mouth, and saw that the bronc was all of eight years old. That made him examine the back closely and discover the marks of past riding. The buckskin had an Indian brand, and then was counter-branded with a Flying A. The Indians had sold him to Flying A, and Hank had just turned him out with the remuda. Knowing the truth, Dewey had no trouble at all. He rode the buckskin three times, and the old education came back and made the buckskin a pretty fair horse. One thing sure, it allowed Dewey to work with two other broncs as the days passed.

And time was going now. The boys worked another slice of the Cherry Creek country, using the same routine, bringing in the cattle. But there was a difference on this second go-round. Hank had caught a good share of the worst renegades the first time out, while deliberately bypassing other cattle they could round up and work like regular pasture cows.

Now, on the second go-round, the boys used burros for just three days and managed, after that, to gather and drive in loose cattle on horseback. You couldn't exactly marcel their hair like barn-fed thoroughbreds; they were still wild, but they would drive. Working from dawn to dark, sneaking extra minutes every day, driving themselves harder than ever, the boys gathered two hundred and eight head in nine days.

"That's enough," Hank said at supper. "Everybody out tomorrow."

They moved faster next morning because the herd left the holding pasture gate without using the burros. Dewey and Squab packed up and followed the high trail, the boys pushed the herd along and made Hole-In-The-Ground before dark, slept six hours, and turned all two hundred and eight into the main ranch pasture at five the following afternoon. It was tough, driving work and the boys had honed down pretty fine in face and body. With the Hole gather coming up, Dewey wondered how long before those little dark hollows began smudging into view under their eyes. A man could take plenty, last beyond belief, but sooner or later the strain left its mark.

They stayed overnight at the main ranch, Dewey packed provisions on a horse, and they rode straight back to the Hole next morning. Dewey saw the impatience in Hank's face that night, the driving urge to beat time, get up before sunrise and chase those cows. Dewey cooked early breakfast and watched the boys ride off into false gray dawn even before the birds started singing. They were going into the true rough country, a flat country as Raymond put it, but all the flats were alaying on their sides. Plus the six center sections of really deep Hole, there were another twenty-some sections from three to five hundred feet lower than the surrounding country, with the same single trail in and out. The cattle in the Hole were no wilder than Cherry Creek cows, but they did seem more like deer. They were shy, they broke on sound rather than sight, and each cow meant a wild chase over water-piled rocks and loose gravel and around sharp canyon turns. But there was one advantage Dewey could appreciate. The cattle couldn't get out, and the boys didn't give up if they missed one loop. They just wound up, kept running, and sooner or later made the ketch.

Dewey cooked his level best that week. He made a roast with cornbread dressing, a pot of beans, and he had stewed fruit at every meal. Squab worked faster with the relays when the boys rode in, but good food and help from camp didn't ease off the work. Dewey saw the strain signs toward the end of the gather. George Spradley took to eating supper and going straight to bed, not to sleep, just so muscle-sore he lay under the blankets and sometimes quivered as his body finally relaxed. Hank got a little dark-eyed but he seemed to be all muscle and bone and worked harder as he slept less. Indian Tom was the only man who didn't change. He just rode in, wolfed his supper, and went off to bed, walking soft and easy, shoulders never slumped in that sign of weariness. On the sixth night Dewey said, "Hank, things are going good, eh?"

"Sure," Hank said. "An' the luck's holding."

"Food all right?" Dewey said.

"Just fine," Hank said. "You keep it up, Dewey. It helps."

Dewey hoped their good luck would last to the finish, but next day he saw the first close one. Toward supper time, he heard the cow running down the canyon, heard and then saw George Spradley chasing, loop up and ready as cow and rider hit the thicket just upstream from camp. The horse went down and the cow appeared with George's loop hung true over the horns. Then the downed horse snapped the rope tight, broke it, but whirled the cow around.

That cow never stopped. She just headed straight for George who was trying to get up. Dewey began running, Squab right behind him, but the cow was a jump in front. George tried to crawl away but one horn caught him in the pants' seat and almost ripped chaps and pants plumb off. George rolled over, the cow wheeled and bored in, gave him some hard bunts and flat horns before Dewey and Squab hazed her away.

When Dewey and Squab helped George walk down to camp, George looked like he'd argued with a sausage grinder. His clothes were ripped and torn and gouged; he was scratched and bruised and covered with his own blood and the dried, caking sweat and dust. Squab got a bucket of water and Dewey washed George until they could see the bruises and the big blue welts caused by the horns.

"You feel all right?" Dewey asked.

"Wait," George said, took a deep breath, and turned white. "I guess so, Dewey."

"Any ribs busted?"

George prodded himself and tried to grin. "Nothin' that feels that bad."

"Then you lay back and take it easy," Dewey said. "We'll tend to your horse."

When the boys came in a little later, George was so stoved up he couldn't move without grunting to swallow the pain. Hank went over him carefully and finally laid down the law.

"Nothin' broke, but you take it easy a couple days."

"I cain't do that," George said.

"You stay in camp," Hank said evenly. "You hear?"

George bowed his head. "All right, Hank."

So George stayed in camp the last two days of the gather. Dewey fixed up a back rest from George's saddle and some blankets, so they could talk while Dewey worked. George never mentioned the spill, but they all knew how close it had been. If the horse had fallen on George, if the cow had rammed a horn home, then preaching sure would have been over.

They talked about bronc riding and bulldogging, and Dewey told all he could about contests while George drank coffee and smoked chain-fashion. The last afternoon George started talking about his wife and two kids, back in Young, and how they didn't see much of their old man.

"Maybe I'm crazy," George said. "Riding out like this."

Dewey said, "Can you get a job at home?"

"Sure," George said, "but it gets so damned tiresome around town."

George didn't elaborate, but Dewey understood. It was just like riding broncs and going from one show to another; it got into a man's blood and sometimes he never did pull clear. George wasn't riding for the Flying A because of money. He could make more money elsewhere. But once a man got the feel in his blood, once he had the country in his eyes, it was hard to quit. And every man had the same idea in the back of his head: if he kept working, some day he might get his own spread. Then the cows would change shape before his eyes and turn into dollars, and those dollars meant all the things any simple man wanted from life. A decent home, plenty of food, schooling for the kids and nice things for his wife. They all had the dream, whether they admitted it or not, and that was part of the reason for staying on. But not all; the big part was all around Dewey as he cooked; it would always be there, pulling strongly at a man.

They had a hundred and forty cattle on the ninth day. Next morning, using a few burros for the wildest cattle, they moved the herd back to the main ranch. George was up and riding, but Hank made him stay with Dewey and the burros. They got back in midafternoon, turned the herd into the big pasture, and rested an hour on the grass outside the kitchen door while Dewey cooked supper. Eating, Hank looked around and said, "Who wants to go over to the rockhouse, get provisions and fifty-one spools of barbwire?"

Nobody answered and Dewey wondered if it wasn't his place to speak up because Hank couldn't spare a rider from the job.

"I'll go," Dewey said. "If you want me to, Hank?"

"Well," Hank said, "we're goin' to lay around for two days and I guess we can do our own cooking that long." Then Hank grinned and ducked his head. "Sure, you can go, Dewey."

"Squab, too?"

"Oh sure," Hank said. "It'll take two of you."

Squab had twenty-one burros all lined for the trip next morning. The boys saw Dewey off, offered a lot of advice on loading wire, and acted like Dewey might not be big enough to handle the job. With Squab leading, they lined the burros out and began the slow ride. The rockhouse wasn't very far, but nothing hurried burros. Dewey half-dozed in the saddle, thinking about the burros, looking ahead at the kinky, curly hair on the moving backs. The hair lay in waves once the burros shed their thick winter coats; the kinks and curls were mostly on the flanks and under the belly, and from the shoulders on the neck sides up to ears. By now they were well shedded and not rubbing so often against trees. Dewey watched them and realized that he'd learned a good deal about burros, and from burros, since the start of the job.

Burros never overdrank or overate like a horse. A burro could go two days without water and not be affected outwardly; and while a saddle horse could go about that long, the horse went crazy when it smelled water, lambed in to the eyes and bloated itself. But the burro took five or six swallows, walked away, and came back to drink real slow. The burro always took his time, it seemed his instincts were better than a horse.

A burro never choked himself down. He didn't excite and he never tangled himself in fences. Dewey remembered one day he saw Benstega grazing under a tree and getting all tangled up when a big rope of brier dropped down over his neck. Benstega worked thirty minutes untangling himself, backing up, pinching down his neck as he moved forward, just taking his time until he worked loose. And burros like Benstega never rushed in soft footing. He'd smell, take a step, smell again, and nine men and three mules couldn't put him where he didn't want to go.

And eat . . . dear Lord, Dewey thought, he'd sure learned about their eating habits. Like a goat, they'd eat paper and dishrags, but again, they wouldn't touch uncooked beef or spoiled food. They were good watch-men, nothing slipped up on them. Their hearing was equal to a mule's and, come to think back, Dewey hadn't spotted one blind burro or even a glass eye among the seventy-odd he'd gotten to know.

Then there was that old saying, "That's a one-man horse." Well, there were one-man horses because only one man could take a certain horse and get the best out of him. Mules were even better friends than horses, and more one-man in some cases. But the burro . . . !

Dewey knew now that the burro was anybody's burro. He'd do what he wanted for anybody, and never a bit more. Burros seemed to do the intelligent things from instinct, like smelling snakes and water, and never getting excited. A horse could be run over a cliff, but never a burro. Nor would the burro learn tricks. And when it came right down to cases, nobody ever saw a burro do anything smart like a good horse standing over his rider if the man fell off and got hurt. The burro would say, "The hell with this," and go off hunting food, water, and somebody with two good legs.

Now that he was getting to know burros, Dewey felt qualified to say they were the most patient, aggravating, goddamned things that God ever watched over. Yet completely trustworthy and untiring.

He watched the burros walking nose-to-tail behind Squab's horse. He grinned for no good reason, rolled a smoke, and rode along easy, feeling rested for the first time in weeks. It was lucky Hank had sent him after the barbwire; this was just like a vacation with pay.

They made the rockhouse at suppertime, cooked supper on the south side, and slept on the grass with the wind blowing softly above them in the trees. Next morning Dewey unlocked the big, iron-lined door and they packed the provisions first of all on four burros. Then they rolled out fifty-one spools of barbwire, found the special canvases in the back corner of the storehouse, and lined up the other seventeen burros and started loading. And right there, remembering the grin on Hank's face and finally understanding, Dewey got all tangled up in the damnedest job he'd ever tried.

The heavy canvases had two holes cut so that the two ends of a pack saddle stuck up through those holes and let the canvas come down snug on each side. They put hair pads on each side, too, to keep the wire from jabbing the burros. They got the pack saddles all cinched and canvased and checked, and then they started loading the wire in the prescribed manner, one spool on each side and one on top the pack-saddle box, three spools to a burro.

Dewey caught a spool by the open ends and hoisted it up a little above his belt and swung it against the near burro's right side. That was fine, he got it almost in the right place, but the burro moved a little, the spool slipped, and Dewey pressed forward naturally and held the spool up and in place with hands, forearms, and chest. The burro gave a little more, the spool slipped down, and the barbs took a nice hunk out of his jacket and cut straight through one glove back. Squab stepped silently on the burro's far side and braced himself, Dewey swallowed a few opening cuss words, and they tried again. Fifteen minutes later Dewey was so mad he couldn't talk, much less cuss. He stared at Squab who was plenty mad but holding it in, and finally Dewey said, "Well, we got to do it . . . let's start heaving these sonsabitching things!"

By the time they packed seventeen burros, Dewey didn't have enough clothes left to flag a handcar. His gloves were torn off, his hands were bleeding front and palm, his pants were shredded, his jacket was ripped fore and aft, his face was scratched and his hat was on the ground, just where he'd stomped it about halfway through the packing.

"Better start," Squab said.

"Sure," Dewey said. "By all means."

He locked the rockhouse door and climbed up on the old sorrel cutting horse and fell into line behind the tail-end burro. He sat all day, watching those spools of barbwire go bobbing down the trail on seventeen brown backs. His hands ached and his clothes flapped against his body, and he wished, right then, he could meet the man who invented barbwire.

When they rode into the yard, all the boys were standing around with after-supper smokes, watching the burros amble in. Dewey got down and headed for the kitchen, tried to pull up the torn seat of his pants, and saw Hank staring sober-faced at a tall pine tree; and about then Dewey finally got his sense of humor back and lost his angry feeling.

"Good trip?" Hank asked solemnly.

"Just fine," Dewey said. "Wasn't it, Squab?"

"Sure," Squab said. "No work, just like two Sundays in a row."

"Why, that's good," Hank said. "Then I don' reckon you had any trouble loading the wire?"

"Listen, Hank," Dewey said. "The next time some little old easy job turns up, you let one of these poor, overworked cowboys take the vacation and get the wire. I'll handle his job and cook to boot, just for the privilege of staying home."

"Tear your clothes a little?" Hank said.

"Oh, just a little," Dewey said.

Still sober as a judge, Hank said, "Well, that comes from being careless. However, the policy of this ranch is to pay for all clothes ruined in the line of duty."

Dewey finally had to let loose his grin. Raymond started laughing and spitting about three feet straight out, and even Squab's dark face cracked in a smile.

"That's the meanest job in the world," Hank said. "We needed the wire and the boys needed a rest. Many thanks, Dewey."

"You're welcome," Dewey said. "What I'm wondering is, when do I get my rest."

"I don' know," Hank said, suddenly serious. "We got to line out tomorrow, Dewey. I'm afraid you and Squab will both have to help out."

CHAPTER SIX

THEY RODE to Hole-In-The-Ground next morning, set up camp, and started the second go-round. Cattle had hidden deep in the canyons and around the smaller water holes, and Dewey knew this chase would be rough all the way. At breakfast after the previous half day's work, Dewey wondered if George Spradley could cut the mustard. Hank was polishing off a last cup of coffee when George limped out to the corral and roped his horse.

"Think he can?" Dewey asked.

"Don' know," Hank said.

George saddled up and fought the horse around a half-circle and finally got up and stayed put. "Well," Hank said. "I guess he can go."

"When you need me," Dewey said, "just sing out."

"Keep your horses on tap," Hank said. "We just might call any time."

"I'll try that buckskin," Dewey said. "He ain't bad."

Hank nodded and went out to his horse. He led the boys down the canyon out of sight, and the second go-round was underway. Cleaning up camp and getting dinner on the fire, Squab shook his head and said, "Be a tough job, Dewey."

"Keep your horse ready," Dewey said. "Hank might yell any time."

Dewey looked at the sheer walls and thought about the canyons and arroyos, the loose sand and the gravel and the cluttered piles of rock, twenty-five sections jam-packed with that type of footing. He began hoping their luck would hold good. George ought to get by, just on the law of averages, but the other boys were sure overdue for spills. All that day, working with two new broncs and watching his fire, Dewey found himself waiting for the boys.

When they rode in at noon he counted until Indian Tom, always the last man, showed up around the canyon bend. Dewey caught himself counting again at sunset, then going out and helping the boys turn the cattle into the holding pasture. George Spradley was in bad shape when they ate supper, and George lay down right away and went to sleep.

"He all right?" Dewey said.

"Just tired," Thornhill said. "Maybe."

Dewey washed the dishes and talked awhile with Raymond before everybody turned in; and then the days passed in a swiftness that seemed to blur, all work and hasty meals and never enough sleep, although no man complained. The luck held; ropes broke and cattle turned on riders; but no one took a bad spill. The cattle were ranging further from camp every day, the boys had to ride out and find them, and that took all the extra strength a man could muster. Even so, George Spradley lasted until the morning of the fourth day.

When Dewey banged a pot for breakfast, George tried to climb from the blankets and fell back with a grunt. He wasn't suffering from any delayed internal injuries, that was plain, but he was all done in. He had pushed himself too fast, his body had been too stoved up to come back so quickly and take the punishment.

"You stay in today," Hank said. "Dewey'll ride with Jim. You rest up and keep the burros out of the flour."

George tried to argue but he was too sore in the bones and body to make it stand up. He grinned weakly at Dewey and lay back down and went right to sleep. He didn't move while the boys rode out and Dewey hurried from breakfast to saddle the buckskin and join Thornhill. He just lay wrapped in his dirty blankets, on the rough ground beside the fire, his hair sticking up in all directions; and Dewey knew that bed felt just as good to George as the best mattress in the world.

Thornhill and George had been scouting out toward Cabresta Creek, and Dewey followed along that morning through a half-dozen canyons that tried to swallow up each other, through a long canyon that grew deeper and finally ended in a box, with a steep little trail going up atop a mesa and on down the far side toward the creek. They were halfway down the slope when Thornhill stopped and pointed.

"Take a look, Dewey."

Dewey saw the Indians down creek, some riding, some afoot, packing all their belongings on the little ponies. The women had on great big skirts that belled out over their ankle-high moccasins, and their hair was braided like Tom's, only thicker, and hung down their backs. The men were dressed in patched, faded Levis and jackets; most were bareheaded, but a few wore old, floppy hats. Dewey noticed three or four wearing boots but for the most part the men had on the same ankle-moccasins. Boots cost a lot of money and these Indians were not like some in New Mexico who had changed a lot and put all their money on their backs.

"How come they're here?" Dewey asked.

"They can cross Flying A any time they want," Thornhill said. "When they come from the other side, they cut through the Hole along Cabresta Creek, and come out on Indian land again on the far side. It saves 'em a lot of travel."

"Apaches?" Dewey asked.

"Yes," Thornhill said. "Some of Squab's outfit. Around forty, I'd say. By God! See that woman, Dewey?"

"Which one?"

"That one droppin' back," Thornhill said. "And that old squaw."

Dewey saw the two women, the younger one on a pony, drop behind the procession. The young one got down, the old squaw came up close, and they seemed to be holding a council of war. Nobody else stopped. The line kept right on going up the creek on the trail that followed the second bench bluff above the bottom. Finally the old squaw and the young one headed down toward the creek bottom.

"Wonder what—?" Thornhill said. "Let's ride down and see. Might be a steer in the creek."

By the time they had ridden a quarter mile around and then down onto the second bench, they could see easily the remaining two hundred feet into the creek bottom. The young one was spread out on her back under a clump of willows, and the old squaw was just hot-footing it to the creek with a pan. The old squaw dipped up water and carried it back, got down beside the young one, and got busy as the all get out, moving from side to side, punching up and down in some way on the young one, and spitting out words they couldn't hear except for the low buzz of the sound rising from the bottom.

"Well, I'll be goddamned," Thornhill said. "Would you look at that."

Dewey couldn't make out what the squaw used for tools; likely she had none other than a knife. He couldn't see how she cut the string, but all at once she had a baby and she spanked it good and it let out a healthy squawl. The young one raised up and took a look; then the old squaw carried the baby to the creek, washed it off in that cold water, and brought it back. Dewey and Thornhill watched them for about forty minutes, holding the horses still, not wanting to disturb the two women who didn't seem excited at all.

Finally they both got to their feet, the young one climbed on the pony and the old squaw put the baby in the pack on her back, and they came climbing up the lower bank, the old squaw leading the pony. They didn't look at Dewey and Thornhill, they never spoke a word. The woman had just had a baby and that was that, nothing to get excited about.

They made the second bench, turned upcreek, and started after the others.

"Well, by God," Thornhill said softly. "I wonder what it is?"

"I couldn't tell," Dewey said.

"Me neither," Thornhill said, "but it ought to be a boy, the way it yelled."

They watched until the two women disappeared up the bends of the creek, and headed downstream to scout the bottoms. Every mile or so Thornhill grinned, shook his shaggy red head, and said, "Well, I'll be damned!"

"A white woman'd die if she tried that," Dewey said. "I guess our breed ain't so tough any more."

"I wonder," Thornhill said. "I been out here quite a spell and I've seen Indians plenty. They can beat us six ways from the jack at lots of things; then they turn around and go all soft inside when they try some others." Thornhill chuckled dryly. "Just like us, eh? We got our faults, they got theirs. Ain't no use trying to add the tally and say which is the best."

"Like Tom," Dewey said.

"Sure," Thornhill said. "None of us can outlast him in this kind of work. An' Squab is just about a top hand now."

"How old is he?" Dewey asked.

Thornhill frowned, thinking back. "Well, Tom brought him over four years ago—maybe a little more—and I think he was twelve then."

"Sixteen now," Dewey said. "I figured he was older."

"You cain't tell," Thornhill said. "All I know, he does a man's work."

Riding Cabresta Creek, Dewey knew that Thornhill was right. You never knew how good a man was until you saw him work a considerable time, and color sure made no difference.

Their scout was a zero day and Thornhill turned back toward camp early, so Dewey could get supper on the fire. Half a mile out Thornhill spotted a burro colt on the hillside and shook out his rope.

"Wild?" Dewey asked.

"Must be."

Thornhill closed on the burro colt, made his cast, and brought the colt down on the hillside beyond the brush. When Dewey rode up Thornhill was cussing a blue streak.

"Broke his leg," Thornhill said. "Damn this rocky ground . . . poor little cuss."

Thornhill got the old .45 from his buttoned-down saddle holster and put the burro out of misery with one shot. There was nothing else to do; it was just bad luck when no bad intentions were meant. Dewey remembered they had nothing but sowbelly and biscuits in camp because the boys hadn't killed a beef. Thornhill always carried a hunting knife in a hip pocket scabbard, and that gave Dewey an idea.

"Jim," Dewey said. "Let's cut off a chunk and cook it up."

"All right," Thornhill said, "but you got to take first bite."

Dewey took the knife and cut out a chunk of round steak from the hip. They rode into camp and Dewey got a Dutch oven, put beef tallow in, and got it sizzling hot. He salted and peppered the burro meat, rolled it in Pet milk and flour, and dropped it into the hot tallow. It smelled good cooking and when they tried a bite, it tasted better.

"Never tried it before," Thornhill said. "We learn somethin' every day, Dewey."

"In a pinch," Dewey said. "That's the only time I'd want to, Jim."

Thornhill smiled and looked over at George Spradley, who was sleeping straight through all their cooking and conversation. "Sure, Dewey. When you hang around them canaries awhile, you get to liking them, no matter how many times they do you dirt."

Thornhill told the boys about the burro meat at supper, but nobody would believe it was good eating. Dewey grabbed the buckskin and rode back to get another chunk, but the flies had already blowed it and it was no good. They had no way of proving their point, and Hank said slyly,

"Dewey, old Benstega's giving you mighty suspicious looks. I wouldn't get too near him for a day or so."

In nine days they gathered two hundred and fifty-six cattle, all wild and subject to run like hell at any time. Squab took the kitchen burros and remuda, and Dewey rode his buckskin and helped the boys drive the herd back to the main ranch. This was the biggest bunch Hank had tackled and nobody dozed in the saddle that day. Dewey let up only when the last cow went into the big pasture and the gate slammed.

"Now we'll stay here about ten days," Hank said. "An' work this home ranch country out."

That was good news and the boys lay around after supper and felt so much better they even swapped a few lies. George Spradley got a bottle of Sloan's from the kitchen and rubbed his legs and arms and neck, and then wrapped up in his blankets to see if he couldn't roast out the last aches and pains. Driver Gobet washed out his dirty clothes and hung them up to dry on the line behind the house, and Benstega and Jim Toddy swiped Driver's Levis and chewed them into thin strips. Even Indian Tom hung near the edge of the kitchen door light and listened awhile before going off to bed.

"Dewey," Hank said finally. "Want a job tomorrow?"

"Sure," Dewey said, half-asleep. "Whatever you say, Hank."

"Well," Hank said. "We could use a few more spools—"

Dewey woke fast. "Hank, you go plumb to hell!"

Hank chuckled and went off to bed, and Dewey felt so good that night he got up early and helped Thornhill kill a beef. When the boys rode out to work, Dewey made a cowboy sonofabitch stew, better known as a "district attorney" if ladies were present.

A cow has three stomachs and where the food comes out of the last stomach there was a double string of gut. If the cow hadn't been run and heated up, the string was full of white marrow something like the gristle cord down the backbone. Dewey cut that out of the yearling steer Thornhill had butchered, sliced it into three-inch pieces, and then cut the fine leaf fat from around the paunch. He put the pure fat in his biggest Dutch oven, rendered it out, and dropped the marrow gut into the melted grease and seared it over.

Then he moved the big oven off the hot fire onto a few coals, so it would simmer at low temperature. He took the butcher's steak, that piece of meat lying between the heart, liver, and lungs, a strip that separated those organs from the guts. The butcher's steak made two pieces half an inch thick, four inches wide, and about eight inches long. Dewey cut them into little pieces and put them into the oven after the marrow gut had simmered five hours.

The boys came in for dinner at that time, ate their beef and biscuits, and sniffed the odor coming from the Dutch oven. Raymond said, "What's that, Dewey?"

"Dishwater," Dewey said.

"Aw," Raymond said. "That's stew. Say, are you afixin' sonofabitch, Dewey?"

"That's how it started," Dewey said. "I can't guarantee what'll come out."

"Oh, by God," Raymond said. "Let's get to work, boys. I'm already hungry for supper."

After the boys left and the butcher's steak had cooked about fifty minutes over the slow fire, Dewey diced up the heart, cut the sweetbread into little chunks, and set the oven over a fast fire. He dropped in heart and sweetbread, and skimmed off all the grease from the top of the stew. Then he cut slices of liver half an inch thick the long way, and laid fifteen slices on top of the stew. He clapped the lid down tight, put coals on top, and let that heat brown the liver. Then, when the boys came in to eat, they could grab one or two slices of liver and a plateful of stew and get down to business.

Dewey would rather have a good feed of sonofabitch before a real long ride than anything else. With black coffee, dried fruit, and a cigaret, no man was going to get hungry in twenty minutes. That sonofabitch really set on a man.

The boys came in that night and settled down to serious eating with no fooling around. They cleaned up the stew and ate some apricots and rolled their smokes in a kind of bloated daze. Hank let his supper rest a while before he said,

"We'll make another pasiano into the Black Brush, then one swing through Cherry Creek and the Hole, just cleaning up. If our luck holds, we'll be ready for general roundup."

"When's that?" Dewey asked.

"June twelfth," Hank said. "Cochrane's spreading the word by grapevine. There'll be fifteen outfits or so, mostly those little two hundred head ranchers north and west of here. We got to be ready."

"How long do we stay in the Black Brush?" Dewey said.

"Not long," Hank said. "Don't take the burros, just pack some grub on a horse. We'll need you and Squab anyway."

Dewey said then, "How's George?"

"All right," Hank said. "Nothin' serious. Guess that's our luck holding fair."

The days began slipping away from Dewey while the boys cleaned up the main ranch. It was always that way when a man got accustomed to his job and his outfit. Work settled into grooves, a man left his blankets at sunup and followed that set groove, did his work, and found night on him before he sensed the passage of time. That was lucky because no matter how good a job, sooner or later the work chafed on a man if he had spare time. Only when he had it rough and tough, from dawn to dark, did a man ride through to the finish and then wonder, almost childishly, where the time had gone.

Dewey and Squab packed beef, biscuits, and dried fruit on a horse and followed the boys into the Black Brush. The boys roped cattle, tied them to trees, and brought the burros around next morning. Dewey and Squab rode back toward the main ranch, acting as a guard for the burros. They always hit the main ranch ahead of the burros and cattle, and as each pair came in, Squab and Dewey unhitched the steer from the burro and turned them into the big pasture.

Squab was pretty good with a rope and Dewey never could throw a good loop, so Squab heeled the steer, stretched him out, and even if Dewey didn't have enough slack on the rope to untie, he just unbuckled britching, strap, and surcingle, and let it come off together. Then Dewey got on the horns and untied the rope from the head. They got along pretty good and managed to keep the cattle from scoring any direct hits with the horns.

One burro brought out an old stag that Dewey never forgot. He was a long-ear at least ten years old. Dewey and Squab got curious, examined the stag closely, and saw that he'd been castrated, but a rough job. Then, because he had no brand or earmark, Dewey remembered what his older brother had told him once.

Van had been working with the biological survey in southwestern New Mexico, trapping coyotes and wolves. Van told Dewey that some coyotes and wolves seemed to get a taste for deer and cattle testicles, and would come up underneath the deer or yearling on the run and actually do the castrating with their teeth. Dewey figured the old stag had been caught by a coyote when he was two or three years old, because a stag has a different head than an ordinary steer when left to run that long. He had more or less a bull's head; and Dewey knew that a lot of those old stags were like a proud-cut horse—they tried to do a little business with the cows but, of course, without results.

That old stag was about the last cow in the Black Brush, for Hank brought the boys in next day and spent the afternoon shoeing horses, repairing leather, and stretching new ropes; and took off the following morning for Cherry Creek with the kitchen burros and thirty-five head of the other burros. The boys rode in pairs to make sure they'd catch any stray missed in the first two go-rounds. Hank knew where all the little missed bunches were hiding out, and every morning before sunup, the boys rode out and sneaked up on those renegades and either drove them back to camp or used the burros for a tie down. Six days of riding cleaned out Cherry Creek and netted them forty-five head that they drove to the Hole-In-The-Ground with no trouble, and on to the main ranch the next day.

They spent half a day shoeing horses, patching up, then headed back for a final cleanup in the Hole-In-The-Ground. Dewey didn't bother with fancy cooking, he just dished up quick meals and went out with Squab to hunt the water holes. When two days of hard searching brought in just twenty head, Hank called a halt. They drove the small herd in and turned them into the big pasture. Dewey walked up to the house that noon, turned around, and looked across the endless stretch of country, and said half to himself, "June tenth! By God if we didn't make it!"

CHAPTER SEVEN

COCHRANE HAD DONE a good job spreading the news among the small outfits, mostly Mormon people who lived to the north and west of the Flying A. Toward midafternoon of the eleventh, Dewey saw the first riders coming in, kicking up lazy dust streamers against the hot blue sky.

"You got plenty of chuck on?" Hank asked.

"For how many?" Dewey said.

"Say twenty-one or so tonight."

"All right," Dewey said. "We'll manage."

Those early riders were the reps from the different outfits, usually the owner himself, with his boys stringing along behind, due to reach the Flying A in the morning with the mixed head of stock. The Circle C sent two men that afternoon, and two came from the Bar Y. Zachery got down, shook hands with George Spradley, and handed over a letter from George's wife. George and Zachery were both from Young, the post-office town in Pleasant Valley southwest of the Flying A, where Zachery ran his three hundred and fifty head outfit.

"Good man," Squab said. "Good roper."

"Good as Hank?" Dewey asked.

"Close," Squab said. "Nobody good as Hank."

Each man had his bedroll and running iron, and two extra horses. They unsaddled, turned their horses into the corral, and stood around outside the kitchen door, talking, the non-Mormons smoking, waiting for supper. After supper, while he washed dishes, Dewey listened to their talk. They compared the size of their mixed gathers, heard Hank give the total for the Flying A, argued about the number of lions in the country, went on into casual discussions of everything they knew and lived with. While the Flying A had gathered hundreds of cattle, these men had done the same job on a smaller scale, work equally as tough for they were small ranchers and two men had to handle the job. Tomorrow some fifteen little herds would be thrown into the big pasture with the Flying A herd, and then the roundup would start. The talk moved slow and easy, voices gentle in the night, not joking much or laughing, but telling old stories repeated countless times in past years around their fires; and then the voices murmured away as they spread bedrolls and slept on the grass.

"Lot of hungry boys tomorrow," Squab said.

"An' don't forget," Dewey said, "we need another beef."

"I'll tell Jim," Squab said. "You want anything else tonight."

"That's all," Dewey said.

" 'Night then, Dewey."

Dewey hung the sopping dishrags on the wire above the Majestic Range, looked at his sourdough keg, and checked up on his remaining beef quarter. Breakfast was scheduled for four-thirty and after that he'd be humping all day long until roundup was finished. It meant cooking for about thirty men, putting out roasts and steaks and stewed fruit and biscuits until he knew damned well he'd be sick of the sight and smell of food. It always happened when you cooked for a big bunch. It wasn't as much fun and a man caught himself caring less about quality and more about dishing the grub out and getting the apron off. He'd have to watch himself the next few days; there was no sense getting sour on the job and giving the outfit a bad name.

Hank and Zachery were lining up night guards and Dewey heard four men head for the pasture to relieve the first four who were holding the Flying A herd off to the side. All night Dewey woke to the sound of men coming and going; morning came fast and gray, pushing him toward the stove and the cooking. And all morning while Hank and three others scouted the pasture for any layouts missed the day before, the others held the Flying A herd intact. Then, after dinner, while Thornhill kept up the stray hunt, Hank and George and Driver just rode in among the herd. The little herds started coming in at noon, all available hands helping to drive each herd through the gate into the pasture. Other men joined Hank and the boys and they all rode among the steadily growing mixed herd, working the cattle, not stirring them up, just easing around, getting cows and calves lined up in their minds.

They'd see a long-ear calf and then find the mother; and whatever brand the mother carried, they knew the calf was that cow's brand. They all kept working and the dust got thicker and the herds came in, and up in the kitchen, sneaking looks between jobs, Dewey kept cooking. Some of those boys, just riding up, brought Dewey food carried all the way from their home ranches. Three big cakes in A-1 condition, pies and cookies. Dewey put everything on the top shelf behind the table and thought of those women, way to hell and gone in little ranch houses, cooking up all these desserts for the boys. He wished he could thank every one, but he never would get that chance, and those women didn't expect thanks. It just wasn't necessary in this country.

"An' you steer clear of them cakes," he told Squab.

"Don't like cake," Squab said, dropping an armload of piñon wood in the box.

"Oh, sure," Dewey said. "You ain't no different from Benstega. He don' like cake either . . . not much!"

"No," Squab said. "He likes pie best."

"And so do you, eh?"

A faint trace of laughter touched Squab's eyes. "Apple pie."

"Well, you're a helluva Indian."

Squab just stared as if saying Dewey was a helluva something or other, and then ran outside to tend to his chores. Dewey poked a fork into the roast, sniffed the biscuits, and went out to clean and cover the fresh beef Thornhill had brought in after breakfast; and working through the day, serving up dinner and starting supper, he watched the work in the big pasture and admired the way those boys did the job.

He never saw a pencil in sight to make a count. He never saw a man make a foolish move or waste time; and during supper, thinking how nice it was of the womenfolks to bake the cakes and pies and cookies, he wondered at the change in feeling. There were thirty-one men present and, during and after supper, Dewey noticed the change in talk and feelings, like wind shifting quarters on a still night.

Hank gave the orders for night guards to change every two and a half hours, four men to the guard, and there was no trouble because the purpose was mostly to get the cattle used to men being among them at night. But Dewey couldn't miss the feeling of unfriendliness. They all wore guns and some carried carbines in saddle boots, and coming off guard to grab a bite, each man loaded his plate, went off by himself, and ate like a coyote. There was very little talk, and what came out was essential cattle talk that had to go on between them. All that night and next day, as the work quickened, that strained and unpleasant feeling went on. Toward evening of the thirteenth, Dewey saw something that made him understand just how everybody felt about the business of so many little outfits having to gather on the Flying A and sort out brands.

Hank came riding through the bunch, struck a three-year old Mormon cow, and made his cast. He went over her right shoulder, picked up both fore feet, and slammed her down hard. Just as Hank got down and loosened his rope, a big Mormon rode up and said quietly, "Don't do that any more, that's my cow. If I think she needs roping and throwing, I'm sure capable of doing that job myself. . . . even if I ain't as good with a rope as you are."

Dewey looked for an explosion and got ready to toss in his two-bits alongside Hank. But Hank never spoke a word in return. He took off his loop, wound and hung it on the saddle, and rode up to the house. Nobody else had seen it happen, and the big Mormon went on into the herd about his business. Hank came into the kitchen, poured a cup of coffee, and grinned.

"Reckon you saw it, Dewey?"

"And heard it," Dewey said. "You just yell if help's needed."

"No," Hank said. "That ain't the way to figure those things. You got to consider their feelings. Flying A is big an' they're little. They got to work off steam somehow or other, like all little fellows always get stuck and have to work it off on the big one. It don't happen but once a year . . . and it don't go any further than this."

"They don't like to come here," Dewey said.

"That's most of it," Hank said gently. "An' I don't blame 'em a whole lot."

Next morning the big roundup got underway. The boys began cutting out and branding the calves belonging to the various cows; and it seemed that the hard feelings simmered down a bit overnight. When the work started there was no argument over the way the jobs were passed out. Hank and Zachery did the roping, the big Mormon and six men held the herd, while ten others tended fires and did the branding and helped out when needed on the rope. Working outside the kitchen as much as possible, Dewey watched the work and listened to the talk. Very often he heard a rider call, "What cow does this calf belong to?"

Then one of the herd riders would raise up and look the calf over and say, "That calf belongs to the Bar Y cow. She's a four-year-old, got a stubby tail."

Those men seemed to know every cow. They kept all the facts in their heads, never wrote a word down, and never made a mistake.

They worked under a hot, cloudless sky, through a day that got hotter toward noontime and turned into the heavy, lay-down kind of heat in midafternoon.

Calves were brought out of the herd, mothers were called off, and the calf went to the branding fire where the irons were ready, cherry red from the coals. They branded the calves and some of the cows and the old renegade long-ear bulls; as the iron went on and the hair burned, the calf was turned right back into the herd and another was dragged up to take its place.

Dust lay heavy over the fires, riders showed up filmy and indistinct to Dewey as he watched from the kitchen door; heat waves danced far out across the big pasture. Time was pressing them all, and nobody gave a minute or an inch to time in terms of muscle used and sweat wiped away. They worked through the long day and finished the job, and rode the night guard with a minimum of talk and the same feeling of unfriendly mistrust.

Morning of the fifteenth was started right on schedule. They cut out the different brands and threw all together into the big horse corral, while Hank and the boys held the Flying A herd off to one side in the pasture. Then the different owners and reps ate dinner and went to the horse corral and began cutting out the individual herds.

Two men waited outside while one entered the corral and weaved in and out among the cattle, like an old lady knitting fancy socks, looking for and finding his own calves and cows and steers, moving them to the gate and on through where the outside men held the growing herd. One by one, the little outfits cut out their herds and pulled away, driving straight for home without a so-long or a backward wave.

Dewey watched them go and wondered if one might say a word; and the only two were the Circle C and the Bar Y. Zachery paid his respects all around before leaving, and Circle C did likewise; and there was a reason for their action. They were bigger outfits, they had a better understanding of the Flying A's position in the country. And maybe, Dewey thought that night, it was because they had grown from little outfits to middle-sized ones and hoped, one day, of getting as big as the Flying A.

And all the time the cutting out and heading for home went on, the boys held the Flying A herd in one corner of the big pasture. The cattle, held two days now, were getting gaunt without their proper grazing. Hank kept them off water through the afternoon, way back in the pasture, and held them all night until five o'clock next morning when the boys turned them down on water. The purpose was to get the herd filled up, so loggy they wouldn't run when the time came to turn them out. Hank rode back to the kitchen while the herd was drinking, had a cup of coffee, and gave Dewey orders for the move.

"Pack up," Hank said. "Head for the rockhouse. We ought to be lined out by nine o'clock."

Hank was gone then, heading back to the pasture. Dewey and Squab packed and hit a side trail just as the boys brought the herd to the main gate. Dewey had fixed a lunch and, at noontime, Squab angled over close to the line of drive, and the boys came in two at a time to eat. They grabbed a slug of beef, biscuits, and a can of tomatoes, stepped off to one side, ate fast, and rode back to the herd. Then Dewey and Squab drove on to the rockhouse and arrived at four-thirty, with just time enough to cook supper. Dewey didn't set any normal ration that night. He just cooked up hell and half of Georgia, because the boys were damned hungry.

When the herd came in, the boys turned it into the holding pasture to scatter out and do some grazing. Two boys worked among the herd all the time, in two-hour shifts, getting the cattle used to people riding around them at night. It had been an easy day and the herd acted fairly normal. They all lay down for a couple of hours; then, after supper, they started to get up, scatter, and graze. The pasture grass was good, so the herd could pretty well fill up around one o'clock, after which, if nothing bothered them, they'd lie down and rest. Dewey knew they'd start getting up at five and heading for water, and this would make it easy for the boys to gather and make a good start on the long road to Winslow.

Dewey got everything ready for a fast breakfast at four o'clock. Indian Tom and Thornhill took the first guard and the other boys rolled up and went to sleep on the grass. Hank took a stroll out and looked the herd over, and came back to smoke a cigaret and drink coffee on the lee side of the rockhouse.

"Everything all right?" Dewey asked.

"Fine," Hank said. "An' you cooked good, Dewey."

Dewey said, "Thanks," and then popped the question he'd worried over considerable the past week. "We're driving to Winslow, Hank?"

"Yes."

Dewey said, "When you reckon we'll hit town?"

"First of the month," Hank said. "At the latest, barring anything real bad."

"That's good," Dewey said. "Real good, Hank."

Hank turned around and recrossed his legs and filled his cup from the pot. He chuckled softly and grinned at Dewey over the fire.

"Ain't cured yet, eh?"

Dewey Jones snubbed out his cigaret and leaned back on his elbows. He thought of the Las Vegas show starting July third, and the train from Winslow that would get him there in time if he left the morning of the second. He could see the bronc riders and bulldoggers and ropers he knew, all the crowd coming into Las Vegas, and the arena and the broncs and the smell of it all.

"Not quite yet," Dewey said. "I sure want to make this show, Hank."

Hank seemed to understand the reasons without going into a long line of palaver. He said, "Dewey, you're sure in good shape."

"Never better," Dewey said.

"Nothin' like a clear head, too," Hank said. " 'specially when a man's in good shape and trying for first money."

"I aim to be clear-headed," Dewey said. "An' I'm going for that first money, Hank."

"What's it worth?" Hank asked.

"Well," Dewey said, "if a man got lucky in bronc riding and bulldogging, he could pick up eight-nine hundred easy, Hank."

"Lemme see," Hank said. "You'll make around three-seventy-five on this job, Dewey."

"Less my tab at the store," Dewey said.

"Call it three-fifty," Hank said. "That's a good stake. And some of that first money and a man could nearly set up in business."

"I'm thinking on it," Dewey Jones said. "You got to get cured sometime, Hank. Maybe I'll make the grade at Las Vegas. That's why I want that first money."

"You'll get it," Hank said softly. "I got a hunch you'll get it, Dewey. 'Night."

CHAPTER EIGHT

WHILE THE BOYS slowly turned the herd toward Cibecue, Dewey and Squab packed up the kitchen and followed along a parallel trail. The cattle drove good and Hank called a halt after eight miles on a little stream of clear water. Dewey was cooking off the cuff now, with no time for roasts or baked beans, and the boys had no time to enjoy a six-course meal. They just ate and went on night guard, and came off and dropped asleep.

Four men stood guard that night because the herd was in the open; and just when the second guard went on and the first boys came off, the night turned still and nothing moved for a long, long moment.

"Get your boots," Hank yelled. "An' get your night horses!"

"God damn," Thornhill said, just settling down in bed.

Then every boy moved swift and silent getting to his night horse tied nearby on a stake, and out in the open pasture Dewey heard the cattle come up like a whirlwind.

"Squab, come on," Dewey called. "We got to help."

They ran into the mixed-up confusion of the remuda, moving foolishly between the roused horses, pushing toward the old cutting sorrel and Squab's black. Something had happened in the herd to send the cattle up a-milling and bawling, ready to take off. Paper, clouds, a coyote, nobody could guess. It just went that way with a herd. They could get all laid down, and just when they were still, the least little thing would touch them off like powder.

Dewey rode for the edge of the herd where the other boys were already riding, talking soft and easy, watching for the first wild jump. Dewey got between Thornhill and George Spradley, and did what he could to quiet down the herd. He rode slowly and hummed snatches of old songs, time passed, and luck was with the outfit that night. The cattle just got up and milled a while; then the scare seemed to drift over. Within twenty minutes the herd was lying down again.

Hank sent Dewey and Squab back to camp, and a few minutes later the early guard came in, finished unrolling beds, and settled down. Hank stayed out with Indian Tom, Driver, and George; and back in camp Thornhill looked across the fire at Dewey and shook his head.

"Now what in hell did it?" Thornhill asked.

"I didn't hear anything," Dewey said. "You, Squab?"

"Nothin'," Squab said. "Maybe ghosts."

"Maybe anything," Thornhill said moodily. "Coyotes, lions, clouds on the moon, wind, you name it and by God if they won't up and run! An' we got to expect it every night from now on."

Dewey thought it over after the boys fell asleep and knew it showed just how much Hank understood cattle. Hank had the boys up, on their horses, ready to go before anything had happened. It was sort of second sight or some unnatural talent, the way a man got after so many years of work with cattle. Hank had that feeling for cattle, he smelled and thought—if cattle did any thinking—and looked at life just like a cow or a rattle-brained steer.

"Dewey?" Squab said.

"Yup."

"The dishrags," Squab said. "Benstega got 'em while we was out."

Dewey climbed from bed and went over to the kyack boxes and found just two dishrags left from the wet ones he'd hung up to dry. Old

Benstega had sneaked in and damned near cleaned house, and now was standing somewhere in the darkness, grinning and chomping like a cow with a big cud of honey. Dewey started to cuss the old devil from hell to breakfast, and then grinned helplessly and lay down again.

"Eat 'em up," he said. "I hope you get the bellyache."

Next morning they drove on across the little creek and made six miles to Cibecue. Hank grazed the herd all day because this was open country with little timber, and he didn't want a break to come where the cattle could fan out and disappear over four horizons. They hit Cibecue at five o'clock and turned the herd into a big corral made up rail-fence fashion. It was zigzagged all around, the rails were old and rotten, so Raymond and Driver started riding around the outside of the corral, and got relieved in two hours by Indian Tom and George. Dewey set up camp, cooked supper, and picked up two cases of tomatoes on Hank's orders.

"We'll need 'em for drinking," Hank said. "Got a dry day comin' up."

Supper was eaten on the run and the boys staked their night horses close to the fire; and sure enough, about eleven the herd suddenly jumped and ran. The old rail fence went down like matchsticks, but the herd didn't go far.

Thornhill and Hank were riding the fence and managed to get out front when they saw the herd wasn't really anxious to make a genuine getaway. It was another scare like the night before, typical of those little renegade cattle who were spooky as the devil. They had broken a hundred-foot gap in the fence and shot outside like a cork from a bottle, and Dewey thought maybe being so close and tied up caused them to stop.

Once the herd was thrown back inside, two boys had to watch the gap while two more rode around, singing and talking to the cattle until they began lying down and getting settled. Thornhill had a nice singing voice and Driver's wasn't bad, but Raymond couldn't carry a tune in a rain barrel. He began singing the "Santa Fe Trail" and Thornhill called out, "Don't jump 'em again, Raymond," and Raymond laughed at himself and whistled instead.

They didn't get much sleep that night, broke camp early, and drove about five miles into a little park in a valley that was subirrigated, with good grass and plenty of water. Hank put two boys on day herd and gave orders to stay all afternoon and night. Dewey fixed up a quick dinner and put on a roast for supper, and kept one eye on his fire and the other on the cattle, expecting any minute to lose the roast and go hot-footing after those spooky cows. But the herd made no trouble on that good grass and water, and next morning Hank told Dewey to cook up plenty of breakfast.

"An' take your time," Hank said. "We got a long drive and no water on it. Let 'em load up on grass and water here, we'll start off easy."

Dewey packed a five-gallon keg of water on Jim Toddy, and saw the advantage of having those tomatoes along before the day was over. They drove along slow and easy, and whenever a boy rode in, Dewey gave him a can of tomatoes to quench his thirst. That night Dewey had enough water left from cooking and making coffee to give every boy a good drink.

"Four boys on guard tonight," Hank said at supper. "Those cows are dry and there ain't much danger of stampeding, the way I figure, but they'll sure make a go at getting up and drifting off, looking for water."

Hank was right as usual. The herd was restless and every now and then a single old cow or steer began moving out, got turned back, and bedded down again. They made an early start and drove to Hebron Creek Ranger Station where Hank rode in to see the ranger and make sure the man would be on tap to count off the herd next morning. The forest rangers, under the Indian Service, charged two dollars a head for any animal over a year old, for grazing through on Indian land.

They strung the herd out next morning and drove through a funnel-shaped double fence. The ranger stood at the narrow end and counted off cattle as they passed, one at a time, by dropping rocks in his jacket pocket. Every time the ranger reached a hundred, he dropped another rock. Hank was right beside him on the fence, double-counting, and Indian Tom, George, and Squab held the herd up as the cattle passed through, just in case there was any argument over the count.

But the ranger and Hank ended with the same tally and Hank signed the tab to send to Cochrane, and they wasted no time driving on seven miles and making camp for the night. During that easy drive Hank came around and grinned half to himself, and said, "Be a nice camp tonight, Dewey."

"Good water," Dewey said.

"Good water!" Hank said solemnly. "Dewey, you never tasted the like."

Good water that night, Dewey found out on the first swallow, was a soda spring. You could inhale a bellyful of that water and belch all over the place; it was just exactly like drugstore soda water. And there were over two hundred acres of seepy land surrounding the spring, with plenty of grass. Dewey cooked up the remains of the roast for supper, made cream gravy and hot biscuits, and the only complaint was how the coffee tasted made out of soda water. It didn't have a real bad taste; it just made a man uncertain how he stood below the belt in regard to holding or losing what he drank.

"By God," Raymond said. "If cows belch, we ain't gettin' much sleep tonight."

Early the following morning Dewey and Squab filled the five-gallon keg with soda water and took off with the pack outfit and remuda. They rode on ahead and Hank caught up at one o'clock and had them make camp on the driest alkali flat Dewey had ever seen. The boys brought the herd up at sundown after creeping along all day, for the cattle were full of water and grass from the soda spring and Hank wanted to keep them that way as long as possible. Two boys came in to eat and change horses, and two rode night guard until nine o'clock.

Then Hank doubled up to four and, while snatching a slug of beef and coffee, kept looking up at the sky and listening, head cocked, to the herd.

"Lookin' for trouble?" Dewey asked.

"Not so much running," Hank said. "Maybe a little moving around, Dewey. We got to hold them close, an' that ain't so good."

And it turned out, that night, as if the cattle were kept too close packed. They stayed restless and nobody got much sleep because Hank didn't like the sound or smell, and had everybody up on guard after midnight. They hit the road at four o'clock, driving slowly, and that was the day Dewey began counting the time left in the month and wondering if they'd make Winslow by the first. Raymond rode in for a bite and coffee, and remarked on how good a bottle of beer would taste, and that got Dewey thinking about beer and maybe a drink, and the day was bad for him. When they cleared the alkali flat he cheered up some, and counted off the miles—twelve long ones—that brought them into Devil's Canyon just before sundown.

That was the damnedest country Dewey ever saw, coming in across flat land and looking down suddenly on a canyon that opened up at their feet. The canyon wasn't deep, only twenty feet or so, but once they dipped down into it and began riding on after Hank, the canyon began veering and circling until Dewey was plumb lost. Hank hit the spot he wanted long after dark and they made camp on the north side beside a little creek that formed a pool of water; and here the boys had to cut the cattle out in bunches of thirty and bring each bunch down for a drink. Then Hank pushed the herd a little way back from the creek, and the boys came in pairs to eat supper.

"How big is this place?" Dewey asked.

"About three sections," Hank said. "It ain't so bad."

"It ain't good," Dewey said. "You figure on any trouble?"

"Could be," Hank said. "I don' like it for holding a herd, Dewey, but we had to use the water."

"What'll you do," Dewey said, "if they bust and run?"

"Let's just figure they won't," Hank said.

About nine o'clock the herd was all bedded down and causing no trouble, and then the luck changed. A thunderstorm came up, the sky went crazy, and the cattle broke and ran. They scattered all over that hell's half acre, and the way they climbed the shallow banks like a bunch of cats, the boys couldn't do a blessed thing during the night about holding or stopping them. No man could chase and corner cattle through those twisty canyon turns and out in the arroyos and ravines. But everybody saddled up and headed right out, and Dewey built up his fire and made ready for trouble.

He cooked plenty of beef and biscuits, and buried the filled Dutch ovens in hot ashes so any boy who got the chance to come in could have hot food ready while he changed horses. Dewey dozed beside the fire, listening to the last sounds of the thunderstorm, and about sunup Hank rode in and got down, just shaking his head.

"Dewey, if you don' mind," Hank said, "you better saddle up and help us get this stuff together again."

"You want me?" Squab asked.

"Think the remuda'll stray on you?" Hank said.

"Little ways," Squab said. "Everybody better help."

"Get down and eat," Dewey said. "There's hot food."

"Later," Hank said. "No time now, Dewey."

So Dewey saddled the old sorrel and took off from where the cattle had run north and east, up and away from the canyon. He picked up the trail of about forty head and followed along, trying to catch up, and during this time ran into the old roan cow.

The roan cow had taken the herd lead right from the start at the main ranch, and now it seemed like the smart old devil was bent on leading every possible head of cattle about five hundred miles into Utah. Dewey spotted her up ahead and took off, and the old roan cow switched her tail and disappeared around a hill. Dewey lost her, kept going around that hill, and couldn't find her at all. He rode on again, and it seemed like every time he rounded another hill, he ran smack into that roan cow.

He finally got her headed back toward camp, picked up a few more cattle, and worked the old sorrel pretty hard, driving the bunch south. He saw Raymond once, way off in the east, and somebody else topped a hill to the west, waved, and disappeared. It took until noon to bring in the twenty head he'd gathered, and then Hank had him stay on herd guard with Squab while the other boys kept up the hunt. That went on all day and night and up to noon of the twentieth, guarding the growing herd, running into camp to cook and feed the boys coming in, going back to the herd, changing horses, sweating under the hot sun and drying off at night in dusty, dirty clothes. And finally, at noon that day, Hank counted up and they were only twenty-three head short.

"The hell with 'em," Hank said wearily. "We cain't spare no more time. They'll get gathered in the fall Mormon roundup, so let's go on."

"I could do with a drink," Driver said.

"An' a bath," Raymond said. "I cain't hardly stand livin' with myself no more."

Dewey still didn't know how far they were from Winslow. He counted up the remaining days before the first of July and thought about Las Vegas and worried over that considerable. When Hank said, "Let's go on," he forgot about his dirty clothes and his beard and the lack of sleep and the lousy water. He was willing, that noon, to drive straight into Winslow without sleep or rest, just to make it on time. He didn't even want to think about missing Las Vegas now; that was something he had to make. If he could hit the show and do some good, and stay sober, it ought to prove something for him. What it was, he couldn't rightly say to himself, but that was how he thought and how he had to go on thinking and living.

Chapter Nine

THEY MOVED OUT of the canyon and drove eight miles northwest on the trail, pitched a dry camp, and headed out early the following morning. Things went along fine until double-damned if the herd didn't break and run again in broad daylight. But the boys were on top of that break and kept the old roan cow pointed up the trail, and nothing was lost except time. That night Hank brought them in to camp beside a lake just twenty-five miles below Winslow. Dewey took one look at the water and said, "Oh, by God!" and tore into his cooking chores.

The lake was formed in some kind of old crater, deep and cool, and fed by springs. Dewey kept smelling that water all the while he cooked, and the boys brought the herd up and spread it out so every cow, calf, and steer had plenty of room to nose down and fill up. There was no danger of stampede and the boys had time to sit down and eat and roll a smoke over coffee for the first time in days. Then Hank looked at Dewey and said, "I guess you all know what I'm plannin'."

Dewey got right up and cut off hunks of the yellow soap. Every boy pulled off his clothes, grabbed a chunk of soap, and took a plunge in the lake. Dewey stripped off his filthy, dusty, torn clothes and walked down into the water, taking it slow, letting it come over his knees and belly and up to his neck, feeling the coolness soak into his body. It was always kind of a shock to undress and notice how white their bodies were from the neck down. Dewey's face had burned and browned deeper through the three months, his body had thinned out at first and then, with the work and plenty of good food, had laid more hard muscle over his stringy shoulders and arms and thighs. He was hard and he knew it now, and he thought of Las Vegas while he scrubbed off from head to foot, and then dived and paddled around a few minutes to wash the soap and dirt away.

"By God, Dewey," Raymond yelled. "Ain't this somethin' like it, huh?"

Raymond was scrubbing and slobbering between his teeth, looking for all the world like a weather-worn head stuck on top a white skeleton. Squab was swimming in deeper water, dark head going up and down as he circled Raymond. All the boys seemed to loosen up and get rid of their old feeling that had lain on them all ever since roundup. Indian Tom was off by himself, but when they crawled out and stood by the fire, letting heat and night wind dry them off, Tom stood close by and stared across the lake and even talked a little with Squab.

"Well," Hank said. "We'll just squat here awhile."

"For whose benefit?" Thornhill asked.

"The cattle," Hank said, wiping his wet face. "You no-counts don' need a bath more'n once a month anyway."

The herd rested easy that night and Hank held them beside the lake all next day and night, letting the cattle get full again. Dewey fretted as time passed but he didn't let Hank see how he felt. They left early on the twenty-third, and just a few miles up the trail began moving into the farming country below Winslow. Hank scouted ahead to pick routes that missed the farms and kept them on decent grass and water. Hank knew every inch of this country, but as he told Dewey, it was building up fast and he couldn't keep track of the new, strange farms. And there were roving bands of cattle the boys had to throw out of the way, so

Hank rented a two-hundred-acre pasture with a strong barbwire fence and they threw the herd in that night on grass and water. Hank skipped the night guard for the first time because it didn't seem likely they'd have trouble with the good fence and the herd on grass and water.

Hank chiseled on the farmer next morning. He'd only rented the pasture for overnight and he signed the tab for Cochrane before the farmer let them turn the herd in. So Hank broke camp late, giving the cattle plenty of time to eat good grass and drink pure water. The farmer came out and gave them a dirty look, but he couldn't do much about it. He stood at the gate and watched the herd move through and up the trail, and Dewey saw him glaring at his nice pasture with the grass all cropped short and the water muddied up.

Hank scouted ahead ten miles that day and made another deal at a farm with a windmill and tank, and open country to the southwest for grazing. They had to put night guard back on, and double up at nine o'clock, but nothing happened and Dewey decided the luck had returned.

They started early on the twenty-fifth and cut out across some open country Hank knew in order to save a few miles. That was a dry day, with cold beef and biscuits, and tomatoes for water, but twelve miles brought them back on the edge of farming country to a good water camp. Hank took no chances and kept everybody on guard that night, and during the next day's drive two boys would ride on ahead and steal a few winks on the hillsides. A man could last just so long without sleep, and they were all pretty well honed down to the breaking point.

They camped on water and had no trouble; and next morning, the twenty-sixth, they moved up within three miles of Winslow and threw the herd into a four-hundred-acre pasture Hank had rented. There was plenty of water and grass, a good camp ground, and time again for a decent supper.

Dewey cooked up everything he could muster, and the boys ate and lay back and slept all night. Nobody did much next day while Hank rode into Winslow and made the stockyard arrangements and sent a wire to Cochrane who had to come up from Holbrook. Hank rode back at suppertime and sat beside the fire and grinned through his dust and sweat and long-gone feeling of bone-weariness they were all packing heavy on their heads.

"We'll move 'em tomorrow," Hank said. "Cochrane's comin' up from Holbrook."

"Got the cars?" George Spradley asked.

"Cochrane'll get 'em," Hank said. "Won't have no delay there."

Dewey remembered all his worries over hitting Winslow by the first. He felt a little foolish and finally he said, "I guess we did make it by the first."

Hank laughed and poured out coffee. "You were gettin' pretty damned worried, Dewey."

"I sure was," Dewey said, " 'specially back in that canyon country."

"Well," Hank said soberly. "So was I."

Next morning, the twenty-eighth of June, they moved the herd into the Winslow stockyards on the south side of town. It took all day to ease the cattle up close and then move little bunches of thirty into empty pens. It took fast work to cut off the old roan cow once she really smelled town and saw those pens. A few steers, including the old stag, tried to break and make a final run for the Black Brush and Cherry Creek, but the boys swung wide and doubled up on those singles and didn't lose a head. They went back to the pasture camp that night and Dewey cooked supper and used his last two ragged dishrags to clean up, and stretched out, dead to the world, then sleeping fitfully because there was no sound floating in from the herd that wasn't in the pasture.

Dewey got up at five o'clock and cooked a big breakfast, and the boys took their time eating. Hank drank an extra cup of coffee and gave out his orders for the day.

"Dewey, you and Squab pack up everything. We'll pick it up on the way back. We'll be cutting out and loading all day, so I reckon we should eat in town this noon."

"By God, yes," Raymond said. "An' I don't mean no offense to your cooking, Dewey."

"I'm tired of it myself," Dewey said. "What I want is milk and butter and lettuce."

"Me, too," Hank said. "We'll go in now, Dewey, an' you come along when you get packed up."

Dewey watched them saddle and ride for town, and then he looked at the camp and the burros. He washed the dishes and began packing everything away, and Squab worked alongside, not saying much. Dewey looked at old Benstega and then, one by one, at Jim Toddy and Tom and Jerry. He thought of all the miles they'd covered, and looked at those little hoofs, not much bigger than a silver dollar, and wondered at how they stood up, unshod, over the sand and gravel and rock. True, burros were never punished like a cow horse over rock, but it was still plenty tough. So it seemed like nature just took a hand and made the burro a little different. Their hoof bone was no bigger than a horse's, but the inside frog was a lot higher up and the hoofs kept grown down all the time to protect that frog. Still they had no easy life.

Then everything was packed and Squab went out to saddle his black and the old sorrel. Dewey picked up the pan of cold beef and biscuits he'd laid aside, and went over to the pasture fence. He said, "All right, come and get it the last time, you ornery devils," and then he remembered that day in Black Brush country. He'd killed a little mountain rattler, picked up the snake for a close look, and gone back to camp and washed his hands good before cooking dinner. Then he'd taken a bunch of biscuits out to the burros, but not a one would come even close. He had to lay the biscuits down and walk away, and even then old Benstega smelled everything careful before they ate.

"Come on," Dewey said. "No snakes today."

They moved a couple of steps, sniffed at the beef and biscuits, and then stopped and looked at him. He wanted to think they did look. For a minute, holding the pan, he watched them and thought of his older brother, Van, who was good in everything but not outstanding in anything. Van would go out and make a fine ride on any bronc, but never a spectacular ride. And come to think of it, the burros were a good deal like his brother. They did everything good, but nothing spectacular. Some humans and animals were that way. They did their best, and it was mighty good, and nobody seemed to care.

Dewey put the pan down inside the fence and said gently, "So long, you old sonsabitches," and walked to his horse.

CHAPTER TEN

IN THE STOCKYARDS the boys were cutting out steers and driving them into certain pens, then dry cows into other pens, cows with calves into others. Dewey unsaddled the old sorrel, turned it into the horse corral, and carried his gear over into the shade of the tool house at the corner of the pens. He went forward to help, but Hank waved him off and called, "Take it easy. We'll all eat dinner together."

"I can help out," Dewey said.

"No need," Hank said. "Well, go up to the depot and see if the cars are comin' on time. They're due at noon."

Dewey watched the boys a minute and then walked down the platform to the depot office and found that the cars were all ordered and coming right on time. He took that news to Hank and sat in the shade of the tool house and smoked until the boys woke him from a doze and damned near tore his shirt off, heading uptown to the restaurant. None of them had changed clothes or shaved, and they were about the roughest looking bunch of boys that ever hit a town. And the best.

"Now you act like gentlemen," Hank said. "You ain't been in a house for some time."

"I'm housebroke," Raymond said.

"Sure," Thornhill chuckled. "I'll keep my boots off the table."

They crowded into the restaurant and took over the big table in the rear. They hung their dusty hats on the wall hooks, rolled up smokes, and looked down at their dirty hands on that white tablecloth. Raymond coughed and reached for the menu, and the little red-haired waitress came running up and smiled and said, "What'll you have, boys?" and Dewey knew they all wanted butter and milk and green stuff after the meat diet of a solid ninety days.

"Don't hurry us," Hank smiled. "We'll figure something out."

The little girl said, "All right," and began pouring water and passing out patties of butter. Raymond reared back in his chair, stared at those little patties, and pointed one big, dirty hand at the girl.

"Hell," Raymond said. "Have you got a capsule we kin take them in?"

The little girl didn't know quite what to make of that, so Dewey spoke up, "Sister, bring us out a good, big strong pound of butter, and lettuce and tomatoes in tubfuls. Then just most anything else you got to eat, it don' make no difference. About the best thing you can do in the way of drinks is bring us a gallon of buttermilk if you got it, and if you ain't, well, bring us two gallons of sweet milk."

"An' cold," Thornhill said. "Real cold, miss."

"You got any watermelon?" Driver Gobet asked.

The little girl said, "I'll see if there's one left."

"Bring it," Driver said. "With a butcher knife."

"Hold on," George Spradley said. "I want a big plate of onions, you got any of them little spring onions?"

"I think so," the little girl said. "I know we've got Bermudas."

"Bring them too," George said.

"Yes, sir," the little girl said, and looked at Dewey as if she didn't think anybody could eat so much. Then she headed for the kitchen before somebody got another idea. When the swinging door closed behind her, Hank lit his cigaret and grinned.

"Watermelon and onions and buttermilk—be damned if you don' all sound like a pregnant woman."

When they finished the last glass of buttermilk and slice of watermelon, they got up slowly and slapped their dusty hats and moved up front toward the cash register. Hank said, "This is on the ranch," and signed the tab for Cochrane. As they started down the street Hank took Dewey's arm and let the other boys draw ahead when they reached the depot. Then Hank gave Dewey a sealed brown railroad envelope. "Twenty-ninth today," Hank said. "Be a good idea if you caught that four o'clock train going east."

"Sure," Dewey said. "If you don' need anything more, Hank."

"Not a thing," Hank said. "That's your pay. Cochrane got in this mornin' and I told him you was in a hurry and he got the cash."

"Thanks," Dewey said. "Many thanks, Hank."

"Less the Holbrook tab," Hank said. "It left you three hundred and fifty."

"I didn't break many broncs for you," Dewey said. "Only eight in all that time."

"That's plenty," Hank said. "You earned it, Dewey. Now we better load up them cattle, and you go buy your ticket."

They walked along down the hot road and Dewey turned into the depot while Hank went on to the pens. Dewey bought his ticket to Las Vegas and walked down to help with the loading if need be, and to say good-by. He was always shy about saying good-by, and he knew the boys felt the same way. He stood beside the end chute and watched the boys push and prod the cattle up the alley and through the chute into the cars. Cochrane came along then, waved at Dewey, and stopped in the alley to talk with somebody from another outfit. Raymond climbed over the chute after filling another car and stood beside Dewey, rolling a smoke while the railroad men moved the car and slid an empty alongside the chute gate. Dewey saw the three boys on the alley fence and said, "What outfit is that, Raymond?"

"OG Rails," Raymond said. "That's a Babbitt Brothers outfit—they got twelve hundred head on the west side waiting for cars. Hey, will you look!"

"At what?" Dewey said.

"Looky down there," Raymond said softly. "See that little old hare-lipped boy coming along toward Cochrane."

"Sure," Dewey said. "What about him?"

"He worked for us last year," Raymond said. "An' when pay time come, he claimed Cochrane shorted him eight dollars. Let's mosey down that way."

Dewey followed Raymond down the alley where Cochrane was talking to the man—probably the OG cowboss—and Raymond went right on past Cochrane, whistling loudly, and turned the corner. The OG cowboss said something and went off toward the depot, fumbling with a sheaf of papers that looked like car orders. Then Cochrane saw Dewey and said, "Hear you're leaving today," and the little harelipped boy came up behind Cochrane and tapped him on the arm. Cochrane turned around and the little boy said, "Don't suppose you remember shorten my check last year?"

"I'm in a hurry," Cochrane said. "We'll talk it over after I get my cattle loaded."

"Oh, we will," the little boy said, talking funny through his twisted harelip. "If you was as low in principal as you are in stature, Cochrane, you could sure walk under a snake's belly with a plugged hat on."

"Oh, go to hell," Cochrane said.

Then the little boy hauled off and hit Cochrane, and Cochrane had no choice. He had to fight back. The little boy let out a war whoop and started swinging punches, jumping up and down like a banty rooster, landing those blows and getting his shoulders into them.

Cochrane was more surprised than hurt. He sort of leaned back and flexed both arms and got down to business, and the little boy seemed to grow six inches and stop swinging wild and really bore in.

Dewey leaned against the alley fence and watched the fight. He thought of roundup and the way that unfriendly feeling was directed toward the Flying A, and now he knew what Hank meant by saying the Flying A's size was just part of it. Cochrane was the other part. If he'd shortchange a boy eight dollars and try to wiggle out of it, how many other times had he tossed his weight around the Mormon country and piled up enemies for the Flying A. Quite a few, Dewey guessed now, and the sad part was, those little outfits couldn't help taking it out on Hank and the boys. Dewey never made a move then. He watched the little boy whip Cochrane to a fare-thee-well, and he watched the three big OG punchers on the fence across the alley and caught a faint, understanding grin from one.

When the little boy had Cochrane staggering and bleeding at the nose, he whipped in a couple of final punches and climbed right up on the fence between those big OG boys and grinned down at Cochrane like a cat full of cream.

Cochrane started down the alley and Dewey followed along. When they reached the corner and Cochrane's jaws were halfway in working order, he turned on Dewey and said thickly, "Well, Goddam you! Why didn't you get in there and help me?"

Dewey had his pay in his pocket, his ticket in his shirt. He'd made good friends and they'd remember him well, but he had to say his mind.

"I hired out to cook and ride broncs," Dewey said. "My gun ain't been out of the bedroll since I hired on with the Flying A, and I think I gave value received. What do I want to get mixed up in this for, Cochrane? Maybe you did short that little boy some money. You want to go back and have me ask him?"

Cochrane looked at Dewey a moment and then walked out of the pens, wiping his bloody nose. Dewey watched him and wondered how a man could have good qualities, and then show up with a lot of the small, no-good habits that spoiled it all. Like the one bad apple in the barrel. Dewey turned down the alley and stood in the shade and watched the cattle go up the chutes into the cars, and heard the now-familiar voices of the boys calling back and forth in the dust-clogged alleys and pens. Time passed and he thought ahead, to Las Vegas, tomorrow morning, and then it was four and he had to go.

Dewey picked up his gear and faced the pens. He saw the boys coming and he waited until they all stood facing him. Hank shook hands first and said, "Good luck, Dewey, an' if you ever want a job, you know where to come."

"Thanks," Dewey answered. "I'll sure remember, Hank."

Then the others pushed their hands forward and Dewey Jones shook them all, Thornhill and Spradley and Driver and Raymond and finally Indian Tom. He said, "Good luck to you all," and Jim Thornhill smiled.

"Get that first money, Dewey. We'll sure be watching the papers."

Then Hank said, "Better catch the train. Dewey, you want a drink?"

"No," Dewey Jones said. "I'll buy, Hank, next time we get together."

He looked at them all, and then he turned and started across the open, dusty ground toward the depot. He heard them shuffle their boots and break away, go back to finish the job and saddle up and head across the old, old country for home. He got nearly to the depot and heard the whistle of the east-bound train just coming in, and saw the boy at the corner in the shadow of the eave. He walked straight over there and took Squab's hand and said, "Good luck, wrangler."

"Good luck, Dewey," Squab said. "Maybe sometime we cook and ride again."

"Some time," Dewey Jones said. "So long, Squab."

"So long, Dewey."

He watched the Indian boy walk toward the pens in that funny little pigeon-toed stride, and then the east-bound passenger stopped. Dewey Jones swung up the iron steps past the conductor and went into the smoking car. He took a seat on the depot side and rolled a cigaret and watched the depot slide past, then the edge of town, and wondered if he'd ever come this way again. He knew better, inside, because he was no different from so many of his kind. They came awhile and worked, and went away, and never said good-by.

PART TWO:

RODEO

CHAPTER ONE

"PAY NO MIND to the bunting, boy, look to the broncs!"

He remembered that saying when the taxi driver said, "Where to?" and he got into the Model T that July first morning. He saw the sleepy cowtown transformed by bunting and decorations and soft drink stands, and he felt the sharp excitement building in his own chest.

"The grounds," Dewey Jones said. "You got a morning paper?"

"Daily Optic, pard."

He sat back and read all about it, how the Eleventh Annual Cowboys' Reunion would offer premier entertainment this year, with McCarty's string of bucking horses the main attraction. Well, he was sober and nail-hard, not even stopping at the hotel for a drink, heading straight for the rodeo grounds to look over that McCarty string. Down through town, passing the carnival outfit, across the wide bowl-shaped valley, its grass dotted with horses and cow wagon camps of folks in to watch the show; and the first thing he saw, telling the taxi driver to wait, was a cow pony race on the straightaway track.

They ran two hundred yards from a lariat rope line, edging their horses up head-to-head alongside the rope, wheeling downtrack and racing for the judges when somebody fired a gun. There was plenty of interest in those pickup races but little money bet, for this was only tune-up time for tomorrow. Dewey Jones walked on, jingling the small change in his pocket, getting the feel of it again, passing the grandstand and coming to the stockpens south of the race track, taking his look at the bulldogging steers and liking what he saw.

They were Texas coasters weighing around six hundred, some whiteface mixed with longhorn, averaged out carefully for weight and horns. That helped him because the days of hooliganning were over, riding hard to hit a big steer between the horns and get him down fast. Today's rules made you stop the steer, then twist him down, and if you accidentally floored him getting off on him, you had to let up on all four feet and twist from there. Dewey Jones couldn't handle a heavy steer unless he hooligan'd; he had more chance with these lightweight coasters.

He went along to the bronc pen, climbed the boot-worn boards, and looked down on the McCarty string: Invalid, Broken Box, Deer Trail, Black Thunder, who weighed 1470 with a halter on, King Tut, Overall Bill, Pretty Dick, Schoolgirl, Done Gone. He knew them all, their colors and bumps and scars and ears and faded brands. This was McCarty's first string, the tops, twenty of the best bucking horses in the world. Any one of them was liable to buck off any rider if he didn't set flat and have luck in his pants. Dewey Jones studied those horses, old friends he'd followed on the circuit for five years. Having the McCarty first string on deck was equal to an ace in the hole.

He was in A-1 condition and he knew just what he could and could not do on those horses. Not many of the bronc riders had ridden those horses or knew much about them. They were accustomed to riding New Mexican horses nowhere in the McCarty string class. Then too, this was a single rein contest, one hackamore rein had to come up on the side of the horse's neck habitually used by a man. Until last summer everybody had used two reins, but all spring he'd practiced single rein on the Flying A, getting ready for this and other shows. He looked at the broncs, twice at old Done Gone, and turned back toward the taxi.

Plenty of time for the broncs tomorrow, after he drew his first day horse from the hat and knew what to expect.

The driver took him through Old Town into New Town, where rodeo headquarters were set up in the parlor room of the Meadows Hotel. Up and down the street the old cow horses stood ground over dropped reins; on all sides Dewey Jones saw the growing crowd, smelled the popcorn and hamburger and bootleg whisky, felt the tension that would knot tighter, every hour, once the first rider booted a stirrup. The street was a ragbag of bright patches, all the dudes decked out in gaudy shirts and pants and boots. Working cowboys didn't dress like the dudes. They wore a new pair of Levis, a Levi jacket, leather gloves in a hip pocket; if they had the cash they bought a new silk or broadcloth shirt, had their old hat cleaned or bought a new Five X Stetson. Their belts were wide leather and it was just coming in fashion to have a big buckle engraved with a bucking horse or a man flanking a calf.

Las Vegas was going all out for this rodeo. Everybody from bankers to soda jerks were sporting shiny custom-made boots, a few good Stetsons, and a lot of those dollar-ninety-eight wool hats you could tell a block off. Some of them passing the hotel were a sight to behold, their hats ace-deuced on one side of their heads, big red bandannas around their white-skinned necks, some wearing hand-me-down spurs—and there was so much difference in hand-me-down store-bought spurs and really good shop-made. Shop-made spurs were cut from battleship steel with the maker's name proudly stamped on the inside. Kelly Spur Company of Pauls Valley, Oklahoma; Crockett Bit and Spur Company of Kansas City. Two of the best and proud of their brands. Most of the boys had begun to have initials raised or inlaid on the outside of their spurs, gold or silver work, and those sets ran high as sixty dollars. Some spurs were beginning to sport inside and outside buttons to kept the spurs from flying up the leg like a window curtain when a man reached forward to make his grab. Dewey Jones thought how you faked with spurs in a contest, the old trick called "locked rowels." If you locked your rowels and made one point longer than the others, you could spur a bronc coming in and the rowels would stick. A small rowel was not apt to roll as much and, whenever you reached up and hit a horse with those locked rowels, and hit him coming down with your heels turned out, your rowels stuck and you could rake all the way through. But the judges would ride up to the chutes and flip your spur rowels to see if they turned free and clear, and if you got caught it was marked against you before your ride began.

Thinking of the broncs and the spurs, of the dudes and their clothes, Dewey Jones was jostled a dozen times entering the hotel. Dudes and cowmen and range women, drunks and kids and Indians, the ladies all dressed up fit to kill. The range women were wearing their divided leather skirts made of light whang leather, those big-legged and seated skirts, some natural brown color, some white buckskin. The range women had that look of belonging no dude gal could ever imitate with trick costumes. The range women brought dresses and boots for the dances, but the dude women had to wear shoes at night because they couldn't dance in boots. No matter what they wore, he thought, he could always tell the dudes, tell his own kind from townsmen.

He stepped aside for a long-nosed girl in fancy red shirt and two-toned boots, and swung inside the lobby toward headquarters. Faces turned, clean-shaven and sun-wrinkled; the shouts reached him from old friends. He began to feel it strong then, all the past years, the sum total of spent time, gone forever but still bright in memory. He shook hands and spoke with men he hadn't seen in months, some in years; Jack Clark was there, and Fightin' Bill Baker, Charley Green from Wagon Mound, O. T. Fore from Tucumcari, presently riding a rough string for the Bell outfit. The show clown, Pecos Coker, slapped his back and joshed him about his flat belly and offered a bottle; and up front, at the secretary's desk, he recognized the sloped shoulders and sandy red hair of Dick Harrell, the Indian from Oklahoma. Walt Baylor was taking Dick's money and signing Dick for roping and the wild horse race.

"You old gut-stripper," Dewey Jones said. "Wastin' your money again." Dick Harrell whirled, grinned broadly, and pumped Dewey's hand in a bear grip. "Dewey, where the hell you been?"

"Flying A," he said, and then thought of bulldogging and the wild horse race. "Will you haze for me?" he said. "Loan me a horse?"

"Sure," Dick said, "if you'll team me in the wild horse race."

"I'll saddle and ride," Dewey Jones said, "if you'll rope and ear."

"A deal," Dick Harrell said. "Say—"

"Holding up the line," Walt Baylor said. "Howdy, Dewey. Long time no see."

Dewey Jones pulled his roll from his shirt pocket and paid his entry fees. Twenty-five dollars for saddle bronc riding, twenty for bulldogging, ten dollars as Dick's partner in the wild horse race. He signed the blanks and drew his number—seven—which was his throughout the rodeo in all events.

Paying the money earned from those wild, rough weeks in the Salt River country, earned so hard and pushed across the desk so easy. When he turned away Dick Harrell had gone off somewhere, so he waved at more new faces and registered at the lobby desk for the last free room in the house.

He walked to the depot, got his gear sack and bedroll, and carried them back to his room; and threw the bedroll into the corner with a grin. For a few nights he'd sleep on clean sheets, with a toilet, bath, and plenty of hot water. He sat on the bed and looked down at the faded rose design in the flat-grained carpet. He was alone in the room now, but somebody would come along tomorrow and make him double up. During rodeo a man shared his room with friends down to the last six feet of floor space. He unsacked his saddle, looked over his latigo straps and cinches for breaks, examined his spur leather, flipped out his bucking rein, gave his old pair of bronc riding boots an extra sharp inspection. You used a horseshoe rasp on the vamp of bucking boots, roughed up that vamp plenty, for it might keep you from losing a stirrup. He checked everything, washed, and went back downstairs into the crowd. Looking for Dick Harrell, he saw old Blatherwick in the far corner and pushed that way to order a new pair of boots.

Blatherwick was a big Dutchman from Dalhart, a blunt and honest old man, one of the best bootmakers in the country, his only trouble being he hardly ever took new customers. When you gave him your first order, that size went into his file, and all you needed do thereafter was send your name and current address and what kind of boot you wanted—French calf, kangaroo, or common heavy calf for range work. Blatherwick had his table set up with a display of boots and different types of stitching and spur pieces. He made only one type heel, but you could order that in different heights, undershot or straight down. Undershot was the bronc rider's heel because it was wider and clamped down tighter on a stirrup. Blatherwick sat behind his table, gruff and scowling, not soliciting any orders, up here mostly to see old friends and watch the show. Dewey Jones leaned over the boot-covered table, saw the thick mustache quiver in recognition, and greeted old Blatherwick the way he liked it best.

"You old horse thief," Dewey Jones said. "You stole enough cattle for hides to make me a pair of boots?"

"Yah," Blatherwick said. "What you want, how you been?"

"Fine," he said. "Working hard."

"Yah, and that's a lie."

He had the money, he was sober, and he hadn't treated himself in a long time, so he fingered one of the best boot models and poked a thumb at the stitching. "Like this, light French calf, tan foot, black top, five rows of stitching, inch and a half heel, an' make that heel pretty well undershot. Now what'll it cost me this time around, you thieving Dutchman?"

"Thirty-five and a half," Blatherwick said. "No busted toes, no change in size?"

"Not yet," he said, and passed a ten-dollar bill, the usual down payment. "Don't know where I'll be. I'll drop you a letter in a couple of weeks and give you an address."

"Yah," Blatherwick said, writing everything down. "Good luck, Dewey. Ride good."

Others were waiting so he shook hands and crossed the lobby and found Dick Harrell waiting at the inside restaurant door. The noon rush was finished so they went in and had coffee, and just sitting down brought Dewey Jones all the way back to the feeling of the days ahead. Restaurants were the same everywhere during rodeo days. During mealtimes a line of two hundred or more waited at the side door off the street. When a table emptied, the doorman let in the same number to grab those seats at counter, tables, or booths. You ate first and paid seventy-five cents at the cash register and went out through the lobby door. The bill of fare never changed. Supper was always roast beef, pork, country fried steak in cream gravy, stewed chicken with dumplings. Back in the kitchen the cook was setting up plates on the ledge fast as he could work. The hashers sung out the bill of fare, took your order, ran to the ledge and grabbed the proper plates and ran back. Two people couldn't have a four-chair table; the next two inside just sat right down. Breakfast line was run identical—ham and eggs, bacon, hot biscuits, hot cakes, toast, one girl walking around steady with a pitcher of coffee in each hand. Six bits for breakfast, all you could eat, and the hotel still made good money. A half-gallon pitcher of syrup on every table, a big bowl of sugar, salt and pepper shakers big as cups, the tables covered with white or red-checkered oilcloth, the lunch counter boards smoothed by a million shirt sleeves. They boiled the coffee on the kitchen stove in fifteen-gallon kettles, coaled that old range like a locomotive firebox. The cook stripped to his undershirt, wrapped a white towel around his neck to wipe sweat, and never sat down once the rush began. His meat was already cut, he just reached around with his hands and slapped meat on the plates, added vegetables and potatoes and gravy. For breakfast he was back there two-hand cooking bacon and ham and eggs, watching a griddle of hot cakes, toasting bread on every open piece of stovetop. Rodeo time was fast-feeding time, and fast-talking time too, for you had to shout in those restaurants as the talk filled the room, every word having something to do with the show.

Con Jackson stopped by the table, and Big Jim Shoemaker. Cliff Neafus slapped Dewey's back and then he felt a ham-sized hand and looked up into Elmo Bray's face. Bray was brand inspector at Antonito on the Colorado-New Mexico line and, long ago, one of the men Dewey rode against in 1915 in his first professional show in Oklahoma. Bray was tough. He stood six-two, he was a curly-headed, good-looking man who always wore a cold grin that turned into a rough frown any time he got ruffled the wrong way. Bray was the only brand inspector Dewey ever knew who couldn't be bought; he knew that, for he saw it tried, and the tryer got slapped so hard it jarred his kinfolk in Utah. Bray took a chair and pretty soon they were talking about that forgotten Oklahoma contest and the old Clay McGonigal horse that bucked Dewey down in the semifinals, arguing that old horse's weight and how much power he put to a man on the curves he shot. "That old horse," Elmo Bray chuckled. "Weighed 1250, an' you on him like a toad-frog on top a mushroom." Bray rose then, smiled coldly, and said, "I'm judging here, you know," and walked away.

"Your old pard," Dick Harrell said, "but just to remind you."

He hadn't known Bray was one of the judges. Not that talking together mattered; it was just Bray's manner of reminding him that friendship ceased in the arena. He finished his sixth cup of coffee and they stepped back into the lobby and there stood Sam Beday, grinning wide, grabbing for his hand. Sam was a little fellow with no prat hardly at all. Sam could wear a pair of Levis and the hip pockets almost whipped together, but a salty hand who went all out.

"Let's eat supper together," Sam said, and in the same breath looked past Dewey at the desk. "By god, there's the wop."

About time, Dewey Jones thought, turning around. Mike Cunico plowed toward them, brown and squat and soft-eyed, ready for the show and, if he hadn't changed, to start giving Dewey another lecture on finding that steady job.

Mike talked fast, his words spilled together, he left the r's off most of those r words, so that in the lobby where noise was louder than a brass band, they were shouting and losing half the talk, not caring by now, just feeling loose and easy as ashes. Sam Beday poked Dewey in the ribs and said, "Well, boy. Here she comes!"

He knew before he turned. Neal Smith and his sister Babe, the trick riders under contract for this show. He took his time shaking Neal's hand before he faced the slender girl. She was so dark she might have Indian in her high cheek bones and big full mouth and glossy black hair. Her Stetson throat latch hung loose under her chin, not for show like the dude women but part of her job, for the first thing she did on trick runs was kick her hat back and let the latch hold it billowing out behind. She was a handsome girl, all wire and muscle, and by now she must be at least twenty-four years old. She grew up on her father's ranch near the Arizona border with three wild brothers; and when her folks sent her off to college she lasted two months, cussed out a teacher, and came home. She began playing rodeos with Neal about that time, she had a knack for trick riding, and now she was stuck with the life worse than Dewey Jones. He had met her at Deming in November of 1918— she was around sixteen then—and the years marched by and they'd been together all over: Cheyenne, Pendleton, Monte Vista, Fort Worth, Amarillo, even the old settlers reunion on the XIT at Dalhart. A wild life for a single girl but she was that kind, wild as the range, wearing no man's collar, earning her own way and doing as she pleased. They had drunk together, danced together, and she was remembering the last time six months ago when it turned more serious than either intended. Thinking of that night Dewey Jones tried to keep things free and easy.

"Babe," he said, "you just can't get away from saddle leather and horse sweat, eh?"

"Who wants to?" she said. "Where you been, Dewey?"

"Flying A," he said. "Impersonatin' an honest man."

"You!" Babe said. "Are you getting religion?" She took his arms and swung him around into window light and looked square at him while the others laughed and moved off a few feet. "By god, I can see one big change. You never been on a show this long before that you weren't drunk and black-eyed."

"Aim to win," Dewey said, and edged over closer to her brother. "You got many contracts lined up, Neal? You oughta teach Babe the rope juggling, too."

"Hard enough learning her trick riding," Neal said. "Seems like she's most interested in what goes on after the show."

"And the hell with you!" Babe Smith said curtly. "Dewey, you want a quick one?"

"No, Babe," he said.

"Let's eat," Sam Beday said. "If you people want to go into life histories, let's do it while I eat."

"Dewey," Babe said again, softer this time. "You want that drink?"

He shook his head and saw the puzzlement rise in her face. She was remembering the last time when they emptied two bottles and walked a forgotten street arm in arm, singing at the sunrise. "I've got a fancy outfit for the dance," she said. "I better go up and change. An' I want to be down here when the draw starts. Dewey, you coming to the dance?"

"I might look in," he said cautiously.

"Hell's fire," she said. "What you going to do if you don't dance and stay sober to boot?"

"Make a million dollars," Dewey said. "Sam, let's eat."

He pushed Mike and Sam into the restaurant, gulped down his food, and trailed back to the lobby for first day drawing. They lined up outside the headquarters' room door and the talk petered off as Baylor, inside, dropped the names into the hat. A young kid was in front of Dewey, nervous and worried, sweating through his blue silk shirt. Dewey Jones, thinking of those McCarty broncs, turned to Mike Cunico and said, "Sure hope I don't draw that Overall Bill."

"He's a good horse," Mike said.

"Too good," Dewey said. "If the good Lord'll keep his arm around my neck and draw me another horse, I got a chance."

The green kid was just reaching into the hat. He drew his slip and said, "Overall Bill," and touched Dewey's arm as he stepped aside. "Pard, what's wrong with this Overall Bill?"

The kid's face was wrinkled up like a prune with sudden worry, the look of any boy trying his first show. Dewey could sluff off what he knew, but that wouldn't help this kid, so he talked straight out, a mixture of truth and some of the old Nick that made a man take dead aim on green kids.

"Lemme tell you," Dewey said. "I've followed this string of horses five years and that Overall Bill has got my goat. He'll buck you off and tromp on you, and it don't take more'n two jumps to get the job done either. Tell your ma good-by before you top old Billy because there's no time after he leaves the chute. Chances are you'll go up and comb Little Eva's hair."

The kid turned pale around the ears and walked off fast. Baylor said, "All right, Dewey," and he reached into the hat and drew the horse he had known long ago as Cockleburr Dun. That was when the bronc started from Tucumcari County, but he made such a reputation at Fort Worth and thereafter, he bucked off so many good riders, they took the

country name away and called him "Done Gone." If Done Gone went
into those head spins tomorrow, as was his custom, there'd be one Jones
in the dust. Stepping aside to let Mike draw, he spoke his thoughts
aloud, "If I can get by on him for a qualified ride, it'll be more than
I expect." He drew number six bulldogging steer from the other hat
and led Mike from the room. Mike had drawn Pretty Dick, and Mike
wasn't singing carols either. Drawing never changed; when you dipped
into the hat you always felt like a green kid.

"Goin' to the dance?" Mike asked.

"You go on," he said. "I'll just set around."

"And stay sober?"

"Aim to," he said.

"Do it," Mike said, "an' you got a chance."

He'd do it. He knew that dance too well and what happened when
a man went in there with the best intentions. You paid a dollar at the
door and kept your hat on if you wanted it later. If you saw a woman you
wanted to dance with, introductions were out of order, it being impolite
for any woman to turn you down unless you were drunk. Everybody wore
their Sunday best and many boys had revolvers loaded with blanks. The
smell of gunpowder got pretty thick when they tried to bring back the
feel of the old days. There was no such thing as disturbing the peace on
rodeo dance nights because there wasn't any peace. When a fight started
folks just formed a circle and after the boys finished the battle the dance
went on. The bootleggers were thick as flies, and the women were always
too damn eager. No, he wasn't going tonight. This was the first time he'd
ever been in perfect condition, absolutely sober, not sparring for a fight
and getting licked. He said, "You go on, Mike," and crossed the lobby
to the stairs. A dozen people called hello and he answered; funny how
many he knew, how the faces and names piled up over the years. He went
upstairs and sat on the bed, happy he was alone tonight. He needed that
good sleep, he felt clean inside, he had a chance tomorrow.

Chapter Two

HABIT WOKE HIM at six o'clock. He stayed in bed until seven but he couldn't sleep later to save his soul after rising so early on the Salt River job. Finally he shaved, put on his clean blue shirt and best pair of faded Levis, went downstairs and ate six bits' worth of ham and eggs. A noisy bunch was sitting behind him but he didn't need to turn around to tag them. He could hear them eating toast; dudes and tourists always ordered toast. He was nervous over coffee, thinking of the day ahead, and his legs trembled going back upstairs to get his gear. When he came down one of Dick Harrell's boys had brought in a horse for him to ride in the parade and later in bulldogging, a nice roan with black mane and tail, all horse and well reined. Just saddling up and swinging aboard made him feel ready for anything.

"Let's go out," he said. "Make a few runs before the parade."

They rode from town down the dusty road, passing the carnival outfit that brought a grin to his face. He knew that show's roll-downs, pick-out joints, and three-shell games; all those games of chance where nobody had a chance. And the soft drink stand that sold bevo near beer, bevo keg on the counter, another keg on the ground. When the sucker pushed his nickel across the board, the owner whispered, "Want a drink of sure 'nuff beer?" and if the sucker said, "You bet," the owner ducked down, filled a small glass, set it up and said, "Hurry now, get it down!"

and while the sucker sloshed it down the hatch, looked around afraid-like for pro agents. The owner charged two bits a glass for that sure 'nuff beer, but it was the same thing, just bevo with a little malt added. Dewey thought of old "Bevo" Brown and smiled all the way to the grounds.

They got behind the starting gate at the bulldogging chute and made a few practice runs down the track before the grandstand. Other doggers were working out, ropers were putting their horses into the chutes and scoring them out, swinging a few loops at imaginary calves, using the leisure time before the big parade started from St. Anthony's Sanatorium on Friedman Avenue.

Fightin' Bill Baker and Jay Miller rode over from the pens and got down to talk. Jay was in charge of the McCarty string, the short-est-legged bronc rider in the business next to Booger Red Rogers. They shook hands all around and, as was Fightin' Bill Baker's custom, Bill said, "Dewey, I drew Broken Box. Think I can ride him or whadaya think?" Bill always talked that way, even in fighting he'd say, "I think so-and-so needs a whipping, do you think I can whip him or whadaya think?" Bill was hard to take after in anything, bronc riding, bulldog-ging, fist and skull fighting. Bill began telling one of his crazy adven-tures in the Osage country just as Mike Cunico rode up; and standing beside the bulldogging chute, smelling the dust and the horses and their own sweat, Dewey Jones was in his world with his kind of men. He understood them all but he knew Mike best, and when the others headed for town he squatted against the chute boards and made talk.

"You know about them McCarty halters?" he asked.

"No."

"Then listen," Dewey said.

All the McCarty bucking horses had their halters put up high on the nose so the halter band rode high and could ruin a rider who missed that little trick. If a man went out to make a ride and held the bucking rein real tight and didn't give the bronc plenty of head, he was a dead stinking fish because the bronc would take that first jump and pull him right down the side of the neck before he let loose. The man who knew that McCarty tight halter business came out giving the bronc plenty of head and dealt himself a better chance on the ride. Dewey warned Mike of this and then, because Mike had drawn Pretty Dick, told all he knew about that old horse.

Dick already had a reputation when he was shipped to London for that Wimberly Park show with the Tex Austin outfit. Dick was drawn eleven times, bucked five men flat off on the ground, and bucked six into day money. If you gave Dick plenty of head and left the chute with him, not one split second behind him, spurred in the neck first jump, you could just go right on through because, once you got started in Dick's rhythm, you couldn't quit until the gun. But woe to the rider who left a split second behind Dick at the chute and failed to give him enough head; for the first jump out Dick would throw his head to the right and, if you were riding with rein up the left side as usual, Dick would pull you right down over his left fore shoulder.

"Don't forget now," Dewey said. "An' you'll make a ride."

"Jay know all this?"

"Sure," he said. "Jay's played nursemaid to this string a couple of years. I figure him hard to beat just for that reason."

"Who else?" Mike asked.

"Baker," he said. "And you, you wop. Come on, time for parade."

They rode into town and took their places in the starting line, up front ahead of the bands and floats, behind the flags and the officials. The parade marshall repeated the route as late arrivals rode in, along Sixth Street and circling the downtown loop, moving thence to the plaza, rounding the placita and dispersing at Fountain Square where the photographer would take a panoramic shot of floats and riders. Order of the day was have your rope out, rope the pretty girls along the way, shoot off your gun and holler loud. Dewey Jones glanced at the floats, big boats and white paper hens, a log cabin and deer head, a bottle of milk, a truckload of Hereford yearlings, floats of all colors and sizes. He saw the bands and lady riders, the important gentlemen from town and the state capital, everybody wearing fancy clothes and sporting six-shooters long as hoe handles, all of them rubbing off a little second-hand glory from the real contestants. He ought to be dressed up, he knew, but he was here to make money, not spend it, and he'd ridden in too many parades to worry about his looks. When the final signal came he reined into line as the bands blared out the march music, and they were off, heading into the biggest crowd he'd ever seen in Las Vegas.

Everybody was here for the rodeo; in that passing blur of faces he guessed that nearly every person knew one or more of the contestants. That personal angle brought grandstand and arena much closer. The revolvers popped, bands played, float trucks began to steam and puff. People were yelling, bottles flashed in the sun, kids were underfoot. The sun got hotter, a truck broke down, somebody roped a pretty girl and she tripped and caused a minor riot; and finally the long march was ended and the panoramic picture taken. Just then the news came of a special Elks train from Ohio, enroute to the national convention in Los Angeles, stopping at the depot.

"Boys," the parade marshal shouted. "Let's hold 'em up!"

Dewey Jones joined the run to the depot platform. A porter was just coming from the possum belly of one car with a big food tray. Sam Beday whipped a loop over porter and tray, swiped the ham, and scared the porter half to death. The Elks piled off their train and got lined up lynch-style on the platform, everybody flourishing guns and acting serious, but the Elks took it fine. Their Grand Exalted Ruler, or whatever the hell his name was, went straight to the office and sent a wire ahead, holding the train until six o'clock so they could attend the afternoon show. Then the Elks and their own band formed with all the riders, and they paraded uptown and disbanded outside the hotel and redoubled the hullabaloo. Those Elks had plenty of liquid refreshment and if they ran out, well, Las Vegas had a bootlegger for every Elk.

Dewey squeezed past a fat woman trying to kiss him, sneaked into the restaurant for his dinner, and by the time he got back to the grounds men were cutting the bulldogging steers into their pens, and other chute men were moving the bareback riding steers, big 1200 pound Brahmas, sure bucking stuff. Brindles, blues, grays, yellows—everything but red, for red only showed when a Brahma was crossed with a whiteface. All those bareback riding steers were nobbed, their horn tips cut off and three-pronged brass nobs screwed down tight over the tips into the fat of the horn. Those old steers were bawling, dust was rising high, important looking officials were riding up and down, yelling at contestants to form up for the Grand Entry.

Dewey took his time going behind the barns and falling into line, and half an hour late as usual, they rode around the race track and lined up facing the overflow crowd. The show announcer introduced the flag bearers, the governor, the leading political parasites, distinguished guests, and outstanding contestants. When the last contestant rode out front and took a bow, the announcer roared, "Disband, cowboys, and let's get on with the show!" and then all extra riders, guests, and tenderfeet left the arena, roping and bulldogging horses were led to their places behind chutes and pens, the three timing judges joined the announcer on the high platform above the chutes, and the three main judges cantered into the arena. The announcer swung his megaphone and began his spiel about the reunion, the top contestants, the amount of day money, the fact that bronc riding would be done with committee saddles furnished by McCarty.

Dewey Jones heard those last words and wondered if Jay Miller had his special saddle ready. Eddie McCarty carried a special saddle for Jay and Booger Red Rogers. All committee saddles had narrow sweat fenders, but Jay and Booger Red were so short-legged that when they put the stirrups up to fit, the sweat fender was run up so high that whenever they kicked back it made a roll under their leg. So Eddie made that one saddle with little short sweat fenders special for them. He had used it when he first started, but over the years he had gained just enough height to use a regular.

He rode behind the chutes, tied his horse, and carried his gear to a quiet place beside the pens. Five bareback riding steers were going into the chutes; on the track a Roman race was run off to get things warmed up while the steers were set and the steer riders gathered. Dewey recognized Arthur Brandley climbing the first chute and wished he had time to watch the ride, but his job was getting ready for the broncs. He did have time to watch old Arthur stand up on the chute with a leg on each side; and that first man in any show, looking over the field, checking the position of judges and pickup men, was always the time every contestant felt the tension clamp down hard—that last moment before the rider, surcingle in hand, dropped down on the steer and gave the word and the gate slapped open.

He heard the announcer call, "Arthur Brandley, out of chute number one on steer number nine!" and the gate opened and he saw the hump of the big steer's back as it left the chute. He turned away then and moved down the line where other bronc riders had gathered to test stirrups, taking no chances on those strange committee rigs. Jay Miller was going over his little saddle carefully. Booger Red Rogers had not made this show, so Jay was all alone on the short-stirrup special. They checked the saddles, bucking reins tied around their waists, cocking an ear toward the arena noise. Everybody used the same type bucking rein, three-strand cotton rope unraveled two feet from the end, then loose-plaited to make holding easier. They were all nervous as a bowl of jello because this was a big show money-wise, and one split second off meant the difference in hamburger and steak.

Behind them the steers left out of the chutes like cats turning handsprings. Word drifted back that Brandley had lasted three jumps; the next boy made a fair ride; things were moving fast and smooth. The arena men were clearing out the ridden steers, number three left the chute and the crowd roared, hats waved, dust rose up above the chutes, it was all there and couldn't stop for three days. Down the line five calves were plugged into the barrier chute for the first roping section, ready to start when the fifth steer rider finished. They all stood now, smoking fast, waiting out the time. The fifth steer went out, the announcer called for the first calf of the day, and Jay Miller left them to boss the chute men who were bringing up the broncs through the alleyway from the pens. Dewey watched those broncs, fourteen today, kicking hell out of the boards, then quieting down, standing easy as the first five were separated and pushed forward into the now empty chutes. Dewey paid close attention to the broncs and the five riders who went forward to begin saddling. Vaguely he heard the announcer call Charley Green's name on the first calf. He was getting too nervous so he climbed the fence and watched.

Charley was a top hand off the Drag Y outfit, riding a little stocking-legged roan horse that moved fast as lightning. The calf broke and the roan put Charley to the mark right quick. Charley made two fast swings over his head and the loop shot out straight and accurate over the calf's neck, but Charley had to make two kicks with his left foot to clear the stirrup, then coming off his horse and going down the rope he got astraddle as the calf tightened it up fast. Charley had to grab rope and swing his right leg backwards, and that cost him time. Dewey guessed twenty-four seconds and the official time, announced moments later, was twenty-four and two-fifths. Not very good time for that bunch of hands who were capable of doing the job in anything from fourteen seconds up. He dropped off the fence, feeling better, and turned to the bronc chutes and climbed up to see how the luck went before he straddled Done Gone.

Jay Miller came out of chute one on Schoolgirl and made a pretty fair bronc ride. That was expected, Jay knowing the McCarty string as he did. Dewey watched Jay and smelled plenty of competition from Bill Baker, Mike, and Miller. Any one of the three was capable of fitting a bronc ride on a good bucking horse. Then he got too nervous again and dropped off the fence and stood, back to the chutes in the sun and dust, while the announcer's voice rolled out brassy loud and the chutes trembled as the broncs shifted weight at the last moment, the gate slapped, and man and bronc raged into the arena. Pecos Coker went out on Black Thunder and stuck till the gun; Fightin' Bill Baker stayed on Broken Box for another qualified ride; Arthur Brandley was tossed fast as Invalid hit the sky. Then the announcer called number five, that was the green kid who drew Overall Bill, and somebody up the line said, "Hell, he ain't showed," and Dewey turned to find Mike grinning at him.

"You gave him too much chow-chow last night," Mike said. "Ain't you ashamed of yourself?"

"Sure," he laughed, and then sobered, for it wasn't right to make fun of any boy on his first show, scared most to death. "Smoke?" he asked.

"You got to roll it for me," Mike said. "Want to watch Neal and Babe?"

"Not today," he said, "an' roll your own. I ain't exactly the rock of ages myself."

High on the platform in the shimmering heat waves, the announcer was starting his spiel for Neal and Babe. Dewey didn't need to watch. He knew their routine by heart, from the moment the announcer gave them the big build-up. Babe rode out first in her fancy show outfit, got down, Neal followed and they went through some butterfly stuff, throwing the loop out and jumping through as it came back. Then Babe mounted and Neal started his loop, timed things to the second, throwing it out, bringing it back spinning in the sun, jumping through, then forward, whipping it out like a live snake just as the announcer chimed in and called a bridle bit catch. Babe rode past and Neal caught her horse on the nose just above the bridle bits. Babe took the rope off and rode on down below Neal, and the announcer called, "Next is both forefeet." Neal was jumping forward and back through his loop as Babe started her run past him, and as Neal jumped through he ran his loop overhand and snapped both forefeet.

He knew how it was in the arena, in this space of time before the next steer riding section. The rope was flashing yellow in the sun and Babe looked handsome on her fine horse. Up in the stands the dudes were eying her and wondering how they could meet her that night after the show; and she was sweating like a butcher under that fancy outfit, turning her horse fifty yards up, timing it, starting her run as Neal began his next spin, the neck catch. That was fast and always drew applause, and then they poured it on for the dudes. The announcer always gave the next trick a big play, how Neal would attempt to catch three horses and riders passing abreast, with his foot.

Two riders came out and flanked Babe while Neal laid a big loop on the ground over his foot; as they passed he whipped the loop out with his foot and his hand for the catch. You had to ride those three horses just so to help Neal out on that trick. Riding past, just before the throw was made, both outside riders caught Babe's saddle horn to keep from spreading out, the loop caught them all, and that was the end of their first show as Neal finished by going the length of the grandstand, spinning the loop and jumping through. Following Neal off the arena behind the chutes, Babe always doffed her white hat and showed her jet black hair, and the dudes watched her go and began figuring angles for that night. And the women in the stands sniffed and said a lot of snide words about big muscles and no brains.

And all this time, whenever a lag hit the arena, the show clown did his stuff. Pecos Coker would come out backwards on a steer picked special to buck or fight. One hand on the surcingle, the other holding his big suitcase. He'd take two or three jumps, the suitcase would fly open, and out would tumble a rooster and a cat. Pecos had one fighting steer that made him a fine act. He'd come out on that steer with a red blanket under his arm, ride about fifteen jumps, throw his right foot over the withers and step off, unfurl that red blanket and get it set for a bullfight pass as the old steer turned and charged him.

Pecos wore a hard-boiled derby hat and every time he passed the steer he'd doff that hat and bow to the stands.

About the third charge he'd look up and yell, "Wonder if the governor can do this?" and after the next pass he'd call on some well-known lady to come down and kiss him for his bravery. On the last charge Pecos would flop broadside and the steer jumped over him, and then he'd come up with his long-barreled Colt and go to shooting blanks at the steer, then pat his ass to the crowd and walk away. Pecos was on top for every lull. He earned his money ten times over, especially during bulldogging when he might appear to be clowning but wasn't.

Then the second round of steer riding was finished, the calves were roped, the crowd settled back from its early jitters. The broncs were up again, and this was the action they came to see. Mike was saddling Pretty Dick in chute one when Dewey climbed the boards and looked up into Mike's face.

"Remember what I told you," he said. "Give him plenty of head."

"Bueno."

Mike took a long hold on his hackamore rein and dropped down into the saddle as the announcer blared his name, and just as Mike gave the word, face white under dust and tan, he forgot himself. Mike's right hand moved down and yanked the hackamore rein through his left hand about a foot. Dewey saw it happen and had no time to yell as the gate cracked open. Pretty Dick humped and the spurs flashed, and Dewey knew he had one less man to beat for final money. Mike lasted four jumps and bucked flat off on the ground, and Pretty Dick went humping across the arena, missing Mike's head by inches with one hind foot. Then Dewey had no time. He swung down and walked shaky-legged toward chute four and Done Gone. He didn't see Omar Meeks buck off on Deer Trail; he was too busy looking over his saddle and getting reacquainted with Done Gone.

He stood beside the chute, studying the big horse, thinking of those head spins. Done Gone would rare right up on his hind feet reasonably straight and then just whip his head down between his forelegs, and any bronc rider who had ridden much would naturally loosen in the saddle, what with remembering to spur and sticking to the leather on the first jump out. But old Done Gone, whenever he rammed his head between his legs and whipped his shoulders toward the ground and kicked out with both hind feet, was apt to loosen you up, then jump once more, do it again, and not many riders were still on top by that time.

Dewey climbed up and looked down on the saddle and the horse. His front cinch was fairly tight and he checked that again to make sure the chute men had followed his directions. He never figured it wise to cinch a saddle too tight on a bucking horse unless the horse had low withers or excess fat. He heard Sam Woody go out on King Tut, and that sure was a light frost and early fall. Sam lasted about five jumps and hit the sky, and the chute men looked up at Dewey Jones.

"Pull it," he said.

They pulled the back cinch while he was straddling the chute. He got up there, with the sun on his neck, and he never could wait. If he faced something he dreaded, he had to get it over and done with. He looked the field over to make sure the judges were set and the pickup men in position. He saw the grandstand from his eye corner, the flags whipping in the breeze, the crowd holding back now as they watched him, astraddle the chute with the dust swirling around his legs. He dropped down on Done Gone and shoved both feet in the stirrups and brought them up into the shoulders and felt the horse tremble and grow silent beneath him, waiting quietly, as much a veteran of all this as Dewey Jones or any man.

"Turn him to me," Dewey said.

He knew that old horse. He had to get past the first head spin Done Gone was almost sure to make, had to get by without loosening in the saddle, then spur Done Gone forward on the jumps he generally made between his first and second head spins, then go to the cinch with both spurs and try to come through without a disqualification. He spoke and the last thoughts were erased as the gate slapped back and Done Gone left the chute.

Dewey spurred him forward two jumps, but Done Gone never pulled his usual head spin. He just threw some curves and plenty of power, and Dewey spurred some more, went to the cinch, and camped one jump. He was setting pretty but still waiting for that first head spin, riding on, staying flat and easy, knowing as the horse moved beneath him that he could make a better ride. But he had respect for those head spins, he didn't want to get caught off balance in the last second if Done Gone finally decided to move out. He heard the gun and spoke to the old horse, and let the pickup man help him off and trot him back to the chutes. When he climbed the fence and dropped over, Mike was waiting, frowning at him, saying, "Dewey, why didn't you eat that damn old horse up?"

"Qualified," he said. "That's what counts, Mike."

"But you could of done better," Mike said. "I figure you no higher than second day money off that ride."

But Mike just didn't know Done Gone, know how a man feared and respected those head spins. Dewey had watched that horse buck off Hugh Strickland, and Bryan Roach, and Bobby Askins; and when a horse bucked off any one of those men, especially Askins, no man had a right to play king on that horse. He had qualified today, he knew that, and he still felt that the man who made three good qualified rides on any three of these horses would end among the top, if not the top rider.

"Second day money," Dewey grinned. "Fifty bucks—I'll settle for that, Mike."

He leaned against the fence and rolled a cigaret and felt his legs and body stop shaking, and Pecos Coker was chasing his rooster and shooting his Colt between the second and third rounds. The dust blew away on the wind and the announcer brought Neal and Babe back for their trick riding. He felt better now so he climbed the fence and waved at Babe as she passed, and watched them do the tough part of their act.

Babe made the first run, the Roman Drag. She had a strap on the right side of her saddle away from the stands and before she started the run she put that strap around her right ankle. When she got a third of the way down the line she just threw up both arms, dropped the reins, tied together of course, and fell back off the horse. The strap held her but a lot of women in the stands turned pea green. As Babe finished her run, Neal came down on his first pass. He dropped off the left side of his horse, both hands on the saddle horn, let his feet touch and bounce, vaulted back into the saddle, went off the other side and vaulted up again. Neal made four vaults on his run; then Babe came across again.

This time she had two straps tied to the saddle fork and slipped her feet into those straps, broke her horse away, dropped the reins, stood up and leaned forward into nothing and rode like a bird all the way. She pulled in below Dewey and Mike, winked as she wiped sweat, and wheeled around as Neal, up above, began his second run.

On that trip Neal came vaulting again, only he vaulted back and forth all the way, never touching the saddle, going over, hitting the ground, coming right back over with hands on the horn and feet giving him the spring. He pulled in beside Babe and she was off, saddle horn in both hands. When the horse broke, she threw her right foot over his neck, flipped her left foot, and turned backwards, threw her foot once more and turned completely around into the saddle as she came off the run; and Neal was ready for his next trick.

He had two hand holds on the back skirts of his saddle and when his horse broke into the run he fell off behind, his feet hit the ground behind the hoofs, he held to those skirt grips, gave himself a little pull and went right up on the horse's hip on his right shoulder and turned a handspring into the saddle; and Babe was out again before the crowd stopped clapping, standing sideways in the saddle with the reins in her left hand, smiling up at the stands all the way across; and then Neal broke out in the toughest trick of all.

He went completely under the horse's belly on the right-hand side, caught the strap dangling on the left, stuck his left leg under the belly, caught his toe in the right-hand stirrup, reached under and grabbed that strap and pulled himself under and up into the saddle. He whirled his horse beside Babe and they took a bow and trotted off. It looked easy, but it had taken Neal and Babe a long time to master those tricks. Babe waved, all sweaty-faced and dusty, grinning at Dewey as he headed for the barns. That was Babe, he thought, go out there and risk her neck and be thinking mostly of tonight's dance and how she'd look in her new outfit. He watched her out of sight as the announcer called for the ropers. Bulldogging was coming up, it was time to get his horse; and while he was moving around to the bulldogging chute and the ropers finished, Pecos Coker put on his wild steer and homemade cart act.

Pecos had a two-wheeled cart with a long tongue that curved up and over the steer's back from the axle, and Pecos sat on a single plank seat hung over that axle. The surcingle he used had an automatic trip so that whenever Pecos was ready he pulled a sash cord running back to his seat from the surcingle ring, and surcingle and all came flying off. Riding around, Dewey watched Pecos come roaring out with that old fighting steer pulling the cart. Twenty jumps and Pecos yanked the sash cord, the surcingle flew, the steer took off, and the cart fell back, tongue quivering high in the air. Pecos's suitcase fell open and a little bitty pig, a Berkshire, black with white shoulders, tumbled out and scooted for the chutes. The old steer wheeled and charged Pecos who was on his belly between the cart wheels. Pecos fired off a blank but the steer kept charging, as he always did, until he was hammering the cart with both horns. Pecos fired again and, when the steer turned off, jumped up and grabbed the tail and ran alongside, firing blanks on one hip, then the other, finally doffing his derby hat as he veered away and came over to help with the bulldogging.

Dick Harrell was waiting on his hazing horse and they stood watching the chute men get the first steer ready. Shorty Kelso was number one, with Cliff Neafus hazing for him. Shorty was a good dogger, riding one of Neafus' fine horses, and when that steer broke Shorty rode down and made fourteen and two-fifths seconds.

"Too damn good," Dick grunted.

"Here's Dibbs," Dewey said. "He's the one to watch."

Old Buford Dibbs, the laughing hyena, swung in with O. T. Fore hazing. Dibbs almost overjumped his steer coming down. Instead of taking a hammerlock as was customary, he just got ahold with his left hand, missed the right horn, and stumbled in front of the steer. But Dibbs held on with his left hand, reached back with his right and grabbed the right horn, and threw that back hold; and when Dibbs put the pressure on, being such a powerful man, preaching was over.

"Twenty-five seconds," Dick said. "An' you was worried?"

"Still am," he said, and waited for the official time. When it came, twenty-seven seconds flat, he felt pretty good. Dibbs was sure to come back tomorrow and next day with fast times, and that long twenty-seven might spell the difference.

Arthur Brandley was number three, with Sam Beday hazing. Brandley got a good jump and turned in twelve and two-fifths seconds; then the announcer was calling their names and they took position at the chute, but there was delay getting the steer ready and Dick said, "Hold off then!" and they made a short practice run to keep the horses from getting nervous. When they rode back and swung around, Dewey on the left, Dick on the right, Dewey looked over at the steer and let himself settle back for a few seconds and then said, "Let's have it!"

The steer broke and Dick closed fast, holding him over. They crossed the dead line, the flag dropped, and Dewey Jones came off the roan horse in the fast jump. It felt like he'd done it right this time, timed everything good today. The speed of his horse, the difference in the speed of the steer and the horse, time those and jump accordingly; for if the horse was faster than the steer by the tiny amount a man could misjudge, he was liable to overjump and miss the steer entirely. But he'd gauged it fine, he knew, as he hit the steer smack on the withers and the speed of the horse carried him to the neck and he hammerlocked both arms under the horns, put on the brakes and stopped the steer cold.

He heard Dick yell, "Watch it!" and knew what he'd done. His right arm had gone in front of the right horn. He was in a tight for a second, pulling that dumb trick, for the steer might stop suddenly and back up, right out from under him. So long as the steer kept pushing forward he was safe, and old lady luck smiled. The steer kept charging and he got his back hold and put on the pressure, left hand pushing down, twisting the steer's nose straight up, then exploding with all his strength, feeling the steer go down in a heap. Dick was yelling when he jumped clear and spit to cut the dust, and he knew it was good time. When they rode back to the chute he heard the announcer roll it out, "Twelve seconds flat!" and then he had to grin. That was the best time so far.

They stood beside the pen and rolled a smoke while Fightin' Bill Baker came in for number five, Shorty Kelso hazing. Bill was bull-strong and awful fast, and Shorty Kelso was hazing on a top horse. They were the two he had to watch now, last man up as only five were dogging, it being something fairly new and not many of the boys with few enough brains to try it yet. While Baker and Kelso were lining up, Buford Dibbs joined them, shook hands, and bummed a match.

"Buford," Dewey said. "How was the roping today?"

In his slow, droll way old Buford said, "Most of 'em had a helluva time, Dewey. You see it?"

"Saw Charley lead out," he said. "What happened?"

"Well," Buford said, "they just don't seem to be able to handle these waspy calves like I would handle 'em if I would make a ketch. But not being able to rope a calf, I guess I ain't got a great lot of say acomin'. Trouble is, these calves are pretty good-sized stuff, Dewey. Come off the Scheele Ranch and they sure picked the calves that come early."

"Make 'em work," Dewey said, and then the gate sprung and Baker's steer was out. He counted time in his head as Kelso held the steer and Bill made a good jump and stop, then lost balance a second and had to make up time. It came out sixteen and two-fifths, and Mike slapped Dewey on the back with relief all over his homely face.

"Well, you got it."

He said, "Guess so," and tried to act unconcerned over winning first day money in bulldogging money, plus first or second day money in bronc riding. A hundred dollars, maybe more, and he hadn't touched a drink yet. Then Dick Harrell called, "Come on, Dewey," and he had to scramble for the wild horse race. He didn't like any part of it but Dick was loaning him a valuable horse for bulldogging, and he was honor-bound to return the favor. Still, going around in front of the bulldog-ging pen where they were turning in the wild broncs, he remembered too many times good boys ended this race with busted arms and legs. A wild horse race never proved one damn thing, but the crowd ate it up and that settled the argument.

A roper and rider worked together. When the gun fired the roper walked into the pen and looped one of the wild bunch, and his partner helped him haul the bronc up short. Then one man eared the bronc down and the other removed the lariat from the bronc's neck and tied it to the dangling halter rope placed on all the broncs before the start. Then, one man in front and one in back, tugging and cussing, they got the bronc onto the race track where the rider grabbed up the saddle. The roper went down his rope and eared the bronc while the rider cinched on the saddle, untied the lariat from the short lead rope, ragged that, stepped aboard and signaled to turn loose.

With fifteen or twenty teams doing the same job in one pen and then on one section of race track, it was a mad scramble. The bronc was apt to go in any direction, even straight up, and broncs were sure to collide and possibly fall. If a man could get headed around the track the right direction his bronc was liable to leave out like a scared rabbit, and just as liable to get halfway around and decide to turn back. A man had to swing his hat down the side of the bronc's head and keep urging him on and trust to luck. And even then, with broncs running wild and whacking together, a man wasn't out of danger. Dewey got away third and finished seventeenth because his bronc insisted on bucking halfway around the track before stretching out. They got nothing for their trouble, but Dick didn't mind. Dick had his fun watching the others cuss and yell and drip sweat, trying to ear down their broncs and cinch up the saddles. Dick was always making bets with anybody available while the race was going on. So he was happy when they walked to their dogging horses and watched the last event of the afternoon, the wild cow milking.

"Should of entered," Dick said wistfully.

"Oh sure!" Dewey said, "an' have me mug one of them cows. No thank you, Mr. Harrell."

"No entry fee," Dick said.

"An' no insurance," he said. "Why, look at them fools!"

There were no entry fees because nobody was fool enough to pay money in that catch-as-catch-can. Twenty head of sniffy black muley cows were turned into the arena corner nearest the grandstand, each cow yanking a twelve-foot drag rope. The milkers worked in pairs. The rope man caught a rope and stopped the cow, went down and mugged her and tried to hold her steady while the milker went in with a soda pop bottle and got enough milk to show in the bottom and then made a beeline for the judges, first man back winning the money. Mike laughed himself teary-eyed watching Fightin' Bill Baker and Sam Beday who had entered just for the hell of it. Bill mugged a cow so hard he knocked her down as Sam dived in, and Sam ended up milking upside down and still making it to the judges for first money. The dust hung thick and the cows bawled, and up in the grandstand people stretched and headed for the gates. The first day was over.

Dick Harrell led them out to his wagon camp where Dick's wife had coffee waiting. Dewey gave a little Mexican boy a dollar to walk the roan horse thirty minutes and cool him slow and easy. They stood around the tail gate then, drinking coffee, reviewing the afternoon: who made this ride, who made that, and if so-and-so had done this how much better he'da finished. Dick's wife scolded Dewey for not making a wilder ride on Done Gone, but he shook his head at those sentiments and said, "Sis, I knew what he could do. I'm glad and lucky he never threw any head spins." Then, because he was no different from anybody else, he said, "How do you figure I stand in bronc riding, Dick?"

"Baker first," Dick said. "You second, Jay Miller third."

Dick had probably hit it on the nose. They wouldn't know until the last day because bronc day money winners weren't announced until the books went to headquarters that last night. That was the time, he thought. The crowning of the King of England never had a better crowd than the bunch milling around, waiting for those final results. Dewey finished his coffee and heard Dick answer a question on the bareback steer riding, "Oh, I don' know, Jess. There was some pretty wild rides made but those steers is not too uniform as to habits. Some are hard to ride, but some put on a good show and ain't hard to ride at all. Just average, I'd say." Dick turned around again. "Dewey, you stayin' for supper?"

"Better go in," he said. "Thanks just the same."

"Well then, take the roan," Dick said. "Jess is goin' in for groceries. He'll bring it back."

He walked out to get the roan and Mike followed and had him stop by the next wagon camp on the north. He met some friends of Mike from the country east of Raton near Des Moines, an old-timer named Johnson and a man named Jim Ashford and his sister Mary. Dewey was dog tired all at once, the afternoon finally catching up with him, and he didn't see or think too straight when he shook hands. The girl wasn't tall but she stood erect beside the wagon with that feeling of motion a man saw in the beautiful wild creatures. She had blond hair and she was wearing a faded old leather skirt and paper-thin blue shirt, and her boots were scuffed from hard wear.

Mike started talking about a job for him with these folks and their neighbors, circle breaking broncs the coming winter. He listened with one ear and the girl stood beside him and gave him a shy, admiring look. That was the way so many girls kited after a man when they knew he was in the money, but this girl was different, she was his own kind of folk and it was almost painfully clear that she'd taken a shine to him. She'd grown up the same way and she knew what lay behind the shining outward show a man put on in the arena; and still she was looking shyly as if she saw something better in him. She was old enough to know just how much his kind were worth; it made him nervous whenever a fine girl felt that way.

He nodded when Mike told Johnson that here was just their man for the job. Johnson said, "Will you keep us in mind?" and he nodded again, making no firm promise, anxious to get away from Mary Ashford, get back to that clean hotel room and soak his aching body in hot water. He tipped his hat when they turned away, and she was still smiling slyly.

They rode in slow and grabbed a bite to eat before Mike went off somewhere to see another friend from Raton. Dewey went upstairs and washed his face, but that was all he could handle right then. He lay down for an hour, not feeling bad so much as tired, and knew he was in shape to go all the way through. Mike knocked just as he was getting into the bathtub, and he called, "Make my draw for me, Mike," and sank down to his ears and just soaked and dozed until Mike returned half an hour later, came on into the bathroom, and said, "Pretty Dick."

"Who'd you draw?" he asked.

"Broken Box," Mike said. "You comin' to the dance?"

"Mike," he said, "I'm too damn tired."

"You ain't that tired," Mike said shrewdly. "You're just gettin' some sense. Keep using it. I'll see you in the morning."

He closed his eyes and stayed in the tub until the water cooled off. He dressed then and went downstairs, and had to buck his way through the lobby. Everybody was getting drunk, whooping and hollering, shooting off revolvers and playing tricks on dudes. Babe Smith caught him at the door, swung him inside, and stood there in her fancy dance outfit, digging her fingers into his arm.

"Dewey," she said. "You can make a better bronc ride."

"Sure," he said. "But you don't know them head spins. He'll pull 'em before this show's over, you watch, an' the man on him'll hit heaven. Savvy?"

"I savvy," Babe said. "I guess I was thinking maybe you got scared."

"No, Babe," he said quietly. "Just being careful."

"Well," Babe said. "Let's go on down to the dance."

"You go on," he said. "I don't feel up to it. I might play a little poker instead."

"Bucking horses and bee-backed cards," Babe said curtly. "That all you think of?"

She turned and left him, half-mad by then, and he thought, Well, ain't that enough? and wondered if those vices were better for a man than too much woman. Babe had always been too much woman for one man. He stood in the darkness just outside the door and felt the night cool off around him. He wanted to go down the street to the poolhall and sit in the poker game. He wanted to dance with Babe and get the feel of a good drink under his belt; but not tonight. Or tomorrow night either. He waited until the lobby quieted down before he went inside and headed for the stairs; and crossing over he found Arthur Brandley sitting on a lumpy bedroll, looking tired and dirty and plumb disgusted. Brandley had arrived late in the morning and missed a room, and his long, broken nose was shining red under the dirt, his heavy shoulders were sagging from the afternoon he'd put in, getting off a train with no sleep and competing all afternoon long.

"Where you sleeping, Art?" Dewey asked.

"Well, by god," Brandley said in his thick, nasal drawl, "I ain't got no place to sleep, Dewey. Clerk said I could bunk in the back hall."

"Come on," he said.

"Oh, by god!"

Brandley followed him upstairs, dropped gearsack and bedroll, and looked at the bathtub. Dewey hadn't seen Brandley in six months but that was how it went, nobody knew when Brandley might pop up at a show. Brandley came from Montana where his daddy had a big ranch, but Brandley had caught the fever eight years ago and now he couldn't quit. His daddy had tried sending him off to school but that was no go. Standing there spraddle-legged, old for his years, Brandley looked like every one of their kind rolled into the same dirty Levis and sweat-crystaled shirt.

"You stiff?" Brandley said suddenly.

"Some," he said. "I already took a hot bath."

"Run that bathtub full again," Brandley said. "Hot as you can stand, and get in it."

Dewey filled the tub and slid in. Brandley made him soak about twenty minutes, dry off, and lay down on the rug. Brandley broke out a bottle of liniment and gave Dewey a rubdown that was sure worth the money. Brandley hit all the sore spots and loosened the muscles until Dewey almost fell asleep on the rug. Then Brandley took a hot bath and lay on his belly and Dewey rubbed him down, but he didn't know all those spots, so Brandley didn't get near his money's worth. Getting into bed, feeling sleepy and rested, he said, "Who'd you draw for tomorrow, Art?"

"Overall Bill."

He laughed, leaning back and reaching for the light string. "That green kid didn't show on Bill today."

"He showed tonight," Brandley said.

"The hell he did!"

"Sure, an' he drew Invalid," Brandley said, stretching out in the darkness. "Ought to be worth the ticket, just seeing if he shows tomorrow."

CHAPTER THREE

THERE WAS NOTHING to hurry a man today. They could lay up and soak, with the clean towels and hot water and bathtub waiting to be used, all the luxuries they so rarely had. Dewey Jones woke at six and dozed easy, thinking of the afternoon, until Brandley sat up and scrubbed his mop of sandy-colored hair.

"You stiff?" Dewey asked.

"Just in my head," Brandley said sheepishly. "I been ridin' that Overall Bill all night long."

"You must of rode easy," he said. "I never heard you spurring. Go wash up."

After Brandley finished, Dewey shaved and got into his last clean shirt and made a bundle of dirty laundry. Downstairs, the desk clerk promised suppertime delivery, barring accidents or the washerwoman getting drunk. The restaurant rush was over so they took plenty of time eating breakfast, going heavy on the ham and eggs, putting an all-day lining in their bellies. They would eat light at noon, facing those second day rides. They stepped into the lobby at eight-thirty; too much time to kill in town when a man's nerves were already banjo-string tight.

"Come on," Dewey said. "Let's go out."

They took a taxi to the grounds and loafed around, watching the match races between visiting cowmen and riders. Dick Harrell stopped by; Fightin' Bill Baker joined them and said right off, "Dewey, I drawed King Tut. Do you think I can ride him or whadaya think?"

Dewey grinned at the big man. "I'm not wishing you no hard luck, Bill, but I hope King Tut bucks you flat off."

"Now ain't that a way to talk!" Baker said.

"Bill," he said. "I know you topped me yesterday, an' so do you."

"Maybe," Baker said. "You drawed Pretty Dick. If you fit a ride on that horse there ain't goin' to be nobody ahead of you. When you start with old Dick, you just cain't quit. But if you don't start with him, you'll quit awful quick. Dewey, I ain't wishing *you* no bad luck but I hope he bucks you off."

"Well," he said. "I sure wish we knew how we stood."

Baker chuckled softly. They were both thinking the same way about the association holding up times and purses until the rodeo ended so cowboys wouldn't be jumping out in the middle of a show and leaving the association high and dry. "Would ease the mind," Baker said, "but they got us tied up tighter'n a steer's ass in flytime. See you at the chutes, Dewey."

Fightin' Bill Baker headed for the barns, big and tough and gentle, but just as knotty inside as the greenest kid. Arthur Brandley had wandered away somewhere and Dewey stood alone in the rising sun heat. He went along the inside track fence, the day's early work building up all around, and climbed over the chutes. Ropers were scoring their horses down the line, a gang of roustabouts were swabbing down the grandstand, everybody in a hustle and bustle, getting things all set for the afternoon. The bareback riding steers were being cut from the dogging steers and pushed along the alley into the pen behind the bronc chutes. The men caring for the bucking horses had finished early chores and were laying out saddles beside the chutes. All the bucking horses had been fed a good breakfast and allowed their fill of water under Jay Miller's sharp eye, and they'd get no more until evening. Jay watched the McCarty string like a bunch of prize fighters, giving them the best feed, pure water, handling them tender. Everybody worked ragged to make this show come off smooth and steady, and it seemed, watching, like every man had practiced his job a month. And all for three days. Then he and his kind fanned out to the four horizons and left nothing behind. That was him and Baker and Brandley, all of them, halfway through one show and dreaming of the next five hundred miles away.

He went down to the roping chute and watched Dick Harrell toss a few loops, and rode Dick's stirrup out to the wagon camp where he saddled the roan and headed for town, more to get the feel of the horse than needing the practice. The streets were crowded worse than yesterday and twice as dirty with bottles and litter. People were getting drunk, kids were all over the place, the town was lucky that Elks special train had gone on last night. Dewey ate a sandwich and drank a cup of coffee, paid his six bits and met Brandley in the lobby.

"Where'd you go?" Brandley said. "Follow some good-looking woman back to town?"

"Went up to Dick's," he said. "But I sure can guess where you'd be, talkin' about women."

"Which reminds me," Brandley said. "I saw Babe."

"How was she?" he asked.

"Hung over and lookin' for sympathy."

"Guess she never learns," he said. "Want me to wait while you eat?"

"You go on," Brandley said. "I'll rest a bit before I come out. I'm worried about that Overall Bill."

Dewey said, "Give him plenty of head, Art," and went on upstairs to get his gear and come back down through the crowded lobby to the roan horse standing patiently at the sidewalk rail. He rode from town, past the carnival booths and shoddy canvas sagging gray in daylight, and tied the roan behind the pens. He stretched out in the fence shade while everything was sleepy silent, hat over his eyes, toes toward the sky. The bucking horses with the sun shining on their backs were quiet, whipping their tails at the flies. The riding steers grumbled and rubbed horns, standing close together on the dusty pen earth. This was a daily routine for steers and broncs, being shipped from show to show, put in the pens and then the chutes, getting fed, living on the same way. Dewey slept until the crowd built up its boot rumble on the aisle boards, and the announcer's voice rolled out the daily spiel.

He walked to the saddles and inspected his, put on his chaps, and looked over his spur leather. He unsaddled the roan horse and put the bronc saddle on and stepped up and down a few times. The roan was a hundred pounds lighter than Pretty Dick which made the stirrup difference small enough to adjust beforehand. But mostly he just wanted to step on and off, then stand beside the horse and lay a hand on the saddle, think of Pretty Dick and the coming ride. The bareback steers went into the chutes, the Roman race kicked up the first brown dust, but he had no longing to watch other contests today. He tied the roan and squatted against the pen fence, smoking, listening to the noise as the steers bucked from the gates and Pecos Coker clowned in the lulls, and Neal and Babe put on their trick act again. He sat alone in the thin fence shade, dust drifting down from the arena, until the first roping section finished and the announcer called for the broncs. Then he got up and climbed the chute boards and put all his mind on men and horses.

Brandley was number one today on Overall Bill. The front cinch was pulled; the chute boys pulled the back cinch while Jay Miller watched. Jay was on the spot to check the saddle on every bronc, because Jay knew those horses, all their tricks and traits, how one bucked better with a tight cinch, and one loose; and unless the rider, like himself, demanded his own adjustment, Jay would fix those cinches to give the wildest possible ride. Jay said, "All right, Brandley," and Brandley looked the field over and spoke more to himself than anyone else, "I guess I'll not have much use for them pickup men, 'cause I don' know whether I'll be there when the gun goes off."

Brandley was still worried. Dewey wanted to call out advice, but Brandley dropped down on Overall Bill and got that wild look in his face. He took a long hold on his hackamore rein and said, "Cut him to me," and the gate slapped and Overall Bill went out like an arrow from a bow, ran about thirty feet and blew the plug.

The first two jumps Brandley was there like a leech, going way high in the shoulders and back to the cinch, but the first time he kicked back Overall Bill was a split second ahead, and from there on out it was just which-is-which. Brandley didn't disqualify, but Dewey saw from six to eighteen inches of daylight under him all the way. Overall Bill was just bucking him off, and jumping back under him. The rules stated that the ride would be judged on the amount of scratching done, also on the rider's complete control of the horse, being master of the situation at all times. And Brandley, after the first jumps, showed everything but that.

He'd watched Brandley so close he didn't notice the green kid getting ready at chute two. He heard the announcement and, sure enough, there was the kid who drew Overall Bill yesterday and never showed. The kid's face was rawhide tight and he was chewing his lower lip, but he gave the field a quick look, dropped down on Invalid, and gave his nod to the gateman. Invalid rammed out and the kid stabbed him three times in the shoulders, kicked back about twice, went to the cinch and camped because it was camping time by then, with old Invalid getting mighty rough. The kid was still on top at the gun but slow leaving Invalid when the pickup man ranged alongside. The kid climbed the fence beside chute four and Dewey, ready to saddle Pretty Dick, gave him a hand down and said, "Kid, that was a good ride. That old horse is tough and if you don't let the bile crowd your liver like you did yesterday with Overall Bill, you'll make a bronc rider some day."

He saw the kid's spirits come right up. All it took was a friendly word from somebody like himself. The kid hitched his chap belt and tried to roll a cigaret. He couldn't get that job done, his fingers were still in the jello bowl, but he did find a smile. Dewey threw his saddle on the chute gate when Pretty Dick came into the chute. His stirrups were all set; all he needed do was snap his bucking rein into Dick's halter rein and look the old bronc square in the eye. He was pulling the front cinch when Omar Meeks went out on Schoolgirl, failed to go to the neck the first two jumps and penalized himself right there. Once Omar woke up, he just made a fair ride to the gun. Watching, Dewey climbed up and straddled Pretty Dick, hackamore rein in his left hand, giving Dick plenty of head. When Meeks finished, the kid looked up and said, "How long's he been riding?"

"Long enough to do better," Dewey said. "Look out, kid!"

He didn't want to wait. He was feeling tighter than yesterday, thinking about Pretty Dick who wasn't a mean horse, but a bronc it was best to get out of the chute as quick as possible. Bucking a man off was Dick's business, and if you held him too long in the chute he got cranky and sure took care of his business. Dewey looked the field over for judges and pickup men, heard the final spiel, "Dewey Jones out of chute number four on Pretty Dick!" When the boys pulled the back cinch and gave him the ready nod, he dropped down on Dick, socked both feet into the stirrups, moved his spurs up into the shoulders, figuring to spur Dick the instant they cleared the chute because Dick could make it troublesome if he ran out fifty or sixty feet before he blowed up.

He said, "Give me the gate," and when it slammed and they broke, he laid the spurs into Dick's neck and busted him in two. He was with the horse all the way and from there on he had easy pickings. He spurred Dick in the neck as Dick left the ground; on the next jump he threw both spurs back but, knowing the horse as he did, never going crazy. He wasn't spurring over six inches behind the cinch, and after those first jumps he didn't spur more than eight inches up the shoulders. Just at the gun he got out of time with Dick, and one big jump did the job. He didn't need to step off Dick although the grandstand might see it that way. He cleared and hit the ground and kept his feet, making it look as if he'd heard the gun and finished the ride in high style. He rode back to the chutes with the pickup man and climbed chute five where Mike was due on Broken Box.

He gave Mike the best smile he could rustle up, and Mike looked down from upstairs and nodded.

"I remember what I forgot yesterday," Mike said. "I'm giving this old bird plenty of head and either I win day money or buck off flat on the ground."

"Plenty of head," Dewey said. "Eat him up, Mike!"

Mike dropped down and nodded for the gate and somebody called, "That wop is ready!" When Broken Box cleared the chute Mike stabbed him right on the point of the shoulders for two jumps, then went to going both ways, kicking back and sliding both spurs right up under the saddle skirts, making a wild bronc ride all the way. Even before the gun Dewey knew it would give Mike the best markings of any one ride during the show. He was standing up there, pounding the top chute board and yelling, it was that good, watching Mike and the big horse climb through dust clouds and hit the ground stiff-legged, looking like a man-and-rider ghost in the bright sun. When Mike came walking back and climbed the fence, he pounded Mike's back and said, "You wop! That's the way to ride!" and kept on pounding until Mike yelled for mercy.

"What you patting me for?" Mike said. "You're in the finals."

"You, too," he said.

"After I buck off yesterday?" Mike said. "I don't know."

"Hell," he said. "Won't be five men left for finals if they count all the buck-offs. You watch, Mike. You're in for sure."

"Lemme squat," Mike said. "That old horse like to beat me to death."

They went back to the pens while the second section of bareback steers came in. Pecos Coker walked up from the roping chute, all smiles, and said, "Dewey, your friend Harrell just done a job a-tying his calf. That wild Injun can sure do this roping if he's right."

"What kind of time?" Dewey asked.

"Twelve and two-fifths," Pecos said. "An' that's some time on these calves. Old Dick tied in twenty-one and a half yesterday, and this about puts him high. If he does any job at all tomorrow, he'll walk away with the money."

"If he's high," Mike said. "Cliff Neafus must be close second, and George Hardesty third. Any one of 'em could take the finals."

"I'll take Harrell," Pecos Coker said. "Dewey, better head for the dogging chute."

"Plenty time," he said. And then he saw Sam Beday coming up the line, carrying a jug by the little finger of his left hand. He said, "What's Sam's number in the next bronc section?"

"Three," Mike said, "an' he was sure on the prod last night."

Sam Beday came up and faced them, wiping the sweat from his red face, looking miserable as could be, sporting a day's growth of whiskers and one black eye. Dewey said, "Sam, what you got in that jug?"

"Buttermilk."

"What you goin' to do with it?" Mike asked.

"Try to get better," Sam Beday said forlornly. "Cain't get no worse."

Sam veered off toward chute three, and Dewey knew there was no competition from that direction. He smoked and waited for the second bronc section and tried to guess the five men who'd make the finals. Mike went to the water trough to wash his face, and Babe caught Dewey Jones alone when she came off her trick riding run. She swung him around, smacked his arm, and said, "You made another one of those cautious rides. No use denying, I saw it. I'd say you're in the finals for sure, Dewey."

"Guess so," he said. "Mike done best so far."

"Best ride of the show," Babe said, and gave his arm a squeeze. "Well, that sure was a fine dance I had with you last night."

"Babe," he said, "I was plumb tuckered out."

"Are you comin' tonight?"

"Maybe a little while," he said. "But I'm sure taking me a good hot bath every night, having me a man to rub me down—"

"Art Brandley," Babe said. "Showing off those tricks he learned from that baseball trainer."

"Yes," he said, "an' I'm beginning to appreciate some of them athletic ideas. They must be all right, for I sure feel good."

"You don't act that way after supper," Babe said sharply, and left him standing at the fence with a foolish grin of apology. Babe went down to the arena gate and grabbed her horse from Neal and snapped at him as she headed for the barns. She'd had one too many last night, that was plain on her face, and she wasn't really mad at Dewey, just mad because he was acting so different. He had two nights to go. He wondered if he could dodge her that long, and then he stopped worrying about Babe.

He stayed in the fence shade until the roping and steer riding sections finished, and the call came for the second bronc section. He climbed the chute and watched Jay Miller get set for Black Thunder, and from Miller's face he knew the little man wasn't happy. Black Thunder was dynamite when he felt the urge, and any cowboy who fit a ride on him then had to be full of beans. The back cinch was drawn and Miller dropped down, and being keyed up so tight, forgot himself. The way he held the bucking rein, Jay was giving Black Thunder plenty of head, but he did just like Mike yesterday on Pretty Dick. Jay reached down with his right hand and pulled that hackamore rein up about six inches, and that was six inches too short. The gate cracked, Black Thunder went out, and Jay unloaded in four jumps.

"Well, by god," Dewey whispered. "Jay's out."

He stayed on the fence and watched the riders come out on the broncs into the sun and dust. Pecos Coker was a buck-off on Deer Trail, Sam Beday went out fighting his hangover and made the balloon ascension on Done Gone. Fightin' Bill Baker shook loose and lost King Tut two seconds before the gun. That was all Dewey needed to see. The last section was local talent and stood no chance. Tonight he would know for sure who made the finals. He wanted to do some guessing but the best thing right now was get up to the bulldogging chute and try for more day money.

Dick Harrell was waiting when he came for the roan, grinning all over himself at his good roping time. They moved around to the bull-dogging pen and stood talking while the last sections of steer riding and roping and bronc riding ran through. None of the local boys in the last bronc section lasted five jumps. When the fifth man went rolling Dick Harrell said, "You're in," and they turned to the chute.

"Second today," Dewey said. "Baker's goin' out first."

"An' a good thing," Dick Harrell said. "Don't take no wild chance today, Dewey. Just hang on and rattle for part of this money."

"Sure," he grinned. "All three parts."

Then Fightin' Bill Baker and Shorty Kelso were lining up and the first steer broke for the dead line. Baker made it in twenty-two seconds flat, good time, and they were riding in and getting set, looking over at their steer. Dewey wanted to get it over and done with today; he was thinking already of tonight's drawing. The steer broke and Dick did a fine job of holding him tight, and Dewey went off and made a fast stop, fumbled and recovered, and finished in twenty-three and two-fifths seconds. Coming back he knew that was good time considering the fumble, but Baker was still on top today. Then Brandley and Sam Beday busted out wild after their steer, Sam let the steer drift and Brandley overjumped and disqualified himself for the finals. Buford Dibbs came roaring out with O. T. Fore hazing the best so far, and big Dibbs hit his steer just right. When the time was announced, eleven seconds flat, Dick Harrell just shook his head. There wasn't much use in Shorty Kelso coming out. Neafus hazed well but Shorty had to make record time or lose his chance at the finals. Shorty overshot and took a header, the steer kicked up its heels and ran around the race track, and that was the end for Shorty. It left Baker, Dibbs, and Dewey Jones in tomorrow's bulldogging finals.

"Be close," Dick Harrell said. "Get a good sleep tonight, Dewey. Busy day comin'."

He knew just how busy, knew it too damn well, he thought, turning the roan over to Dick and leaving out right then before the last events. He caught a taxi and rode back into town and went straight to the room. He washed the dirt from his face and hands, was pleased to find the package of clean laundry on the bed, and lay down in his underwear to rest until supper. Mike Cunico woke him just in time to put on clean clothes and get downstairs to the restaurant before it closed. They ate a big supper and stepped into the lobby where everybody was keyed up tight as fiddle bows.

The boys who had bucked off and roped out were the only carefree, happy-go-lucky birds. Most of them were half-drunk and raising all kinds of harmless cain, flirting with the dude women and aching for trouble from any precinct. But not the boys who were drawing for finals. Dewey saw them clustered outside the headquarters door, joking back and forth a little, not talking too much, trying to hide their feelings. The ropers and bulldoggers knew their times so nobody was in doubt about those finals, but the big question that brought so many people into the lobby tonight was which five men would qualify for bronc finals. That part never changed. Cheyenne, Pendleton, Fort Worth, the Garden—it made no difference whether the biggest show or the smallest tank town, a man stood in the same atmosphere, the smoky lobby, the nervous hands rolling Durham, the same crowd in the background watching their faces, waiting for the pick. He'd gone through it a hundred times and it hadn't calmed him down. He was still nervous as a cat on a tin roof.

Dick Harrell and Dibbs had already declared he was in the money both days and sure to be in the finals. But who the other four would be nobody knew for sure. The judges had added up their total markings by this time and decided who deserved the chance, and those judges were honest. Nothing influenced a man like Elmo Bray. He watched a ride and made his marks, and that was final. The only thing Dewey knew, standing outside that door, was the hope he didn't draw Overall Bill. He wasn't afraid of the horse—he never saw a horse he feared—but he always dreaded a bucking horse like old Bill. Any of the horses they were bound to pick for the finals were capable of bucking him off, but tonight he wanted no part of Overall Bill. Maybe it grew up inside from watching Bill handle Brandley that afternoon; maybe it was remembering other shows when Bill had given him trouble.

"Here we go," Mike said softly.

Headquarters door opened and Sid LeMay waited for the lobby to quiet down, and then sang out the five names.

"Coker, Cunico, Jones, Miller, Baker! You all step in and draw your horses for the final ride. If there's any one of those boys not here, somebody go get 'em quick as you can. I want every man to draw his own horse, an' be a-watching you cowboys to make sure there's no fudging. Now come on in!"

They trooped inside and Sid LeMay left the door open so folks could crowd up and listen. The joking stopped, nobody fired off a gun, the door behind them was full of faces, breath coming small-sharp in the sudden silence. Sid LeMay dropped five numbers into the hat, this first draw tonight being for positions.

"All right," he said. "Jay, take your pick."

Jay Miller drew number four. Pecos Coker drew one. Dewey pulled three from the hat, Mike got two, and Fightin' Bill Baker didn't bother to draw the last number which was five for sure, last man out tomorrow. Then Sid LeMay dropped the five big numbers into the Stetson, mixed them up good with his right hand, and glanced over his shoulder, across the desk, where the three judges stood sober-faced, watching everybody closely.

"All set," Sid LeMay said. "Pecos, try your luck."

Pecos Coker wasn't doing any clowning tonight. He drew and looked at the name on his slip, and Dewey saw the worried frown tighten his thin face. "Goddam," Pecos said. "That Overall Bill. But hell, if I can fit a ride on him, I still got a chance for some of the money."

They all understood Pecos' way of thinking. Pecos was down toward the bottom in markings, and he had to make a wild ride to smell the cash. Dewey felt like a new man, now that Overall Bill was gone. He pushed Mike toward the hat and said, "Go get one, Wop."

Word had gone straight through the door into the lobby. Dewey heard those people passing it back, "Coker drew Overall Bill," and somebody out there laughing, "Bet Pecos don't come out backwards tomorrow!" Then Mike pulled his slip and turned with that wry grin. Drawing, they were all releasing their pent-up feelings in their own kind of understanding company. "King Tut," Mike said. "The tough old bastard. Don't put on too much show, but if the judge'll give me a break, I'll make you all sweat."

They laughed and glanced at the judges. Elmo Bray cracked his cold grin, looking into Dewey as if he wasn't standing there. The truth was, Mike did have a chance. He'd bucked off, sure, but he had first day money from today, and a good chance tomorrow, depending on how Dewey ended up.

"All right, Dewey," Sid LeMay said.

Out in the lobby he heard people push nearer the door. They were all waiting to see which horse he drew, knowing he stood high and could take the finals if he drew a horse he liked. Dewey went into the hat, read his draw, and tried a smile that came off weak.

"Deer Trail," he said. "An' I sure know what he can do. Step up, Jay."

Jay Miller read his draw and shook his head. "Broken Box, boys. You can count that a buck-off if he opens up."

Jay was remembering his afternoon ride and still pestered with the doubt that had to come out in tonight's talk. Jay was so nervous he had to do some talking, and the words showed plainly how he felt: "Maybe I ain't man enough to fit a ride over him that'll get me into the money. The good lord better be with me, an' I think he better be in a hurry if he stays with me as fast as that old horse leaves the chute. Bill, take your punishment."

Of course, the judges and Sid LeMay knew the last horse. As Baker made his draw Sid LeMay grinned and said, "You going or coming, Bill?"

Baker opened his slip and dropped it back in the hat. "I've got that old Done Gone, boys." Then he turned to Dewey and pushed his hat high and smiled, "Little man, do you think I can ride him or whadaya think?"

They were alone, with no reason to make false talk or pass the buck. Dewey said, "Watch them head spins, Bill. He ain't tried 'em yet. An' if he don't tomorrow, you got a good chance."

"Yes," Baker said soberly. "But we four boys are ridin' for second and third money. You've got first cinched."

"I wouldn't say that," Dewey said. "Preaching is never over till they pass the box and sing the last hymn. My last hymn sure will be sung on Deer Trail. What the collection amounts to—well, that remains to be seen."

Elmo Bray lit a cigar and spoke for the first time. "Yes, that remains to be seen, but you know, boys, it's the first time I ever saw this little bastard come to a show, stay sober, and not get whipped. Which goes to show you what a man can do if he tries to do."

When Bray spoke that way, Dewey knew he was high coming into the finals. He hadn't been certain before, now he knew. And so did the others, for Bray would not come right out, being a judge, and admit the fact. But he had to say words that meant one thing in the open and something else for nobody's ears but their own. Then Bray said curtly, "Well, let's break it up," and they all went through the door into the lobby.

The crowd parted to give them room and the dudes looked at them, one by one, like they had two heads. Everybody started yelling and shooting off the guns. The tension was off for tonight with the draws made, and each man was showered with advice from half-drunk amateurs as to what they should and should not do tomorrow. A man mounted the staircase with a megaphone and announced the start of the Cowboys Dance in exactly thirty minutes, one and all invited. Mike said, "See you there," and headed for the street door, and Brandley pulled Dewey toward the stairs.

"Well," Dewey said. "You goin' to sleep with me tonight, or sleep on the street?"

"Why, man," Brandley said happily, "I don' know how I can beat that hot and cold running water and that toilet in the same room. Guess I'll just impose on you. Come on upstairs and loan me a clean shirt."

They went up and Dewey ran a tubful of hot water. He soaked awhile and Brandley rubbed him down; and while he dressed Brandley soaked and came out red as a baby's behind except for the big blue bruise splotches on his skinny frame where Invalid and Overall Bill had left their calling cards.

"Belly down," Dewey said. "I'll give you a rub."

"I don' need no rubdown," Brandley said. "That damned old Invalid did a fair job of rubbing, an' Overall Bill almost rubbed me out. Just hand me a shirt."

His shirts were some too small but Brandley could get one on by leaving the cuffs open. Brandley did a little jig around the room and said impatiently, "Let's go swing the prancing fillies, boy."

"I might stop by," he said. "But I want my sleep tonight."

"You worried about Deer Trail?" Brandley asked quietly.

"Some," he said. "If he turns on a full head of steam, he's liable to buck me down. I'm goin' to get my sleep."

"Now, boy," Brandley said easily. "You've rode 'em just as good as Deer Trail. Go out there and fit that ride to him, but for god sakes, don't buck off before the gate opens. Now come on."

Brandley took him downstairs and through the lobby to the street. They walked slow and easy to the dance hall, paid their dollar, and went upstairs. Dewey hung back but Brandley grabbed a girl right off and swung away in a fancy step.

Dewey saw Mike dance by with the girl from Johnson's camp, the girl wearing a yellow dress and town shoes, her blond hair tied up neat with a red ribbon. Mike swung her over and introduced Mary Ashford again, and she said, "Good luck tomorrow, Dewey."

"Thanks," he said. "I'll sure need it."

"Johnson's wondering if you'll break them broncs this winter," Mike said. "You ready to make a promise?"

That was Mike, looping the apron strings around his neck. He pulled back inside, thinking of tomorrow and all the shows ahead through the season. He was coming to that time of making the decision and he knew Mike was pulling hard for his own good, but still he couldn't say the words. He said, "I'll let you know tomorrow, Mike."

"So you're goin' on?" Mike said.

"Don't know yet," he said. "Thinking it over."

"Do that," Mike said. "See you tomorrow."

Mary Ashford smiled as they danced away. He watched her a minute, trying to guess her age, knowing she was good stock and solid all the way through, a real range woman. Then he smelled the perfume and whiskey mixed, and knew it was Babe before he turned. She was all decked out in her fancy trick outfit and fine boots, and no woman in the hall looked better. Babe never said a word, just grabbed him and swung him onto the floor and made him dance.

She came up close against him and held him as tight as he held her, not being brassy because she wasn't that kind, she was simply showing she liked him and she was happy he'd come. He finished that dance and made her stand out the beginning of the next near the stairway. She tapped one toe to the music and finally said, "Let's go get a drink."

"Not tonight," he said. "I won't tangle with old John Barley until the show's over."

"Tomorrow night then," Babe said. "Can you unbend enough to dance twice and take a drink? Just as soon as you come off that high wire?"

"This time tomorrow," he said, "I'll either celebrate on winning some money, or be ready to drown my sorrows. All right, Babe. We'll have that drink tomorrow night."

"An' now you're going to bed?"

"You win the kewpie doll," he said. "Straight to bed. Thanks for the dance. And Babe—"

"Yes?"

"Stay sober," he said. "Ain't no sense fighting it every night."

"I'm not fighting anything," Babe said. "I'm just living on, Dewey."

For a moment, facing each other, Dewey read the same wish in Babe's face that he kept deep inside his own heart. She was thinking of some other life, too, but she was going on the same way because it was so hard to change, it was always half-past too late. She started to say something more, but Brandley took her arm and danced her away, and she looked back at him with that funny, half-sad look on her face. Dewey stood a minute watching the dancers, hearing the music, then went down the narrow stairs and along the quiet street. The hotel lobby was empty when he crossed to the staircase. The night clerk looked up and waved an ink-stained hand.

"Good luck tomorrow, Dewey."

"Thanks," he said. "Good night."

CHAPTER FOUR

HE WOKE and lay half-sleeping, unwilling to get up. Brandley had gone downstairs; wind fretted the veined green shade, throwing irregular dabs of sunlight over his face. He slept again and woke to find Brandley standing beside the bed, laughing, fanning him with a towel.

"Eight-thirty," Brandley said. "Rise and shine, boy."

"Clear day?" he asked.

"Clear and hot," Brandley said. "Made to order."

Dewey shaved close and held a hot towel over his face. Brandley watched him through the doorway and finally said, "Why shave? It won't make no difference with old Deer Trail."

"Well," he said, trying to sound cheerful, "when Deer Trail has a colt I don't want it to look like a bum. Want him to feel like he's brought somethin' into the world he's not ashamed of."

"You're awake," Brandley grinned. "Now come on down and eat."

"What you doin'?" Dewey asked. "Playing momma to me?"

"Somebody has to," Brandley said. "You cain't go out there today feelin' like a motherless calf."

They went down to breakfast and Dewey ordered three slices of crisp bacon, coffee, and the old cowboy standby, one bowl of oatmeal. Then Brandley took him for a walk, up one side of the street and down the other, meeting people who ate up the morning in idle talk. Dewey felt

time pass that way, talking cattle and horses and weather, rolling ciga-
rets, moving along the crowded street under the candy-striped awning
shade. At eleven o'clock they returned to the hotel for ham and eggs,
which gave the food plenty of settling time before his ride. He was eager
by then, aching to get it over and done. He got his gear from the room
and they grabbed a taxi and headed down the dusty road, and the Model
T gave him a fair imitation of just how rough Deer Trail might be. They
arrived early but little groups of people were already squatting in the
grandstand, carrying cushions and lunch, grabbing off the choice seats.

"There's Harrell," Brandley said.

A pony race was forming up on the track and Dick Harrell was waving him over, holding a greenback in plain sight. Dewey paid the taxi
driver and climbed the outside fence onto the fresh-floated dirt. Dick
crooked the wrinkled bill at the ponies and said, "All right, you lucky
devil. Which one?"

"You pick," he said. "I'll take the other one for a five spot."

"Taken," Dick said, "an' I pick the sorrel."

Just as they made the bet, the two ponies broke away from the lariat
rope and headed downtrack: Dewey's pony won by two lengths and
Dick just shook his head and paid off.

"An' that settles it," Dick said. "Lucky as you are, I don' think any
horse could buck you off today, not even Overall Bill."

"I've been on him five times the last year," Dewey said, "an' don't
think I rode him five jumps put together. If I'm lucky, Dick, it's because
I never drawed him last night."

"Well," Dick said. "Keep your head and fit that ride on Deer Trail."

Dick headed across the arena toward the roping chute, and Mike
waved from the bronc pens. Dewey walked over and squatted in the
board shade and rolled a smoke while sun heat beat against their hats and
dust tickled their noses, rising from the bone-dry earth. Everything was
going on the same way, all the work and talk and action, saddles laid out,

bareback steers going into the chutes, the water wagon wetting down the straightaway before the grandstand. Mike didn't say much, just stared narrow-eyed toward the east, out where the little mountains pushed up from the plains. Time loafed along, the announcer climbed the platform, the grandstand filled and overflowed, noise was a heavy, damp blanket spilling across the arena. The Roman Race was run, announcements were made, and the first bareback steer rider began the afternoon.

"Dewey," Mike said then. "Are you goin' on from here?"

"Guess so," he said.

"But you're coming back to Raton this winter?"

"I don' know," he said. "Depends on how I do, Mike."

"Saying you come back," Mike said. "Can Johnson depend on you to break those broncs? There ain't a lot of money in it, but it's a good steady job."

"If I get there in time," he said, "I'll do the job."

Mike looked around at the grandstand roof, at the flags and bunting, at the next steer breaking out of the chute. "Dewey, it's time to quit."

"You're here," he said defensively.

"Just a local boy havin' fun," Mike said gently. "Remember what I told you in the spring. I saw the light, that last time we went around."

Yes, he thought, Mike had licked it in the spring while they were finishing out the tag-end crumbs of the circuit, tired and hungry and almost broke. Mike had sat down with himself and reasoned it all out, and now Mike had pushed that weight off his heart. Mike was after him now, knowing what was best, speaking the twenty-four karat truth. Sooner or later he'd see the light. Maybe this summer, maybe in the fall. If he didn't get hurt, if he rode in the money, if he made all the shows from now till November, then he could save a thousand or more, have that stake, that bank roll. But he'd gone out a dozen springs and had the same dream, and come dragging back in the fall with never enough cash to carry him beyond Christmas. Come back hurt, bruised, once with a busted ankle, once with two hundred cash, other times with less than coffee money. Then work through the winters and save up for the spring, and try it again. Mike wanted to help, but one man who broke away couldn't help another. He had to do it on the lonesome, the way any man made or broke his own life.

"Well?" Mike said.

"I know," Dewey said. "I been thinking on it, Mike."

"You keep thinking," Mike said. "Stay sober like you been, stop fighting, stop—" Mike got up and flipped his cigaret away, leaving the last words unspoken. Mike meant stop seeing Babe Smith and all her kind, the kind that went on until they couldn't go back. "Better get ready," Mike said. "Broncs before roping today."

He followed Mike to the chutes and bent over his saddle, adjusted the stirrups, checked spur leather, felt his belly muscles tighten under his belt. The announcer was calling, "Pecos Coker on Overall Bill out of chute one!"

He went to the front of the chutes, just in time to see the gate crack and Overall Bill take off swift and wild, like smoke over hot water. Bill went about fifty feet, then blew the plug; Pecos hit him once in the neck on the first jump, went to the cinch and camped one jump with both spurs, and on the third jump Pecos hit him in the shoulders and kicked back—and popped both spurs together on top of Overall Bill's back as Bill unpacked. Pecos took the dive and old Bill headed for the catch pen. One baby up, he thought, one baby down!

He ran back, got his saddle and bucking rein, and returned as the announcer called, "Mike Cunico out of chute two on King Tut!"

Deer Trail was already in chute three, but somehow King Tut had been put into chute two backwards, and there was King Tut and Deer Trail facing each other. One of the chute men said, "Dewey, your horse is in the chute," but he waited, looking up into Mike's face. It was all there in the thin, wide lips and the hardness that came so seldom to those soft eyes. Mike was going for a buck-off or a terrific bronc ride. And if Mike fit a ride on King Tut it sure would put him somewhere in the money; and more, it meant that Dewey must fit a top ride on Deer Trail. Even knowing as he did that up to then any kind of decent qualified ride would put him over the hill. Just as he got the front cinch tightened on Deer Trail, he saw Mike nod to the gateman, and there came King Tut.

That old horse broke fast and went to throwing curves at Mike that was subject to buck off any bronc rider. Mike was fitting a ride to him until the seventh jump, and then Mike lost a stirrup and the gun went off and the pickup men ranged in, and that was all for Mike. It could happen so fast and easy, a man making a fine ride and then lose a stirrup and that was the end. He wanted to wait and say something to Mike, but time had run out.

He had tightened the front cinch just as easy and gentle as he could on Deer Trail. No rough stuff with this horse, for if you treated him right in the chutes and got out on him with no fighting at all, he was liable to ease up just a little. And ease up was what he wanted, for he'd seen Deer Trail buck off the best. He climbed the chute astraddle of Deer Trail while the boys tightened the back cinch. He rubbed the big horse down the neck, telling him what a good horse he was, saying inwardly how he'd like to get along with him, and he wasn't lying either, he meant every word. When the back cinch was tightened, Deer Trail never moved a muscle.

The grandstand had turned silent, everybody was waiting and watching, for this was the ride of the show. All the boys around him understood, knew that all he had to do was make a good qualified ride and he was in. And a lot of them up in the grandstand understood. They knew he could make a careful qualified ride and win the finals, but they knew, too, that a man bucked off just as easy making a careful ride. It was all that big chance, that gamble he took every time he dropped down on a horse in the chutes. It was feast or famine for his bread, and nothing in between. The finals money or the dribble that passed for third—and zero if you bucked off. He could hear Mike talking earnestly, brown face screwed up with the feeling of his words. He was a damn fool to go on. He had argued it out in his mind and his heart, out there in the Salt River country beside the fires, through the long days. But it was different away from everything he knew. A man could swear that promise then, and come back, and see and smell and hear all this, and could he be a liar because he clung to something so few men ever knew?

"All right, Dewey!"

Dewey Jones took his time. He looked the field over for judges and pickup men, eased down into the saddle, socked both feet in the stirrups and gave that old demon enough head so he sat straight in the saddle and could wipe his chin with the hackamore rein, because Deer Trail had that habit of coming out, throwing his front feet to the left and swinging his head to the right. If you had too close a hold on the hackamore rein, that meant you were pulled off or bucked off pronto. He wanted to break Deer Trail right out of the chute, more or less like Pretty Dick, not wanting him to run and then break in two. He looked down at the hackamore rein again, making sure he hadn't forgotten and shortened up, wiggled his legs, and gave the nod.

"Turn him to me!" Dewey said.

They broke out fast and Dewey stabbed Deer Trail in the shoulders right out of the chute, kicked back to the front cinch, and when Deer Trail left the ground on the second jump Dewey went in the shoulders again, but not too high. He was filled with that wild urge to make it a crazy ride, but he had enough sense to know he couldn't throw a wild ride and last on Deer Trail. He spurred forward on the fourth jump, came back about eight inches behind the front cinch, not trying to kick the cantle board or leave spur marks on Deer Trail. He went to the cinch and camped for one jump as the blood pounded between his ears, all that pounding a man took between body and head, through the neck, all the pounding of the years that finally got a man. He went into the shoulders and came back behind the front cinch, and from there on out spurred about eight inches in front and the same distance behind. It seemed like a good half-hour till he heard the gun, his head was spinning and the big horse was pounding blood flecks into his eyeballs, and the gun sound through the dust and the crowd roar was music to his sunburned ears. This was his year, by god! He had the big start, the money, nothing would stop him now. He kicked both stirrups away, dropped his left hand down by the horn, gave himself a little shove, and stepped off Deer Trail. He lit on both feet and kept his balance, feeling hot and clean and happy, knowing as he made the circus step-off that he had it, he had the championship, he had to come off and finish this way with everything bubbling up inside. Deer Trail ran toward the catch pen, and Elmo Bray rode out of the dust and called down,

"Little man, want a ride back to the chutes?"

He was feeling wonderful, and some huffy too, thinking Bray had let him ride way past time. He looked up and said, "Hell no, pard. I rode down here, I can walk back."

Elmo Bray leaned over his saddle horn and laughed louder and wider than Dewey could ever remember. "Go on, you bastard!" Bray laughed. "Go on then an' take your bows!"

He made the walk and heard the applause lift up around him all the way. When he reached the chutes there was a delay, and Pecos Coker came out on a Brahma steer with his surcingle backwards. Pecos had his suitcase, and the third jump it busted open and out flew the cat and a chicken. Pecos had a red sash around his waist that he unwound as he stepped off the steer. Pecos was wearing a high-topped silk hat and a claw-hammer coat; he swung that red sash out and really put on a closing show. He passed the steer, turned to the grandstand, bowed and doffed his high hat, turned and threw the red sash to the right as the steer passed. And when it passed, Pecos kicked it right in the prat. On the third charge Pecos wasn't so lucky, or else he'd planned it that way for this final show. The steer hung a horn in his shirt and by the time the dust cleared, Pecos didn't have enough clothes above the belt line to flag a handcar. Climbing the fence, Dewey thought how the fun ranked with the serious business, and who would remember Pecos' skill and his own bronc ride a year from now, or even tomorrow. All that people would remember was the steer and sash and cat and chicken. They always remembered that.

Jay Miller had the saddle on Broken Box by then, front cinch pulled and back cinch ready. Jay worked fast because Broken Box was easy to handle in the chute, a smart old horse saving his strength for the curves he'd sure pitch his rider. Jay dropped down and nodded, the gate cracked, and Jay hit him one time in the shoulders and went to the cinch, bogged both spurs right in there and sat tight. Spurring one time under the rules made it a qualified ride, but it didn't give Jay any markings that amounted to much. But Jay Miller knew he couldn't catch Dewey now, all he wanted was second or third money. Jay rode to the gun, and that left number five.

Dewey went over to help Fightin' Bill Baker all he could. Everybody liked Bill because he would fight or fight for you, it didn't make no difference, just so he was fighting something. Bill got the front cinch pulled and stepped over Done Gone, saw Dewey on the top board, and grinned.

"Well, little man, do you think I can ride him or whadaya think?"

"You've rode better bucking horses," Dewey said. "Eat him up, Bill."

"Yes," Bill Baker said softly. "But I was younger then."

Bill looked the field over and then he threw his hat away and showed his big, round head where the hair was getting scarce on top. "Gimme the gate," he called, "an' let's see where we go from here!"

Bill failed to break Done Gone right from the chute. Done Gone ran out before he broke and went to bucking, and then he went into those head spins he'd failed to try before. Bill went to the cinch after spurring him in the neck about two jumps, and just sat down hard. Both spurs in the cinch, and that was where Bill kept them all the way to the gun. And Bill was lucky to last that long, the way Done Gone was going. Bill was a big, strong man and while he made no outstanding ride he stayed on top. But just on top, no more. He never had Done Gone under control after the third jump. That meant poor markings and a tossup for second or third money. Bill stepped off and the crowd began clapping as the judges came trotting up to the platform and turned in their books to Sid LeMay.

Dewey waited for Bill and shook hands, and headed for his bulldogging horse just as the call came for the roping finals. He followed the boys to the fence and climbed up just as Charley Green swung the first loop and made reasonably good time, seventeen and one-tenth seconds.

Cliff Neafus was next, standing five seconds behind the top man for two days, Dick Harrell. Cliff made a short swing, one time, and whipped his loop out like lightning. He caught and stepped off clear, stumbled for a second, and missed the possible record time he had in his hands. Cliff tied in sixteen seconds flat, which meant, as they all knew, that Dick Harrell had to tie under twenty-one seconds to beat Neafus for final first money. George Hardesty came out, took long chances being fourth over all, shot a long loop and watched it fall short. Hardesty had no chance with his second loop so he offered up a few well-chosen words and coiled his rope.

Dick Harrell rode his little iron-gray horse behind the barrier, shook out his loop, and looked over into the chute at his calf. He saw Dewey then and called, "Little man, does that look like under twenty-one seconds?"

"You gut-stripper," Dewey said. "Bring home that bacon."

Dick's big mouth widened as he grinned at the gateman. "Cut him," Dick Harrell said, and leaned forward.

Horse and calf broke together, and when the flag dropped the big Indian was right there. He whipped out a loop that fit the calf's neck like a Stetson and when he stepped off his horse he let out a war whoop, ran down the rope with the calf still running, and then it' was fine to see.

Dick had his left hand on the rope and when he reached the calf's neck he went under neck and belly to grab that right off forefoot and hit the calf with his shoulder as he yanked the foot up. The calf went down in an awkward position, pointing the wrong way for a fast tie. Dick stepped over, holding that foot, his right boot going in between the calf's fore- and hindlegs, and slapped his piggin string on that right forefoot, threw his right boot behind the calf's hindlegs and pushed the calf forward and pulled on the piggin string, hindlegs above his knees, shoving hard, still yelling, squatting then, right foreleg between the two hindlegs, hands moving so fast everything was blurred, making his two wraps and a dally and throwing up his arms, grinning all over, yelling loud, knowing before they announced time that he was in.

Dick rode back coiling his rope and when time was announced, fourteen second flat, it meant first day money and finals, just about eight hundred dollars for the roping. Dewey said, "Well, what you goin' to do with the money?"

"Get drunk, I guess," Dick said. "Why not, I ain't got no sense anyhow. Who in the hell ever heard of an Indian havin' any money?"

But there was a grin on Dick's face like the wave on a slop bucket. Dick might not care much about the money, but he sure was proud of his record, and the way he rubbed the little horse down the neck showed that he was more interested in the horse than in all the wisecracks he made about spending the money. Dewey got the roan and they moved around toward the bulldogging pens, and Dick said, "If you can do as well in dogging, we'll walk out of here with enough money to buy all of Jim Poe's bootleg whisky."

"We'll give it a try," he said.

He was feeling better every minute after proving to himself that he could ride broncs if he stayed sober and didn't pick fights he always lost. Dick Harrell caught a whiff of that cockiness because he grinned and said, "You'll probably lose your steer, being high as the flag on the Fourth of July."

"Hell," he said. "This is the Fourth."

They rode up to the chutes in time to watch Bill Baker and Shorty Kelso make a run down the track, and riding back Bill swung over and winked at them.

"Dewey," Bill Baker said, "if you beat me bulldogging, I think I'm ready to admit that size don't count in bronc riding, bulldogging, or I might add fightin'."

"I won't argue fighting with you," Dewey said. "Good luck, Bill."

Bill swung around the chute, glanced at his steer, and gave the nod. The chute men were using an electric prod today and when the gate cracked they lifted the Brahma out in high gear. Bill and Kelso closed just as the flag dropped. Bill caught his steer in record time and might have gone down in twelve seconds, but his bridle rein wrapped his right ankle as he came off and that yanked his left foot forward. Bill fumbled a tiny bit getting balance before he put on the pressure, but even so he was down in twenty seconds flat. The chute man called, "Come on, Dewey," and turned to prod the steer going into the chute.

Riding around, taking their time, Dick Harrell talked serious. "Dewey, you've got to get out in a hurry to beat that time."

"I know," Dewey said, "but I'm thinkin' mostly about old Dibbs."

"That's what I mean," Dick said. "You can beat Bill, but if that laughing hyena don't fumble he's liable to go down awful fast today. Don't let it worry you, just go out fast and I'll be right there."

Dewey rubbed the roan's neck as they swung in. The roan was very quiet and gentle at the chutes. He was tender-mouthed, too, and Dewey was riding with a hackamore and no bit because he knew his own fault of riding his reins pretty heavy. By taking a short hold on his hackamore rein, he could give a strong pull and slow the horse without hurting that tender mouth. He looked down at the steer and over at Dick Harrell.

"You ready?" he asked.

"Any time, Dewey."

Dewey gave the nod, the gate cracked, and they closed in just as the flag dropped. Dewey jumped high on the neck and the roan's speed today was a bit faster than the steer. He slid right down the neck and hammer-locked under the horns and went for the back hold. He was taking that long chance again, but taking chances for final money was all in the day's work. He dug in and put on the pressure and went down; and when the time announcement came, eighteen seconds, Dick Harrell did some fast calculating.

"About a second ahead of Bill," Dick said. "If Dibbs blows, you're in, if not you got second for sure."

They rode back to the chutes and watched big old Buford Dibbs move in. It never seemed like Dibbs was really riding a horse, he was just up there hanging loose and easy. Dewey called, "Buford, that's the best loose pack that horse ever had on him," and old Dibbs threw back his head and roared with laughter.

"Little man," Dibbs called. "I'm goin' to beat you."

"Don' care if you do," Dewey said. "Bulldogging money'll help buy your wife beans and bolts, an' you can steal the beef."

Dibbs had a steady horse and O. T. Fore, hazing, was swinging in just as steady. Dibbs looked down at his steer and spoke more to himself than anybody else, "Not much horns to work on," and glanced at Fore and nodded to the gateman.

"Cut him to me!"

The steer sailed out and they overrode just a wee bit and checked it early, and for an instant it looked like the steer might cut behind the hazing horse. But the steer came on through and Dibbs hit him forty feet from the flag, and it was just like a woman knitting. Dibbs threw both feet forward, went down the side of the face with his left hand, threw that big right arm in front of the right horn, almost in the same motion, and when he slammed down with all his brute strength, the steer dropped like he was shot with a .30-30.

"Dewey," Dick Harrell said. "I think you're whipped."

"Close," he said. "Buford sure deserves it."

They waited, watching the timers, saw the pencils working on the notebooks, then the megaphone lifted and they heard the time, eighteen and one-fifth seconds. Final money to Dibbs by one-tenth of a second over Dewey Jones, and Dewey second over Baker by a tenth. Dewey could feel the loss in cash, but he never could feel bad losing to a good man. He handed the roan over to Dick and said, "Dick, many thanks," and walked around the chutes while the last events were coming off and the crowd began flaking away at the edges. Elmo Bray rode up and gave him a hand behind, and he rode toward town and didn't look back. Come to remember, he never had looked back. He hung to the cantle and licked his dry lips, and Bray never spoke a word all the way to the hotel, just rode silent and let Dewey down and smiled that cold, flinty grin when Dewey said, "Thanks, Bray."

"Good show," Elmo Bray said. "See you tonight."

He carried his gear through the lobby and took the stairs, and heard somebody at the desk say, "He just won all the marbles." He was straightening out his gear when Brandley came storming in, holding a pint bottle, and said, "How does it feel to be champ?"

"I ain't yet," he said. "I just rode in with Bray and sort of hoped he'd say something, but he never opened his chops."

"Oh hell!" Brandley said. "There's not much argument, Dewey. You're the only man that qualified on three horses. I got to admit that last ride wasn't too hot, but it was a fair ride on a good horse. You're in, boy!"

Dewey smiled and wondered how many drinks Brandley had downed. "Since you're so damn certain, maybe you'd like to pound on the muscles of the champ bronc rider, not to mention second in bulldogging."

"Why, yes sir," Brandley grinned. "I figure it an honor. Just run that tub full of hot water and soak twenty minutes by the watch—but who in the hell's got a watch?"

"Count it," he said.

"I'll drink it," Brandley yelled. "One sip a minute, an' don't get stuck in there or I won't be in no condition to rub nobody."

Dewey ran the tub and took his soaking as prescribed, lay belly down on the rug, and let Brandley give him a hell-for-leather rubdown. When he sat up, feeling fine, Brandley silently offered the bottle. He took it, thinking of the three days behind him, and drank fairly deep. He'd earned one drink, but that was enough. And he knew, feeling the whisky warm his belly, that he was already lying to himself.

"Now, by god," Brandley said, "get dressed and we'll eat before the rush."

Dewey put on clean clothes and dug his black bow tie from his gear and snapped it on, thinking how it was the only sign he ever had to show he was all dressed up. Brandley had bought a new pink shirt to go with his best pants, making them a real well-dressed pair. They had another drink and went downstairs, and Dewey called the best-looking waitress over and said, "Sister, I want the best steak you got back there, an' give this dude here the same thing."

"You won, didn't you?" the waitress asked.

"Yes," Brandley said, "an' smile real nice so he'll tip you double." Then Brandley set the bottle on the table in full view and leaned back with a sigh. "Glad we got here early. I'll need some rest before the dance."

"Doin' what?" he said. "Resting or drinking?"

"A little of both," Brandley said. "I recommend the same for all my friends."

Dewey didn't take another drink because the two shots were working on him fast. He ate his steak and drank his coffee, and when they stepped into the lobby he felt just right, all his feelings eager to come out in words.

"I been keyed up too tight," he said. "Three days of it, Art. I'm goin' upstairs and read the paper and just lay awhile."

"You go on up," Brandley said. "I'll get the paper."

"An' another bottle?" he laughed.

"You're readin' my mind," Brandley said.

Dewey took the stairs and undressed and stretched out on the bed and closed his eyes. When Brandley came up and dropped the paper over his face, he didn't move, just dozed away the time while Brandley sipped from the bottle and hummed a few songs. He had the sweat off his back, the dust cleared from his eyes, the sun wasn't beating down through his hat and frying his brains, the broncs had pounded him again but he was still adding two and two, waiting happily for the best part of it all. Supper hour passed, night came on outside, boots whacked on the hall floor as somebody called, "Shake it up, Ira, they're writin' the checks!"

"Dewey," Brandley said. "Time to go down."

He sat up grinning. "Bring me a basket," he said. "To carry home that cash."

"Want a drink for the road?"

"Not now," he said. "Where'd you get that rotgut, Art?"

"Right off the El Paso boat," Brandley said. "Come on, moneybags!"

They walked downstairs into a jam-packed lobby, everybody watching the headquarters' door where the judges and officials were writing out the checks. That door was locked, nobody could get inside, and it seemed to take longer to write a check than ride a bronc. They pushed through to the door and stood with Mike and Bill Baker and all the boys. Dewey smelled whisky on their breath, and saw the flat lumps in their hip pockets. Everybody had met that El Paso boat. Fifteen long minutes later Sid LeMay opened the door and waved a handful of checks in their faces.

"Ropers," Sid LeMay sang out, and called off the day money winners and passed out those checks, then called off the finals and passed the three big checks, first finals going to Dick Harrell. Then LeMay called off bulldogging and Dewey took his two checks for first and third day money, and second money in the finals. And then LeMay called, "Bronc riders, gather round! Dewey Jones, Bill Baker, an' Jay Miller especially."

Dewey saw Elmo Bray inside the room, grinning out at him. Old Bray had tickled him all the way to town, not saying a word, knowing very well he'd won. He grinned at Bray, and the big man just shook his head and made a motion of counting off bills. Sid LeMay started with day money winners, and as he called the first name, everybody quieted down because at last they'd know the markings.

First day money went to Bill Baker, Dewey second, and Jay Miller third. Mike drew the top for second day money off his fine ride, Dewey again was second, and Pecos Coker had landed third. Then LeMay held up the last three checks and said, "First in the finals, Dewey Jones. Second is Bill Baker. Jay Miller is third!"

When LeMay gave him the big check, Elmo Bray called, "Don't forget the chow-chow," and presented Dewey with a bronze statue of a bucking horse and rider that weighed ten pounds and got him all confused, grabbing check and statue and smarting as the boys slapped his back. He got the statue under one arm, pushed all the checks into his shirt pocket, and then everybody was crowding around, using language that wasn't permissible in Sunday school. He was called everything but a gentleman, all in good-natured fun because the boys were happy and the tension was off. The biggest dance of the three nights started in a few minutes, and that was sufficient reason to send folks singing and yelling down the street. But around him, among the boys, they might laugh and joke but nobody was really as gay tonight after three hard days in the arena. Dewey edged his way toward the desk and there was Babe dressed up like a million dollars. She stopped him, her eyes bright, her skin gleaming tight and smooth tan over those high cheekbones.

"Remember?" she said. "We were goin' to have a night out whether you won the money or not!"

"I seem to recall." He smiled.

"An' now," Babe laughed. "You being champ bronco rider and second in bulldogging, I suppose you got too much money and stand too tall to remember?"

"No," he said. "I'm just the same as I always was, Babe. But I sure proved to myself I can lay off whisky and ride bucking horses."

Babe came right up close to his face and sniffed. "By god, you've had a drink."

"Yes," he said, "an' I might take another. I want to stick these checks in the desk safe. You go on down to the dance, I'll be there in a few minutes."

Babe moved as if she wanted to kiss him. Dewey ducked around her toward the desk and heard her laugh, high and wild, all the way across the noisy lobby. He saw two dude couples turn and stare at her with that nose-in-the-air look, as if they were too good for her kind. And tonight, feeling like he did, that made him draw closer to Babe and his kind than before.

He put the seven hundred dollars' worth of checks in the envelope that already held his Flying A bank roll, and took out fifty dollars in cash. He didn't need a lot of money tonight, and he wasn't about to blow his fresh stake. He went back then and joined the boys and listened to the talk that never changed, with the one question that always touched every mouth after a show ended, "Where you goin' from here?"

"Back to the ranch," Sam Beday said. "Back to punchin' cows. Bill, are you goin' on to Plainview, Texas, to play the show down there?"

"Have a drink," Fightin' Bill Baker said. "Don' bother me yet, I ain't drunk enough to make them rash promises. Little man, wrap that big mouth around this high grade lamp oil."

Dewey took a drink and listened to the talk and felt at home, knowing how those who didn't draw down money were feeling, how they sang the same old tune Sam Beday was singing now.

"Oh hell," Sam said. "I've got to go back and work awhile before I make another show."

"Sure now," Meeks said. "Them McCarty horses has put my head in the mud. Goin' to have to draw forward pay from the boss to buy a quart of whisky to take back to the ranch with me."

"An' no more fancy uniformed waitresses," Buford Dibbs chimed in. "Rather get me a tin cup and plate and get what I want when the cook hollers, 'Chuck,' an' if it ain't cooked right, why, I can look at the cook like a mule at a motherless colt and think what I want to think even if I don' say a word out loud. Little man, what was your take?"

"Seven hundred," he said.

"Reckon it'll last you?" Dibbs said.

"Maybe," he said. "If I squeeze the buffalo, Buford."

"Then have a drink," Dibbs said.

Brandley came up behind him with a fresh bottle and let him drink from Dibb's, then grinned silly and pulled him to one side and made him try the new one. He was feeling the raw whisky now, and before he took the drink he said quietly, "How much money you got, Art?"

"Oh hell," Brandley said. "Enough to eat on a few days."

"Listen," he said. "Let's go down and make that Plainview show. I'd just as well take you along, for them rubdowns is worth money. An' you know, if you get off of center right, you're liable to win a dime one of these days."

"All right," Brandley said.

"But don't say nothin' about this," he said. "Understand?"

"I savvy."

Bill Baker wheeled around and grinned at them. Bill was feeling no pain, happy as a lark, ready to fight with you or against you. Dewey took a drink from Baker's bottle, knowing better than to say no, and said, "Bill, where you goin' from here?"

"I'm heading for a show in Kansas," Baker said. "Up where this McCarty string is goin', because I'm convinced if you follow these old horses around awhile, you'll either come out on top or finish up in the hospital. Be a good show at Dodge City, plenty of stiff competition. Hugh Strickland, Paddy Ryan, Bobby Askins, all the boys'll be there. But hell, if you're goin' to beat anybody, beat the best."

That was the first he'd heard who would be at Dodge City, and right then he knew he had better duck that show and make a smaller one. He had a bank roll and he wasn't hurt, and it was easier to be a big duck in a little pond for a few more shows until he rode himself back into top form. It sounded like Dodge City would be rough not only in bronc riding but bulldogging as well. Paddy Ryan was a good bulldogger, and he'd bet his shirt Mike Hastings would show, not to mention Slim Caskey and Jim Massey. And sure enough, he heard Baker saying they'd be on top, dogging from Jim Massey's Stranger, one of the greatest bulldogging horses of all time. Dodge City would have big steers that cut down his chances, and those other good men dogging off that great horse put him square behind the eight ball. And every bronc rider up there knew as much, if not more, about the McCarty suing.

He kept silent, not mentioning the Plainview show for fear he might change Bill Baker's mind. If Bill went to Kansas that was one less tough man to beat at Plainview. He waited until the bottle was passed around twice more and the boys began thinking about the dance; then he nudged Brandley and eased away, outside on the veranda, where they were alone.

"You hear all that?" he asked.

"I'm not that drunk yet," Brandley said. "Dodge City ain't no place for this country boy."

"We'll go to Plainview," he said. "But don't say nothing about it, Art."

"I can get there," Brandley said, "but I'll be eatin' off you if I don't win some money."

"We can manage," he said. "Now if we're goin' to the dance, let's be on our way."

"Long dry march down there," Brandley said.

He took the bottle and held it a moment, looking across the street, knowing he'd had too much already. He was feeling that warm glow, and Babe was waiting with another bottle. Then he thought of the three days behind, and what lay ahead, and took the drink. He swallowed too fast and coughed, and Brandley pounded his back.

"Second one goes down easy," Brandley said.

"Hell," Dewey said. "That's about the tenth."

"An' what are you doin' with that?" Brandley asked.

He looked down and found the statue in his hands. Brandley started laughing, and all at once it was funny to him too, carrying around ten pounds of bronze that was supposed to represent so much and meant so little. Then Brandley said, "Hell's fire, you're liable to lose it, Dewey," and ran inside. He stood alone, holding the statue, wondering what was wrong with Brandley now. He was already a little unsteady on his feet, and the weeks behind him in the Salt River country were sneaking up, pushing him toward all the things he had fought against. Brandley was back then, carrying the bucking rein, snapping it around the statue, tying the long end around his waist.

"Now, by god," Brandley said. "Just keep a tight rein on that bronc."

They headed down the street and Brandley doffed his hat to everyone they met, slamming his boot heels against the sidewalk so hard the store windows shook. He held the statue under his right arm and followed Brandley up the stairs, hearing the music come blaring down, and he still had time to do the disappearing act. But Brandley turned and yanked him away from the stairhead and yelled, "Go on, boy. I know she's waitin'."

Babe was right there, grabbing his arm, swinging out on the floor in her fancy white buckskin skirt and red shirt. She smiled up at him and pressed close and said, "Champ!" in his ear, and then looked down at the statue and laughed until the tears squeezed from her eyes. He saw Mike dancing with Mary Ashford, but he had no business in that company tonight, not with the boys stopping him every other round and passing the bottles. Neal pushed through and shook hands and asked Babe to dance, but she wouldn't dance with anybody else and said so real loud. That made Neal mad, not at him, but at his sister, because Neal knew too damn well how these nights ended. When Neal wandered off, that made him think to ask, "Babe, where you goin' next?"

"Dodge City," Babe said. "You coming up?"

"I'll think about it," he said.

"You better," Babe said. "Here, have a drink."

She pulled the bottle from her skirt pocket, but another woman called and Babe left him for a minute. Mike showed up then and led him over against the wall near Johnson and the Ashfords.

"You ought to dance with her," Mike said.

"No," he said. "I'm half-drunk now."

"She's smelled a bottle before," Mike said. "She won't bite."

"Mike," he said. "She's too nice for me."

"A-number-one," Mike said gently, "an' I think she sort of likes you."

"Not tonight," he said stubbornly.

"All right, but where you goin' next?"

"Plainview," he said, "but keep it quiet."

"Then I won't see you come morning," Mike said. "I'm leaving out tonight. About this winter. Can Johnson depend on you?"

"If I get back," he said.

"You won around seven hundred," Mike said. "An' you had some cash from that Flying A job. What's your bank roll, Dewey?"

"About a thousand," he said.

Mike nodded soberly. "Enough to keep you goin' all summer. I'll expect you come fall."

"Mike," he said. "I just may triple that."

Mike just smiled at him and shook his head. "Little man, don't con me. Remember when we went out and made the roll and always come home broke. No, I'll expect you come fall, and good luck."

He heard Babe coming, calling to him, and they shook hands quick and hard. Mike said softly, "You damn fool," and then Mike was gone and he was dancing again. His clothes were wet on his back and Babe had sure downed one too many, but so had he for he was getting that don't-give-a-damn wild feeling. Babe said, "Let's go down and get a drink," and he let her swing him toward the stairs.

Just as they started down he saw Mary Ashford look at Babe, and the smile went stiff on her face. Then they were down the stairs, on the street, walking arm-in-arm toward Clancy's. When they stepped inside Clancy came around the bar and shook hands and called out, "I want to buy the house a drink in honor of the champ bronc rider of the Southwest, an' the best woman trick rider in the business."

Two dudes were next to them at the bar, wearing those straight-brimmed straw hats. The nearest dude walled his eyes back and spoke to the other, "Champ bronc rider! Wonder where he picked up the old rip with him?"

"Pard," Dewey Jones said. "Is that any of your business?"

"I can make it mine," the dude said, and stepped back to give himself elbowroom.

Dewey stepped around Babe and hit the dude in the belly, ducked under a roundhouse swing, and slammed home another punch. He was all set to absorb punishment when the dude suddenly doubled up like a jackknife and dropped flat on the floor; and Clancy was between them, holding him back, lifting the dude to his feet.

"That's enough," Clancy said, and grinned broadly at Dewey. "I'll bet my pants this is the first time you ever done that?"

"By god, yes," Dewey laughed. "An' no hard feelings."

The dude was growling and looking for his straw hat, but the boys had tromped it into pieces hardly fit to gather up. Clancy patted both dudes gently and spun them toward the door.

"Outside," Clancy said, "an' don't came back tonight. This ain't the place for you nohow. Outside!"

Then everybody was buying them drinks and Babe was hugging him, and he wished he had stayed at the dance where he could sweat out part of the whisky. Babe said, "Come on," and they broke away from Clancy and made it to the street. Babe started laughing and pointing to the bucking horse statue, and made him put it on the sidewalk and pull it along behind them by the bucking rein. He stopped in the midblock shadows and leaned against a building, and Babe pressed into him and laughed up into his face. "Where we goin'?" she said.

"Dance," he said. "Might as well dance some more."

"Dance is over," Babe said. "Nobody wants to dance."

She was kissing him then, pushing him up the street toward the hotel. He knew they were both staggering along, pulling that damn statue, and they must look a helluva sight. But he didn't care, nothing mattered after three months on the Flying A, and three days that left him sore and tired and uncertain inside, but holding a new stake. He tried to walk faster and Babe lifted her bottle and drank, passed it over and spoke impatiently, like a greedy child, "Come on! Come on!"

CHAPTER FIVE

A MILK WAGON woke him, rattling past. He didn't know how he got there, but he was sitting on the curb outside the hotel with his head in his hands. The bucking rein was still tied around his waist, but the bottom ten inches and the snap were cut off, the bronze statue was gone. He could remember dragging it along the sidewalk last night, meeting some of the boys on the way to the hotel, Babe calling something about fitting a ride, and that was all.

He was not looking too bright a world in the face. He wanted water and he wanted sympathy and he wanted another drink. A hand came down on his shoulder and he tried to look up and his head seemed to break off sharp and fall in his lap.

"Pard," Brandley said gently. "You just couldn't take it, could you? What happened to the woman?"

"Brandley," Dewey Jones said miserably, "you've been a pretty good boy so far. Do you know what you can do for me?"

"I can guess," Brandley said. "The first thing you want is water. The next thing you want is a drink. I'll get the water and while that soaks in I'll get you a piece of a pint somebody dropped in the hall. I don' know what it'll consist of, but I reckon that makes little difference."

He heard Brandley move across the sidewalk into the restaurant. He looked at the gutter between his boots and dropped his head in his dirty hands. Then Brandley was back with a glass of ice water and he nearly swallowed the glass getting it down.

"God," he said. "I want *water!*"

Brandley made another trip and this time brought a metal half-gallon pitcher filled with ice water, so cold it was sweaty on the outside. Dewey poured and drank three glassfuls and laid his cheek against the pitcher's round side.

"Brandley," he said. "You're one of the best boys I ever saw."

"Now I'll go get you that whisky," Brandley said, "but I'm warning you, little man. You'll get just one big drink and if that comes back—an' it sure won't taste as good comin' back as goin' down—then you can have another. But quick as a drink stays down, then we eat. There's not going to be any of these prolonged drunks. You got to stay in condition if you keep me and yourself a-makin' contests. How much money you got left?"

He fumbled in his shirt pocket and spread the wrinkled bills. "Forty-two dollars," he said. "Had fifty last night. Know I drank a hundred dollars' worth. How come I got all this left?"

"Friends," Brandley said quietly. "We all got so many friends. Now after we eat I'll get our gear together and we'll buy a ticket to Plainview. Once we're on the train you can have a few short drinks, an' I mean short. If I'm goin' to take care of you, an' keep you in shape to make us a living, you got to do what I tell you."

"Stop the preaching," Dewey Jones said. "Just get me that drink."

Brandley shuffled his boots a moment and then said, "Dewey, you still want to go to Plainview?"

He lifted his head and looked at the gray sky. He caught Brandley's hand and pulled himself up; and turning across the sidewalk he saw yesterday's program on the dirty cement. He kicked it aside and said, "We got to go on, Brandley. We can't stop now."

Part Three:

THE RED DRESS

CHAPTER ONE

LATE NOVEMBER SNOW had capped the high peaks and sifted white beneath the trees on the pass slopes between Trinidad and Raton. Dewey Jones got down at Raton depot and limped across the street toward the Rock Hotel, gearsack and bedroll heavy on his arms. He was ganted out again and the wrinkles along his sharp jawbone and neck wattles were deeper, burned from another season of summer sun. His broken fingers showed white-knuckled against the rope-burn scars and calluses of the hand gripping the bedroll strap. He walked slowly on his bad ankle and his stoop was more pronounced, but his eyes were still that happy gray flecked with hazel.

He entered the Rock Hotel, the cowboys' home away from home, and felt the damp warmth from the steam radiator under the front bay window. The Rock was a second-rate rooming house with first-rate rooms and warm beds and clean bathtubs in the two bathrooms on the twin halls, heaven for a man fresh off the range. Dewey signed the register and heard Mike Cunico say, "Just like the birds, come home to roost," and turned to shake hands and grin foolishly at Mike's round face.

"You got my wire?" he said.

"This morning," Mike said. "Come on up."

Dewey followed Mike down the east hallway to a middle room, dropped his gearsack and bedroll, and sat quickly on the iron bed. Mike squatted down and pushed a thumb against the wrapped ankle and said, "Well, Ay-rab. Where you been?"

"Mike," he said. "I been all over."

"You never wrote," Mike said. "I wouldn't know if you been to Africa."

"Texas and Oklahoma mostly," Dewey said. "I played some pretty good shows, Mike."

"Start from Las Vegas," Mike said. "When you had that big bank roll."

He reddened under his tan, remembering how he had bragged of coming home this fall with a real stake, of making a clean sweep around the circuit. He wasn't broke, that was true, but neither did he have the cash to prove that Mike was wrong.

"I played Plainview, Texas," Dewey said. "Win second there in bronc riding. But me and Fred Atkinson and Harper was the only three doggers and they wanted four to make it a legal contest. None of them amateurs would volunteer so we dug up an old boy to take fourth entry and agreed to split the money four ways. Bad part about that was, I win the bulldogging and had to divvy all that easy money. Well, I went from there to Frederick, Oklahoma, win some bronc riding and dogging, jumped over to Duncan and bucked flat off on two broncs. Mind you, they was nothin' compared to McCarty's. I guess I just took the round ass. Then I went down to Denton, Texas, and played a little show and won it by mistake."

"Mistake," Mike said. "You mean nobody else entered?"

"Go to hell," he grinned. "The way it was, Bill Baker showed up unexpected, it was just a one-day show, and when Bill come out on a good bucking horse I overheard two of the judges a-talkin'. They were a pair of cotton farmers and one said to the other, 'I didn't like his bronc ride much, you see how his feet was swinging.' So when I come out on an old straight jumping horse that most anybody could of rode mane holt, I bogged both spurs right in the cinch and went to lookin' back at them judges and laughin'. An' just when the gun fired I yelled, 'How do you birds like this?' An' I won the bronc riding and Baker like to threw a fit. He cornered me afterward and said, 'You little bastard, you couldn't of paid them judges very much because this show ain't worth much money, but you either paid 'em off or got something on 'em because I know damn well I made a better bronc ride.'"

"Then what?" Mike asked.

Dewey stripped off his shirt and kicked his boots into the corner and wiggled his toes. He dug the bottle of dago red from his bedroll and they took a short drink and rolled smokes before he went on. He felt good, just coming back to Raton and sitting with Mike, knowing it was all over once more.

"Well," he said. "I hit Wichita Falls next an' had a ride at the old original Crazy Snake. You know that old horse that's been bucking off top hands for quite a few years around there. Mike, there's a bucking horse. Not as powerful as the McCarty horses, but the first thing he does is sort of on the order of Done Gone's head spins. He rares up pretty well, swings his head to the right, and then does kind of a head dive; then he throws you about ten jumps that are damn hard to stay with. But if you can ride him and knock on him, you can sure get plenty of money called if you want to gamble, and there's a standing offer of a hundred from the man that owns him if you stick. I had a go at him and done reasonable well, but I didn't get the hundred because the judges said I never kicked him the first two jumps. An' you know, they might of been right because I was sure busy. Want another shot?"

"Of this?" Mike said, looking at the dago red. "Too damn sour. Where'd you go then?"

"Tulia, Texas," Dewey said. "I rode at that famous little Preacher Dun horse, and there's the freakiest bucking horse I ever saw. He run at stud till he was nine years old and then bucked off everybody that got on him for a year or two, an' I mean he does something to you and I still don't know just what. Every man he bucks off goes right down his right foreshoulder. Maybe you'll ride him three jumps, maybe eight or ten, then it seems like your front cinch breaks and your saddle comes square up in your face, then you make your exit over that right shoulder."

"So you just rode at him, eh?"

"I rode him the first time I got on him," Dewey said. "An' if Brandley and me had any idea I could of made that ride, we might of carried all the money in that town off in a sack. Brandley wanted to bet the roll, I vetoed the idea. So I bet fifty and got three to one, an' then I rode the horse and Art wanted to cut out my liver."

"How many times you ride him?" Mike asked.

"Well," Dewey said. "I went out of there with a little Wild West show Preacher Dun was on. I stayed with them about three weeks, rode at the Preacher nine times, and he bucked me off every time. Mike, I want to repeat, he's a freak bucking horse.

"Then I jumped up to Kansas and made a show, win some bronc riding, jumped at my steer the second day, got off to the right and didn't clear my left foot from the stirrup and hung up. My horse drug me about a hundred feet before my boot came off and turned me loose. Mike, I had gone and got out the comb to comb Little Eva's hair by the time that boot come off. I wasn't hurt bad but it did take something out of me. I couldn't ride or bulldog the last day, so I went out to Fat Hanlon's ranch and rested up and won a little money playing cooncan with the boys.

"Well, by then it was time for the Kansas City Royal. I was fed up and rested so I went for all I was worth. I rode broncs, rode bareback steers, bulldogged, got in the wild horse race and the wild cow milking. All told, I win three hundred and fifty dollars, no big money in anything but some in nearly everything. But I could see I was slipping. That drag I took back in Kansas might of scared me but I wouldn't admit it.

I got tired, I wasn't thinking fast. The last day of the Royal I come out on a steer and made a good ride, an' when the gun went off I stepped down and turned my right ankle. Inside of thirty minutes it was big as a pickle barrel. All I could do was lay up and rest and poultice this damn ankle. I missed two shows an' that was when I sent you the wire and grabbed the train."

"That's all?" Mike asked.

No, that wasn't all, but Mike knew the rest. No use crying over spilt milk. Mike knew how it went, the poker games and drunks, meeting Babe three times at different shows, going on through the summer heat and driving himself as he lost weight and strength at the grind. Getting bucked off and feeling the blood pound in his head and redden his eyes. Riding the branch line trains, eating in the greasy spoons, sleeping wherever he could find a room. Parting from Brandley in August, teaming up with other boys, going on again, saying so long as they went their own split ways. Over four months since Las Vegas and he told it all in a few minutes, sitting on the bed in the warm room, holding the bottle of dago red between his hands.

"That's about it," Dewey said. "Well, Johnson and them ranchers still want me down around Cerro Grande?"

"Sure," Mike said. "He's got four, five of 'em lined up."

"I guess I promised," he said. "Better do the job. What they paying this winter?"

"Three dollars a bronc," Mike said. "How's your bank roll?"

"Around two hundred and fifty," he said. "I ain't broke by no means."

"No," Mike said softly, "but you sure as hell made and spent plenty since the Fourth. Never mind that. I've got something to tell you. What would you think about taking old Jim Tully's horse outfit up in Moreno Valley? Tully's in town right now, an' he knows that you know horses. He's got a little spread up there with two, three hundred head of horses and a few cattle. He wants to turn the outfit over to somebody who'll handle it right, so he can stay in town during the winter. Of course, he'd be up on the place some and sure to be there in the summertime. Why don't you talk to him, it just might develop into something worthwhile."

"Moreno Valley?" Dewey said. "Five foot snow on a level and forty below zero! I don' know whether I'd want to live up there or not."

"What the hell you care about deep snow and cold weather?" Mike said sharply. "If it's a decent living and gets you off the road an' away from these rodeos. Dewey, you left out from Las Vegas with a thousand dollars, you won plenty more, and you come home with practically nothin'. You ain't getting anywhere, Dewey, and you damn well know it!"

"So you set this up for me?" he said.

"Sure," Mike said. "Tully wants a good man, an' you qualify in a left-handed fashion."

"All right," he smiled. "I'll see him. But you know, them hot biscuits and that woman cooking I'll get down there breaking horses, an' them good old featherbeds, it all looks good to yours truly. I can just smell them baked beef ribs and Mexican beans right now. Hell, let's go eat. I been on that Santa Fe train since yesterday."

"Wash up," Mike said. "I'll wait downstairs."

Mike slapped his back and left him digging clean clothes from the bedroll. He soaked and shaved the train soot away, and felt like a new man when he walked downstairs. They ate supper at Mary Forina's boardinghouse and came straight back to the Rock Hotel, into the little sitting room just off the office, where a short, stocky man got up from a rocking chair and shook hands with Mike.

"Here's Dewey," Mike said. "He ain't broke or hungry right now, just had supper and he's got a little money, but catch him with a full belly and a good humor."

"Hello, Jim," Dewey said. "You don't look any different to what you ever did. When was the last time I saw you?"

"Spring of '24," Tully said. "In Taos. You was drunk."

"An' you were drunker." Dewey grinned.

Jim Tully was about five-eight and almost bald. When he shook hands he popped a man's fingers, and his steel-gray eyes looked straight through. Tully's once-over was swift and final, his opinion of a man was formed right there, and whether good or bad he demanded a strong demonstration before changing his mind. Tully was an Easterner by birth, from Massachusetts, but he'd been in the West fifty years and nothing remained from childhood but his Irish brogue. He wore flat-heeled boots with legs clear to his knees, and spur marks were deep and worn on his boot-heel spur pieces. He stood bowlegged and leaning forward a little, thumbs hooked in his belt, and he spoke with direct bluntness.

"Set down, Dewey. I want to talk to you a little."

"Fire away," Dewey said.

He and Mike took the empty rockers. Tully passed cigars and wasted no time on small talk.

"I've got a little 1480 acre ranch in Moreno Valley," Tully said. "Some of it fenced, all the outside country you want, plenty of grass when it ain't covered with snow, plenty of water, a cow's paradise and better for horses. I've got about two hundred head of grown mares, eleven studs, and the colts. About eighty head of pretty good cattle. But I'm a-gettin' too old to stand the gaff. I was out in thirty-five below zero weather last winter and had a spell that gave me pneumonia. The damned croaker says I frostbit my lungs and I should get out of that high country for a winter or two anyway. An' I'm looking for a man that can take that horse outfit and bring it on through, an' I'll make him a good proposition. When Mike told me you was due back, I says to him that sounds good. I've known you quite awhile in a roundabout way, Dewey, an' I think you savvy horses."

"Well," Dewey said, "I already promised to break out some stuff in Cerro Grande Valley, an' that woman-cooked grub sounds good to me for this winter." He grinned then. "I can work as I want to, an' I'm not goin' to work too hard at it."

"Regular rodeo bum," Mike said softly. "Listen, Dewey. Why don't you go on up to Moreno Valley with Jim and look his spread over before heavy snow? You ain't got no set date to start that horse breaking."

"I'm goin' up tomorrow," Tully said. "We'll stop over at Cimarron with Jerry Chanceller. He's the banker and a good man to meet. We can drive on up to the ranch next day, look the place over next day, and I'll bring you back on time."

"I don't know," Dewey said.

"That ankle ain't strong yet," Mike said. "Why don't you go on up?"

Mike was pushing him and Tully seemed fairly eager to take him along. Even if he made no promises, the trip might do him good. And it would sure please Mike.

"All right," he said. "You want me to take my saddle and stuff along?"

"No need," Tully said. "I've got saddles and beds and plenty to eat, by Gawd. I just sent the freight wagon to Ute Park last week for winter supplies."

"Ute Park?" Dewey said. "What in hell is there at Ute Park where you can buy groceries? Somebody start a store there?"

"Hell no," Tully said. "I ship my stuff in from Montgomery and Ward, wagonload at a time. For meat we eat mostly deer, turkey, an' somebody else's beef." Tully grinned dryly then, and Dewey knew he was kidding on the square. "I'll see you at breakfast," Tully said. "Six o'clock."

They got up and said good night to Tully, and loafed awhile in the little sitting room. Mike stood in the window and watched the switch engines in the railroad yards, and finally pointed his cigar at Dewey.

"Don't blow this one," Mike said. "Even if you don't take him up till spring."

"I promised to break broncs," Dewey said. "You got me into that, remember?"

"Sure," Mike said. "But Tully'll wait till spring. Now you soak that ankle and get a night's sleep and go up with him. I'll be here when you get back."

Mike dropped his cigar into the spittoon, smiled faintly, and went off through the lobby into the night. A settled man, Dewey thought, going home to sleep and go about his good job that was steady and had a future. Dewey Jones took the stairs slowly, feeling the dull ache in his ankle, and carried a bucket of hot water from the bathroom to his own room. He sat on the bed and soaked his foot and drank from the bottle of dago red. Here he was facing a good proposition that could mean all the future for any man, and already he was thinking of next spring when the bands played and the broncs came out of the chutes.

CHAPTER TWO

TULLY WAS WAITING at Mary Forina's boardinghouse next morning at six o'clock. They got outside a breakfast of hot cakes with blackstrap molasses, home-cured ham, and coffee that would float a wedge. Tully took him up to Lloyd Brothers livery stable, harnessed a team of mares, and headed south on the long haul to Cimarron. False dawn lifted behind the plains peaks to the east and shone westward against the snow tips of the Cristos.

"Robes in the box," Tully said.

Dewey pulled the buffalo robes from the box and they huddled down facing the wind and early chill. Tully didn't talk much, just chewed unlit cigars and drove, intent on the road and his own inner thoughts. They ran hard and steady through the short fall day and came into Cimarron at sundown with the Cristos throwing long black shadows across the town. When they stopped at the banker's house Dewey hung back while Tully and Chanceller shook hands for about five minutes and called each other names that wouldn't sound good in Sunday school.

"Well, pard," Tully said finally. "We're here for the night. Get that lazy boy to unharness my team, put 'em in a warm place, and feed 'em good. An' it might be a good idea to tell your cook to put on another pot of coffee and four good big extra steaks, for me and this boy is hungry. We ain't had no dinner, an' we're goin' to make them groceries of yours do the disappearing act."

"You got any more orders?" Chanceller asked.

"Well," Tully said, "not right now, but I'll probably think of some."

Dewey grinned at the way those two old-timers were greeting each other. Chanceller was just Tully's size and shape, a mighty strong man with gray hair and friendly blue eyes and a solid jaw that pushed out like granite. Then Tully said, "Hell, Jerry. I forgot all the manners I ever had. I want you to meet the man that's goin' up to look over the ranch with the idea of running it for me. Dewey Jones, this is Jerry Chanceller, the biggest interest hound in New Mexico. Jessie James used a gun to rob people, but this old badger uses half a pencil and does a better job than Jessie ever thought of. If you stick around this country, Dewey, you'll have to get money from him because he's got all there is."

Chanceller shook hands and said, "Dewey, I saw you ride a couple of times, never got to meet you before. Now come on in, supper's ready."

Chanceller led them through his entrance hall to the dining room and they tied into beefsteak and gravy, sourdough biscuits, and stewed prunes for dessert. Everything was cooked to a turn by Chanceller's Mexican cook, the coffee was extra good, and Tully hadn't misrepresented when he said the groceries would disappear. After supper Chanceller shooed them into the big living room and they dropped into stuffed chairs before the fireplace where Tully and Chanceller went to talking over the past season as to grass and horses and cattle and people. Dewey kept his mouth shut, remembering other years and other houses where settled men talked and laughed over the small pieces of a life he had never known. He dozed in the fire heat and heard the words as if his ears were stuffed with cotton batting.

"Who's Tom McHibben workin' for?" Tully asked.

"A-6."

"Sure would make me a good man," Tully said. "He savvies horses and there ain't a lazy bone in his body, but he just can't stay sober. I don't mind a man gettin' drunk, but I do mind him staying drunk. How is Stan and Mason Chalmers gettin' along?"

"Just fine," Chanceller said.

"Who'd they sell their cattle to this year?"

"Kansas City firm," Chanceller said. "They made good money."

"Say," Tully said. "How is old Captain Adams? I ain't seen him since early summer."

"Same as ever."

"Which reminds me," Tully said. "Has old Dickens come over from England this year?"

"Not this year, Jim."

Dewey knew of Dickens and Captain Adams. Adams was general manager of the DS Land and Cattle Company, and Dickens was the owner who came over every year to inspect his property. Dickens built the railroad from Colfax to Cimarron, and Dewey remembered the time the conductor threw Dickens off his own train because he wouldn't pay his fare.

"Has Charley swallowed up Sanchez's little ranch yet?" Tully asked.

"Not yet," Chanceller said gently. "But he's workin' at it, Jim."

"Oh, he'll get the job done," Tully said. "That's the way it goes, the whales always swallow the minnows."

They talked on and Dewey listened until nine o'clock. Then supper and the soft chair and the fire made him sleepy. Chanceller's cook showed him to an upstairs room, smiled good night, and padded away. Dewey undressed and fell into bed and didn't remember anything until the door opened and Tully began cussing at him loud and happy.

"Wash your face!" Tully shouted. "What you want to do, sleep your whole life away? You're not makin' rodeos and laying up till ten o'clock, you're back in cow country."

"No," Dewey said, "an' I don't set up chewing the fat till midnight."

"Wasn't midnight." Tully grinned. "Was only eleven-thirty."

Tully stomped downstairs and Dewey could hear him growling at Chanceller over breakfast. Tully was just feeling good because he was going home again; his kind was never happy in a town. Dewey washed and hurried down to eat breakfast with them while Chanceller's boy drove the team and buggy round front. They downed the last bite, reached for their hats, and Tully said, " Jerry, you treated us too nice. We'll be back day after tomorrow night for the same treatment, an' ain't no use for you to grumble and growl, an' not a doubt in my mind this beef we ate is either stoled or you foreclosed a mortgage on some widow woman."

"With eight kids," Chanceller said. "Dewey, you stop by any time."

"I will," Dewey said. "Many thanks."

Chanceller followed them to the buggy and when they got settled he looked up at Dewey and smiled faintly. "Take a good look at Jim's ranch," Chanceller said. "It's the place for a man like you."

Then they were heading out of town up the first slopes of Cimarron Canyon, driving into a clear day between the rising walls that narrowed as they followed the rocky trail beside the river. The narrow gauge railroad track followed the twisting river, shadowed by the trees that dropped from the high peaks in a flood of green and blue. They reached Ute Park at noon, passed through the valley, and dived into the wildest section of the upper canyon. Tully fingered his reins and watched for rock slides and spoke to the mares as they climbed toward the blue sky beyond the rim. In late afternoon they topped the rim and looked down on Moreno Valley, the lake to the south and Therma, a bunch of ragged cabins, off to the north on the E-Town trail. Tully drove off the rim and swung around the lake toward his ranch five miles below; and reaching the boundary of the ranch, pointing with one hand, Tully told Dewey Jones about his land.

The long part of the 1480 acres lay east to west, one thousand acres on Six Mile Creek, a good stream that ran almost the full length of the ranch. Tully had two hundred acres of viga land that cut a half-ton of hay to the acre, with plenty of grazing in the fall of the year after the cutting. That piece was fenced and used as a holding pasture in the fall. When horse buyers came up Tully could keep his stock in the pasture and not go to the trouble of rounding up. There was timber on the south side for firewood, big log timber for houses and sheds and posts. A hundred-odd acres pushed into open country that gave Tully grazing access to the whole valley. It was beautiful country to Dewey's eyes, ankle-deep gramma grass and fine trees and good water. The cattle were so fat they had combs, all the horses were rolling fat, and the six-month old colts were like butterballs. He could tell right off that if you went to corral those little colts and they broke away, you'd need a good horse to head them off.

They drove into the yard just before darkness, enough time for a good look around. Tully had all kinds of corrals made mostly of cedar stakes set in the ground with woven wire wound in between. Tully's bronc pens were big cedar posts eighteen inches thick set in the ground with long logs laid flat for the walls. The main bronc pen would defy a bull elephant to break it down, with a two-foot cedar pole in the middle for the snubbing post. Tully had cowpens for roping and branding, other pens for overflow work, a long horse shed with hay stacked on the roof. Tully kept his riding horses in the corrals at night and probably fed them plenty of hay, but hardly any grain, it being too far a haul from the railroad for expensive oats and corn. About fifteen feet from the southwest corner of the house Dewey saw the well, and Tully explained proudly that it was only twenty feet deep but water stood six feet from the top, good soft water for drinking and cooking. Six Mile Creek handled the problem of stock water.

"Strong house," Dewey said then.

"Built to last," Tully said. "Hey, Pablo! Juan!"

Tully's cowboys came from the horse shed and took the team and met Dewey Jones. Tully rubbed his backside, gave them orders for the morning, and limped up the path toward the house.

"Come on in," Tully said. "An' you can bet supper's cold."

He followed Tully inside and ate his share of supper cooked an hour ago. Dewey drank coffee to keep his eyes open and looked at the house while Tully talked about the weather and getting up early to ride out the ranch.

"Build it yourself?" Dewey asked.

"Every damn log," Tully said proudly. "Four rooms, cut and snaked them wall logs down off the hill, dovetailed an' laid 'em. Chinked 'em with mud and straw mix."

Inside, the walls and ceilings were lined with rough-cut timber, the floor was six-inch planed pine lumber shiplap cut for a tight fit against draft. Bear rugs were scattered around, and Tully pointed out the fawn hides tanned by Taos Indians. Tully lived in one room, another room was for storage, they sat in the kitchen, and the fourth room was supposed to be the bunk room but seldom used in winter, being so cold. The cowboys usually bunked in the kitchen beside the big stove. It was a good house, solid built, but nobody had swung a mop or scraped a broom for months.

Like every place Dewey had ever seen, it needed a woman to make it come alive.

"You asleep?" Tully asked.

He opened his eyes and grinned. "Damn near, Jim."

"Then go to bed," Tully said gruffly. "Grab a bunk in the spare room, blankets on the shelf. We'll get up early."

Dewey crossed the hall into the musty-smelling bunk room. He dragged blankets off a shelf and sat down to toe his boots off. He was sleepy and he knew why, coming up from low country to nearly ten thousand feet altitude, and only two days making the change. He fell back on the lumpy mattress and pulled the blankets to his chin and closed his eyes. The last thing he heard was Tully cussing out Pablo and Juan for not keeping supper hot on the stove, telling them to have horses ready at the crack of daylight.

CHAPTER THREE

DEWEY WAS ROUSTED OUT before the first rooster crowed to help fix breakfast on the old Home Comfort cookstove. While Pablo cooked deer steaks with water gravy, Dewey made sourdough biscuits and let them raise in the warming oven, then served them up golden brown just as the steaks were done. Juan ground Arbuckle coffee that had come in a hundred-pound green bean sack and had to be roasted first in the oven over a slow fire. They ate fast, racing the sun, and Tully gave orders for the day before Dewey downed his second cup of coffee.

"Got the horses ready?" Tully asked.

"Sí," Juan said.

"Hitch up the work team," Tully said. "Haul in a load of hay and put it on the horse shed. Dewey and me will be ridin' out so if anything comes up, handle it yourself. Savvy?"

"Bueno," Pablo smiled. "Dewey, you full?"

"Plumb full," Dewey said. "Good meal, Pablo."

"Good biscuits," Pablo said. "Better'n mine."

"You can kiss later on," Tully growled. "Come on, Dewey."

Tully led him outside to the waiting horses and headed southeast around the lower part of the lake, crossed a creek into timber, and right off spotted two bands of horses and some cattle up Turkey Canyon. Riding close, they saw that one bunch was Tully's and the other practically all TG brand. Tully just pointed them out casually, not looking for anything in particular, taking plenty of time so Dewey could see the horses and the lay of the land. But all the time they rode, up and down ravines, across grassy meadows, around deadfalls, Tully talked about horse breaking and breeding, castrating colts, haying, making up road bands, feeling Dewey out as to his knowledge of handling a horse outfit. Tully wasn't quite ready to begin serious talk, and Dewey could tell that from the way Tully cracked dry jokes and even grinned once in a while. Stopping to blow the horses on a crestline in the midmorning sun, Tully felt so good he told the story of how he bought the ranch, something Dewey had only heard through vague second-hand rumors.

"After that Dutch Syndicate bought the Grant," Tully said, "it seemed like they got their fit in the wringer for ready cash at the time I was fixing to buy this piece of their land. I got down to brass tacks with their lawyer and he advanced the idea to me that I had to sign one of their standard sales contracts that reserved all mineral and timber rights. Now what that meant, I wasn't sure, so I pinned him down and asked just where them rights started. Then I found out I was buying eighteen inches down from the surface, and no timber or mineral rights at all. Well, I knew they needed cash money so I said, 'No, by Gawd! If I buy from you, I buy just as goddamned high as I can see, and just as low as I want to dig down. Take it or leave it, an' right now!' Well, they took it, an' I'm about the only one who bought land from 'em that way."

That started Dewey off remembering other stories about Tully in bygone years, and one in particular that had gone the rounds. Tully had taken a bad cold that turned into flu and was brought down to Springer in a buckboard more dead than alive. There was no hospital so the doctor put Tully up in the hotel, and along toward nightfall it looked pretty black for Tully. The doctor brought the padre up just in case. The padre went through the rigamarole and finally got down to brass tacks. He wanted to know if there was anyone Tully wished to forgive. Tully said,

"I don't know anybody I owe, I don't know anybody I done anything to."
But the padre knew better. Everybody knew the old quarrel between
Tully and Pat Meeker that had been going on for years and almost come
to the shotgun route three times. The padre asked if that old hatred was
patched up, had they made friends, had he forgiven Pat Meeker, or to
be blunt about it, was Tully going to forgive Pat tonight in case he died.
"No, by Gawd!" Tully said. "It ain't been patched up. I'm still as mad at
him as I ever was." So the padre asked once more if Tully would forgive
Pat. "If I die," Tully said, "I'll forgive him. But if I live, I'm still the
same old fightin' James Tully!" That was Tully all right, every day and
through the years, tough as an old boot and honest as the day was long.

They rode on and finally Tully said, "Dewey, I know you understand
cattle, and there's every reason to believe you understand horses. But
mind ye, there's many a man will work horses and cattle all of his life
and still never learn the art of how to use a pair of spurs or turn a wild
calf. Fact of it is, they just don't think." Then Tully grinned. "An' there's
a lot of 'em ain't got nothing to think with—Hey!"

Tully saw the turkeys and yanked his old .30-30 from the saddle
boot and knocked down a big gobbler. Dewey rode into the trees and
got the turkey, and they rode on again, talking easier now. Most of the
stock was down in the valley this time of year, for Tully was cutting
both horses and cattle, getting ready to road them to the Ute Park railroad. Tully explained all that while they made a full swing around the
ranch and came back to the house at two-thirty. They were just sitting
down to eat when Colonel Bateman, the cow foreman of the Bateman
Cattle Company, and one man rode in and joined them at the table.

"Tully," Bateman said, "I'm sure glad you got something to eat."

"Set," Tully said, and waved at the empty chairs.

Pablo and Juan came up from the horse shed and Tully told Pablo
to clean the turkey and bake it for supper. Dewey said, "I'll handle the
turkey, Pablo," and Pablo grinned, happy to get out of that detail. When

Pablo and Juan went outside to clean the turkey, Bateman got down to the purpose of his visit.

"Tully," he said. "I want sixty head of your top broncs for saddle horses. What are they goin' to cost me?"

"What age?" Tully asked.

"Three-year-old past," Bateman said. "We want to break them out next spring and put 'em to work next fall."

"They'll cost ye fifty-five dollars apiece," Tully said. "When you go to cuttin' that many of my top horses out."

"Tully," Bateman said, "I think you're a little high."

"Well, by Gawd!" Tully said calmly. "You don't have to buy them. You know I've got the best horses in the country and it just don't pay to buy nothing but the best, an' there ain't no use of arguing any more providing you want to pay fifty-five a round. We'll round 'em up in the morning and you can go to cutting them. If you don't want to pay the price you're sure welcome to stay all night and travel your road home tomorrow."

"Well," Bateman said. "I'll ride out in your pasture and look that bunch over now. I'll give you my answer while we eat that turkey."

"Well, by Gawd!" Tully said. "Eat my turkey and then don't buy no horses!"

Bateman winked at Dewey and left with his man to make his riding circle and get the general run on Tully's horses. Dewey shooed Juan out of the kitchen and took over the job of cooking the fresh-cleaned turkey because he knew, from the way Tully was getting settled, that he was in for an afternoon of cross-examination to see if he was capable of taking the outfit and making it pay. While he got the turkey ready Tully sat at the table with a cup and the coffeepot and began talking about the business, telling how he sold his horses mostly to ranchers in the area, like Bateman, and shipped some mares and stallions to the Kansas City market.

"Dewey," Tully said then. "I understand that your method of breaking horses is with a hackamore, no spurs, an' no rough treatment. Mike tells me you rope 'em by the forefeet and as soon as you get a hackamore on 'em, the rough treatment is over."

"That's right," he said.

"And I understand you use that method of tying them up to a rope between two posts with a spring tied in to keep 'em from pulling their head down. I like that because I've had half a dozen horses in the last two years with their head pulled down by tying them to something solid. An' I don't like tying 'em to a drag for the simple reason they get over the rope and rope-burn themselves and if they don't burn their legs it still takes years to get 'em over being afraid of a rope dragging on the ground or getting tangled in their hindlegs some way."

"That's the way I do it," Dewey said. "I like the idea of not being rough on broncs because you can break a horse without breaking his will power."

Tully looked up sharply. "I never thought of it in just that light. But I sure like the idea. Dewey, what's your general ideas on breeding?"

"Well," Dewey said, "my belief in breeding horses is the fact to try to keep a stallion with a bunch of mares not over two years, for you don't want inbreeding, and the fillies is liable to breed back the spring they're a two-year-old. Talkin' that way, what's your deal on trading stallion with other outfits?"

"I don't do that," Tully said. "I breed steeldust and when my stallions ain't no more good I just ship 'em to Kansas City and buy new ones and bring 'em up here. There's not much to breeding these half-wild horses anyway. Just watch 'em and take care of 'em."

"Oh, there ain't?" Dewey said. "Then you sure don't need anybody as high-priced as me."

Tully grinned and pushed his nose against the rim of his coffee cup to hide the smile. "Well, you've seen the country and the general run of my horses. I've got around sixty mother cows I'm going to keep over this winter, already shipped the calves out. You can see the way I sell my horses, an' I wasn't putting on no show for your benefit. If Bateman don't take 'em somebody else will. An' with these horses being broke out, which can be done some during the wintertime on sunshiny days, especially halter broke and broke to lead, them horses will be worth fifteen to twenty dollars a head more money. Now I'm looking for a man, but I don't want him to work for wages. I want him to draw wages, sure, plus a percent of what the ranch'll make because if you give a man some interest in what he's a-doin', he'll make you a better hand, come nearer saving you money and doing a good job. I'd like to hear how you feel about this, Dewey. How does the country suit you?"

"Fine," Dewey said. "I never saw any country I ever liked better, Jim."

"Are you ready to get this roaming rodeo stuff out of your head?" Tully said. "And them periodical drunks I hear you throw? Mind you, I don't care about you gettin' drunk, but I'd hate to hear of you staying drunk."

"Jim," he said, "I don't know. I'm just a little bit confused right now. I don't know yet if I've got the bug out of my system. I got hung up and drug this fall; I wasn't hurt very bad but it could have been bad on a bronc instead of that gentle horse. To be frank with you, it's got my bile crowding my liver. But I can't be sure yet. I don't want to believe there's very many raw broncs that'll buck me off unless they catch me nappin'."

"Now hold on," Tully said. "I'm not doubting your ability as a bronc rider. You ain't answered my question; you was just thinkin' out loud about things I ain't got time for."

"An' I can't answer you right now," Dewey said. "Not no honest answer. Besides, you ain't told me your proposition. This is your spread and, mind you, here I am a-comin' into it if I do without any outlay of money, in fact the only belongings I've got is my saddle and bedroll and two hundred and fifty dollars. That ain't much to offer. Maybe you better shoot first."

"Well," Tully said, "I've done and got my proposition figured out, has been since we was on the road yesterday. I'll give you forty dollars a month and twenty-five percent of what the ranch makes. You to hold the stock as they are now, keep the breeding done, and after the year's expenses are took out we split seventy-five and twenty-five. I'd want to keep you out here one year, and listen, sonny boy, I'm goin' to keep a pretty close eye on you for that year. Then, if I think you can handle the job, we can work out a better deal. I'm a-gettin' old and these hard winters and the riding is telling on me. I'd like to go to Raton during the winter and stay in one of them places with a toilet and kitchen and steam heat, just set there easy and know that things was right on the ranch. So that's it, Dewey."

"I believe I can handle the outfit," Dewey said. "And the deal is sure fair. But you know I've got that obligation to break horses in Cerro Grande, and I can't break my promise to those people. You've got two good men here, it looks like, and not too much work till spring. I'd appreciate it if I could give you my answer in the spring."

"No," Tully said. "You can't break no promise. One more thing—if you do come up and make the right kind of man, in time to come you know that I'd be selling you the ranch."

"With what?" he said.

"Never mind a lot of cash," Tully said. "You could make yearly payments on it. I've got no living relatives I care anything about, an' all I want the rest of my life is a decent living." Tully looked down at his cup. "Of course, I'd like to spend the summers up here and do what little work I wanted to do. So it might be, some day, that you'd wake up with the spread and wonder how you got it."

"Thanks," Dewey said gently. "That's more than fair, Jim."

"So I'll tell you," Tully said. "Wait till we get back to Raton. I'll let you know then if I figure I can wait on you till spring."

CHAPTER FOUR

THEY PULLED INTO Raton after dark and put the team and buggy away before eating supper at Mary Forina's. Over the pie and coffee Tully got down to business.

"All right," Tully said. "You still of a mind to give me an answer come spring?"

"Maybe sooner," Dewey said. "Depends how fast I finish my job."

"Well," Tully said, "I'll wait on you. But not past March."

"You'll know before then," he said.

Tully seemed to be reading his mind, how he liked Moreno Valley and knew it was the big chance, but hated the thought of winters up there alone.

"You're young," Tully said abruptly. "You figure on staying single?"

"I never met the right one yet," he said.

"If you take me up," Tully said, "you ought not to be alone up there."

Dewey said, "You got by."

"Never found the right one," Tully said gruffly. "Guess I never took the time to look. Wish I had now. Well, I'm tired and I want to sleep. Good luck to you, Dewey."

"The best to you, Jim."

He shook hands and watched old Tully go slowly from the boarding-house. He felt lonely tonight, thinking of the old man who had never allowed loneliness to get the upper hand. That was himself forty years from now, if he lived, if he kept on the way he was going.

"Well?" Mike said.

He turned in his chair and shook hands, and told Mike how much he'd enjoyed the trip and Tully's company. They walked down to the saloon and had a drink, but he wasn't in the mood for drinking. The noise bothered him, all the cussing and talking and sound of bottles on the bar and table tops.

"So he gave you till spring?" Mike said.

"I couldn't promise now and mean it," Dewey said. "An' the way I feel, I better start for Cerro Grande in the morning."

"How long will the job take you?"

"Depends on the number of horses," Dewey said. "I guess about two months."

"That's in January," Mike said. "You can give Tully his answer then."

"Sure," he said. "Ought to have it decided by then."

"By the way," Mike said quietly. "Watch your step down there."

"Trouble?" he asked.

"More like friction," Mike said. "Nothin' that can't be handled with common sense."

He knew what was happening down in that country. The little fellows were having a tough time getting started in the cattle business, so they were busting up grass to plant pinto beans, raise a few cows, and dream about growing bigger. That section had always been cow country and he was a cowman himself, first and always, but he'd gone hungry too many times to get prejudiced against the little man. Knowing the cause of friction, he said, "Since when has old Jerome and Stinett got common sense when some sod-buster starts breaking up good grass?"

"Never," Mike said, "but them little fellows has got to eat. They're plantin' beans, sure, but they're starting cows and horses fast as they can. What I mean is, things down there are sort of in a change-over.

Nothin' like the old days, but don't stick your nose into other folks' business."

"I won't," he said. "I'll just concentrate on pattin' those broncs on the butt."

"Well," Mike said. "Let's have one for the road, then you get to bed."

"Can you find me a horse?" he asked.

"Sure," Mike smiled. "Just don't forget where you got it. Now drink up, an' I'll see you at breakfast."

Chapter Five

DEWEY JONES RODE south and east next morning toward Capulin Mountain and old Cerro Grande, into the valley where the big outfits had run cattle for years: the J Bar J owned by John King, the El Torres LT which was sheep, the XIT further on south, Jerome's Laxy J, and Buck Stinett's Big S. Back at Raton it was all railroad and mining, but out here, where folks traded in Des Moines and Capulin, it was honest-to-God cattle country.

But the little fellows had started fencing in a few acres for farm land patches, trying to make a fortune growing pinto beans and running some cattle on the open grass. They got three and a half cents a pound for beans, and averaged about five hundred pounds to the acre; and doing this with walking plows, planting open furrows by hand, and praying for rain. They had a rough row to hoe and nobody understood their troubles better than Dewey Jones.

He rode into that country, thirty-two miles from Raton, facing a cold wind that could change overnight to winter's sharp knife-edge; and easing under the shadow of Capulin Mountain, near the old Clayton stage stop, he saw a house and barn and windmill, and a woman plowing two work horses under the pale yellow fall sun. Here, where open range had rolled on not long ago, another family had put down roots.

He stopped beside the barn and watched her make the far turn and come plowing back; and when she gave him a friendly wave and he saw her dress, his jaw dropped six inches. For she was out there plowing in a red silk dress, tromping along in the dust behind that walking plow, her blond hair tied up behind her ears with a piece of store string, and that red dress shining in the sun. Dewey thought he'd seen everything, but this was absolutely new. And then, when she got closer, he recognized the girl he'd met at Las Vegas.

"Water in the bucket," Mary Ashford said. "You got time for coffee?"

"Water'll do fine," Dewey said, and then he stared open-mouthed at that red dress.

"Oh," she laughed. "I guess it looks mighty odd."

"It sure does," Dewey said honestly. "You looked like a sensible woman at Las Vegas, but I never heard of plowing in go-to-town clothes before."

"Listen," Mary Ashford said. "I've got two dresses to my name. One's dirty and soaking with all my pants; the other dress is this. That field has got to be turned over before snow, and I've got to do it. And besides—" she laughed again —"it makes me feel happy rich inside, plowing in a red dress, just like we had a million dollars. I know it won't last long, but it was gettin' ragged anyway and it's fine while it does. How you been, Dewey?"

By that time he remembered his manners, such as they were, and took off his hat. "Just fine," he said, and then he got mad, wondering what kind of a brother let a girl plow up buffalo sod. "I'd be pleased to help out."

"Why?" she said.

"Why?" Dewey said. "On account that's no job for a woman."

"My brother fell off the barn yesterday," Mary said. "Busted his arm. He's in Des Moines gettin' patched up. Ain't no choice, Dewey. We got to plow this field before snow."

"Oh," Dewey said, and reddened up and felt like a fool, misjudging her brother that way. He turned to mount and ride on, but she said, "I'm not refusing help, you understand," and made him feel right at home without a lot of fancy explanations.

"You go on inside," he said. "I'll give that plow a whirl."

He was no great shakes with a plow, but he grabbed those handles and plowed through the balance of the afternoon, making up for crooked furrows with plenty of elbow grease. He put a fair-sized dent in that proposed bean field, and Mary Ashford had supper on the table when he put the team away and came up from the windmill.

There wasn't too much to eat so Dewey minded his appetite and got the conversation going to cover up their being alone in the house. He told her about the rodeos and where he'd been during the summer. Then he mentioned the two ponies he'd seen beyond the barn, and Mary admitted they ought to be broken and hoped he could do that job along with the others. Thinking back, remembering how happy she'd appeared in Las Vegas, he guessed those rodeo days were the only vacation she and her brother had taken all year. He would have broken the two ponies for nothing, but she asked about the price and agreed to pay the three dollars each and found for the job. Dewey helped her wash dishes and hated to think of her plowing next day, but it was already dark and he had to make Bob Johnson's tonight.

"I'll be headquarterin' at Johnson's," he said. "Case you need anything."

"I'll make out," Mary said. "The neighbors are good. Jack Stinett stops by every now and then, too."

"Old Buck's son?" Dewey asked.

"Yes," Mary said. "You know him?"

He didn't know Jack Stinett, but he knew old Buck and that made it hard to imagine anything real decent about the son. Stopping by, as Mary put it, was quite some chore when it meant riding forty-odd miles up from Big S headquarters. Plus the fact that he could almost bet Jack

Stinett was a chaser. Dewey didn't answer right away, and his face gave his thoughts away.

"You know Jack?" Mary asked again.

"I know his daddy," Dewey said. "Well, I got to get along."

He rode on down to Bob Johnson's place through the cold, windy night, and Bob had six head to break and figured there were enough others to make it a paying job for two months. Dewey steered the talk around to the Ashfords and Johnson said they had come up from Nacona, Texas country, were hard workers, but short on cash. Then Johnson stroked his handle-bar mustache and said, "Pretty girl, eh?"

"Sure is," Dewey said. "An' I bet she's got plenty of company in the kitchen."

"Yes and no," Johnson said. "Plenty would like to set with her, but Jack Stinett's the big ramrod."

"Old Buck's son?" he asked.

"The spittin' image," Johnson said. "One of them big fellers who tries to impersonate a bronc rider and big-time roper, an' the truth is, Dewey, he can't stick a tough bronc past the third jump. If you're entertainin' thoughts about Mary, don't let him bother you. Just boot him aside."

"I've got no time for women," Dewey said. "I was only askin' questions."

"Then why ask," Johnson said. "I'm sleepy."

Dewey rolled into his blankets on the spare bunk and thought of Mary Ashford in her red dress, and next morning, helping cook breakfast and getting ready for the job, he put those thoughts from his mind. He had to hit the saddle and work, and he knew why he had kept his vague promise to come down here and earn a few dollars. He was thinking of that dragging back in Kansas, that turned ankle in Kansas City, and wondering deep inside if his nerve was gone.

Chapter Six

BREAKING BRONCS on a circle job was no joy ride. Dewey rode around that day and got five customers with a total of twenty-eight ponies. Plus the two Ashford horses it gave him thirty on the job, worth ninety dollars pay off at the finish. Coming back to Johnson's that night, he couldn't help think that ninety dollars was just ten seconds' work in the arena when a man drew first day money. But that was the way he had to stop thinking.

He started at Johnson's, working two days with Bob's ponies, tying up forefeet, putting on rope hackamores and drag ropes, taking off the hackamores, saddling and unsaddling, riding each pony around inside the corral a few minutes, just getting the rough top off them before he moved outside. Then he began the circle, spending two days at each place duplicating that kindergarten work, moving from Johnson's five miles to Rube Weston's, then four miles to Walter Mills', four miles to Minot Prince's, three miles to Ben Brouther's; and that brought him around to Ashford's, his last stop, with a little worry in his mind because Mary might be alone and it wasn't proper to stay overnight.

When he rode into the yard, a tall man with one arm in a sling came from the barn and shook hands warmly. Jim Ashford remembered him from Las Vegas and they got along fine from the start. Jim invited him up to the house, and Dewey saw the big palomino at the gate and the man talking to Mary on the porch. There was no call to feel put out but Mary was wearing that red dress, fresh washed and pressed, and somehow it seemed like that dress ought to be reserved for his eyes alone.

"Dewey," Jim said. "Meet Jack Stinett."

Jack Stinett was on one of his stop-by visits, dressed fit to kill, white Stetson in hand, acting like he owned the place and everything on it. Jack teetered back on his high, undershot heels and grinned at Dewey.

"Oh, the busted-down bronc rider," Jack said. "I see you survived another summer, Jones."

Some dogs and humans rubbed wrong from first look. It jumped up between them, for no good reason, but it was there and nothing would ever change that mutual suspicion.

"I lived," he said. "Mary, how you been?"

"Fine, Dewey."

"What you doin' out here, Jones?" Jack asked.

"Breakin' a few ponies," he said.

"Now that makes sense," Jack laughed. "You practice up on these barn-broke broncs, maybe you can stick those tough ones on the circuit."

"I get by," he said gently.

"Sure," Jack said, "an' you're rolling in wealth to prove it, eh?"

He wanted no trouble, but trouble built up like a mountain storm, with the reason standing in her red dress, smiling deep in her blue eyes behind a sober face. Jim Ashford said, "Suppertime," and eased the tension.

Jack lifted his hat and said, "So long, Mary," and rode off toward the Malpie post office-store, big-roweled spurs jingling the sweet silver music that should come only to the ears of a worthy man. Then Mary said innocently, "Dewey, can you stick the tough ones?"

"You saw me," he said.

She grinned. "Just one show."

"Did I do all right?" he asked.

"Sure," Mary said. "Say, I've heard Jack's pretty good on the broncs."

"Don't know," he said. "Never saw him ride."

Jim gave her a flat stare. "Put it on the table, sis."

Dewey washed up and ate supper with them, and wondered how a girl in Mary's boots would judge a man like Jack Stinett. All Jack could offer a girl was one hundred thousand acres and twenty thousand cattle and a big bank roll. Against those things, just for comparison, Dewey had his saddle and bedroll and two hundred and fifty cash money. If he wanted to take a hand in this game he was sure giving Jack good odds. He drank coffee, smoked, and talked pinto beans, wondering why in the world he even thought about such an idea.

"How many horses you get?" Jim asked.

"Thirty," he said.

"I appreciate you takin' on our two ponies," Jim said quietly.

Mary turned from the stove. "Kind? We're paying for the work."

"That ain't the point," Jim said. "The others got five or six ponies each, an' Dewey has got to ride them out regular. He'll be ridin' our two ponies twice as often as them others. We get more for our money."

"No trouble," Dewey said. "Got to make a full circle anyway."

Jim looked down and swallowed a grin, and he knew what Jim was thinking, that here was another one with the hat set toward Mary. He got up and took his bedroll down to the barn loft and slept warm under the hay, and woke to eat breakfast and start on the Ashford ponies.

Jim rode off south on some business. Mary did her housework, hung out a washing, and came down behind the barn to take a look. She watched him tie up a forefoot, put on a hackamore and drag rope, saddle and unsaddle, work patiently with those two ponies. She began to look as if she suddenly realized horse breaking wasn't just driving a team to town.

"How long do you do this?" she asked.

"Two days," Dewey said.

"An' then what?"

He came over to the corral fence and rolled a smoke. "First round's just takin' off the rough top," he said. "Then you start the circle. Saddle a pony at Bob's, ride it to Rube Weston's, turn it into the corral an' ride one of Rube's to Mills's, and so on around. Try to make a complete circle every day, give every pony one ride every fifth day."

"That figures out about ten rides per horse," Mary said. "Two months total time."

"Discounting bad weather," he said. "An' accidents."

"All hard work, Dewey."

He said, "You mean for ninety bucks?"

"It takes plenty of savvy," she said. "You don't get what the job's worth."

"It don't matter," he said. "I like it."

"You really mean that?" she asked.

"Don't go putting me in a tight," he said. "Sure, there's times I'd chuck it all, 'specially when a norther hits you in the open, or you draw a mean horse—then you wish for most anything else."

"You goin' on this way forever?" Mary asked.

"Which way?"

"Like Las Vegas," she said. "Staying on that rodeo circuit, this kind of work."

"I never give it too much thought," he lied gently. "I'm doin' what I like. That counts with anybody."

"You sure?" she said, and went off toward the house.

She was worse than Mike, and she made him pull up and look close at himself. She knew a man couldn't chase the rainbow forever, dreaming of something he reached for and never quite cupped in his hands; and even if he did catch it, he'd look down quick as his hands opened and see only the bright colors as they melted away. Yes, experience was a great teacher. It lay doggo in a man while his dreams ran wild, but if he had one grain of sense the experience finally stood up and gave him a fair warning. Experience said he was a damn fool to keep riding the circuit. He'd already seen one generation of bronc riders end up poor in body and soul in all the backwaters of the West. It wasn't finishing broke and hungry; it was meeting those old-timers and knowing, after the first minute of talk, that spirit and courage had left them. That was the big chip, courage in the heart, and the man who lost it could be worth a million and still be poor.

He'd come out here to do plenty of serious thinking, and Mary had got him doing it faster than he liked. He worried all through the two days he worked over the Ashford ponies until he was glad to head out for Johnson's. He met Jack Stinett, pulled up to speak civil, and Jack called, "They buckin' you off, Jones?"

"Now and then," Dewey said, and nudged his horse on. But Jack reined over, blocked the trail, and made a big show of pulling that white Stetson over his eyes. Jack didn't need a pair of tied-down Colts to give him that madman look. He'd practiced it so much, probably in a mirror, that it came natural.

"Ain't much profit," Jack said, "breakin' two ponies for Ashford."

"It all helps," he said.

"Sure," Jack laughed, "for you bean-and-bacon boys. But seeing as how it's only two ponies, I don't see no need of you hanging around here."

Dewey Jones said quietly, "I hang my hat where I please."

He spurred and rammed his horse against the palomino, broke clear, and headed south; and riding for Johnson's he knew that Jack was pushing him into something he hadn't given much thought to. Jack figured he was making a play for Mary, and maybe he was and didn't know it. Well, he had no chance with such a girl, but he couldn't wag-tail to Jack Stinett. When he pulled into Johnson's and came up from the barn, Bob gave him one quick glance and got real busy with the frying pan. Dewey washed, kicked off his boots, set up to the table, and rolled a smoke.

"I'll start ridin' circle tomorrow," he said.

"How they comin'?" Johnson asked.

"Fair," he said. "That blue roan of Minot Prince's is goin' to give trouble."

"I know him," Johnson said. "His daddy was all horse."

"So?" Dewey said. "Was old Minot night ridin' the mare?"

"Stinett's black stallion," Johnson said. "Sort of an accident couple of years back. You know, Minot never did get 'round to paying Stinett the stud fee."

"Stinett's got top horses," Dewey said honestly. "I can't say the same for his other stock."

"You mean two-legged?"

"Could be," he said. "You goin' to get any supper cooked, or do I show you how?"

CHAPTER SEVEN

FROM THEN ON Dewey was in the saddle dawn to dark, seven days a week, riding out those ponies on the circle. He began at Johnson's and headed for Rube Weston's, ran Bob's bronc into Rube's corral, changed hackamore and saddle to a fresh pony, put the drag rope and spare hackamore back on Bob's horse so the horse's nose would stay sore and keep him tractable; and then he'd head down the line again. Into the saddle and out the corral gate, watch for those kinky backs and those sidewinder bucks that jarred the brain and made the red spots dance before the eyes; and keep it up all day around that endless circle.

Some of those ponies were half-barn-raised and not so difficult to halter break and then ride out; a few were already halter broken when Dewey started. But even so it was no cinch riding six different ponies every day, six more the next day, and on around the entire remuda. He had the tough ones labeled by the end of the first week, and the worst of the bunch was the blue roan owned by Minot Prince. That roan weighed around seven-fifty and always gave him trouble when he saddled and took off for Mills'. The blue roan jumped and bucked a long mile every time Dewey forked him, and those were the bad days. He rode that blue roan and five other ponies, and fell into his bunk sore and tired and disgusted. A man in his right mind wouldn't take that punishment for three hundred dollars a horse.

He tried to make full circle every day. He always hit Ashford's late in the afternoon and never had much time for talk. Not that he had patience for sweet talk, he never had learned how to please a woman. All he did was talk at the barn or once in a while over coffee in the kitchen. Jim and Mary were curious about the neighborhood and Dewey tried to keep them up-to-date on the doings.

He told them about Rube Weston, who was a bachelor living in a cut-bank dugout; how Rube talked mostly to himself, using a big tomcat for an excuse. Dewey heard Rube yelling at the tomcat one noon, "Yes, yes, you dadblamed old sonofabitch, you stepped on my foot a while back and I never said nothin', but now I step on your foot and you raise a howl."

He told them about Brouther's house built from green lumber and now dried out until you could throw a cat between those wallboards. Brouther's wife had inherited some money the year before and they bought a baby grand piano and kept it in one corner with a tarp over it to keep snow out when bad weather came. That always tickled Dewey, thinking of Brouther's rawboned daughters sweeping snow off that tarp come a February day, flipping the tarp back and whanging out a tune on those jangled wires.

"That's mighty brave," Mary said. "Not everybody would want music that bad."

"I reckon not," Dewey said, and changed the subject. He had learned, by accident, that Mary was sensitive about whatever pleasures a woman could bring into this country. So he talked of things that hurt nobody, rode his circle, and almost ran dry of news in two weeks. The next Saturday afternoon, coming around to Ashford's, Jim met him at the barn and said Mary had gone to the dance in Des Moines with Jack Stinett.

"Want to go in?" Jim asked.

Dewey said, "Ain't got time, Jim," and headed for Johnson's. He was in a bad humor all night and just grunted at Bob when he started next morning. When he got to Ashford's that day, Mary came down to the corral and told him what a fine time she'd had at the dance.

"Good," Dewey said, and began changing saddle and hackamore to one of the Ashford ponies. The least he could do was act decent, but there he was like the little boy who couldn't reach the big red apple on the top limb.

"What's the matter?" Mary said bluntly. "Don't you approve of people goin' to dances and having fun?"

"Never said that," Dewey grunted.

"You sure couldn't," Mary said. "Not the way you acted at Las Vegas."

"That was different," he said.

"Different?" Mary said. "Because you were hanging onto that trick rider?"

"She's an old friend," Dewey said.

"She sure must be," Mary said curtly.

He got the saddle and hackamore on the pony. Mary opened the gate and Dewey used his spurs, something he ordinarily didn't do. The pony squealed and bucked across the yard, around the barn, kicking high and handsome, letting him have it hot and fast. He rode the pony out, calmed it down, and stopped beside the tank. Mary walked over and grinned up at him.

"Nice riding, Dewey."

"My own fault," he said.

"How come?"

"I treated him wrong," Dewey said. "He's a good pony."

"Got mad at yourself," she said. "Taking it out on the horse. I know. I've felt that way."

"Won't happen again," he said. Then, because he felt stingy inside, like a miser afraid to give anybody one kind word, he yanked his hat down tight and said, "Glad you had a good time at the dance."

"Well," Mary said, "I didn't have too good a time, Dewey."

"You wear that red dress?" he asked.

"No," she said. "I wore the blue one."

He found his grin and said, "I got to move along," and rode for Johnson's, whistling all the way for no good reason. Bob sneaked one quick look at him and set up the checkerboard after supper. Johnson hadn't caught him in a decent mood very often, and Bob was no man to pass up a chance. Bob beat him eighteen straight games before bedtime, and after they sacked in Bob spoke across the dark cabin.

"Feeling foxy, Dewey?"

"Just good," he said.

"Stay that way," Johnson said. "Better for a man, easier on his friends."

"Guess so," Dewey said, and sniffed the wind filtering through the chinks. "Weather comin', Bob."

"Past due," Johnson said. "Get out your long handles tomorrow, Dewey."

And sure enough, the weather started going sour, slowing him down. He had trouble making a complete circle each day. He dug out his winter clothes and on those mornings dressed beside the stove, shivering in the cabin cold, drinking half a dozen cups of scalding coffee before going outside to face the ponies. He wore long-handled underwear and a pair of fleece-lined drawers over the underwear, and regular Levis over them. He had a soft deerskin sleeveless sweater he wore over the underwear top, then a turtle-neck sweater, and finally his Levi jacket. He pulled a silk stocking over his head and ears, slapped on his hat, snugged his bandanna close around his neck, and was ready to go.

It was tough getting up at dawn and throwing a cold saddle on a sulky pony, then riding that cold seat from place to place in the bitter wind. Light snow dusted the country and made it look colder; all a man could do was hunch deeper in the saddle, cuss the ponies, and ride on. He was never warm but he didn't freeze, and the only mistake he made was coming into Ashford's with that silk stocking down over his ears.

Jim yelled from the kitchen door and he went on the run to work the stiff cold from his legs. When he entered the kitchen Mary turned from the stove and eyed that stocking. Then Jim saw it and said, "Now there's a smart trick, Dewey. Does it help much?"

"Good deal," Dewey said, happy as a hog in summer to sit down and drink hot coffee, not noticing the way Mary was reacting. "Cuts the wind an' you stand less chance of freezing the ears."

"You're mighty smart," Mary said sweetly. "Where'd you find the stocking?"

"This one," he said absently. "Cheyenne. No, it was Fort Worth."

"You can't remember?" Mary asked.

Dewey spooned sugar and cream into his coffee, breathing deep in the stove warmth. "Yes," he said. "It was Fort Worth."

Mary came over and rubbed a finger against the silk. Dewey saw her eyes and realized he was not exactly taking first money for smart action.

"That's fine silk," Mary said. "How did you do it, Dewey? Just cut the stocking off short and pull it down?"

"Sure," he said cautiously.

He yanked the stocking off and dropped it on the table. "Ain't nothin' wrong with doing this to keep from freezing."

"Who said there was?" Mary asked, still as sweet as sugar. "But you being such a shy and bashful man, I just wondered who gave it to you."

He remembered very well who gave him that silk stocking. A fat lady behind the store counter in Fort Worth had sold him that pair of silk stockings, and helped cut them off to fit his head and snug down over his ears. But he got stubborn then, thinking she had no business asking such questions. Friends like Mike never wanted explanations. Friends never doubted a man's actions. Otherwise, they wouldn't be friends.

"A woman," Dewey said. "In Fort Worth."

"Was she pretty?" Mary asked.

"Sure was," he said. "Doggone pretty."

"Black hair?" Mary said. "Kinda skinny and smelled of horses?"

"No," Dewey said. "It wasn't Babe."

"Somebody like her, I reckon," Mary said.

Then he had to get smart and multiply the damage, compound the felony. "Red hair like a sunset," he lied. "A mighty pretty woman."

"Red hair!" Mary said. "That's interesting. Where'd you say you met her?"

Right there he almost bit his tongue off. He was showing fine judgment, talking about red-haired women. Red hair was associated with ladies who were far from being ladies. He choked down his coffee and mumbled, "Gettin' late," and half-ran to the barn and saddled up an Ashford pony. He just cleared the corral gate when Mary came down and handed him the silk stocking.

"Put it on," she said. "Don't freeze your ears."

Dewey tucked his hat under one elbow and began pulling the stocking down over his head and ears, holding the pony with his knees, fumbling for his hat while the pony trembled with calculated malice; and all that time he saw the laughter in her eyes and wondered what was so funny about him getting embarrassed half to death. He finally got his hat on, tightened the hackamore, and said, "Thanks."

He moved off and she called, "Dewey, she couldn't of been so pretty."

"Was," he said stubbornly.

Then she was grinning openly. "Not from the size of that stocking. That's the biggest size in stock."

"What?" Dewey said.

"Legs like nail kegs," Mary yelled. "Red hair!"

She ran for the house, her shoulders bouncing with laughter. He hadn't fooled her a minute; she'd seen right through his stubbornness. But she had to let him dangle before she took him off the hook. He grinned at the darkening sky and rode loose all the way to Johnson's and lost sixteen games of checkers after supper without batting an eye. All he could think of was, she was a fine girl and the man that got her was going to be plenty lucky.

CHAPTER EIGHT

TWO MORNINGS LATER Johnson took a look outside and suggested they sit tight for the day. Dewey looked up at the north and shook his head.

"Got to chance it."

"Then pack your bedroll," Johnson said.

He strapped the bedroll behind his saddle, dug into the cold leather, and headed out against the icy wind sweeping down from the northwest. He got to Brouther's just as the first snow tapped his face. In that country the wind came low and strong, it seemed, and snow was always sleety in the beginning. It sailed parallel to the ground, sharp and gray-colored, cutting a man's vision to yards. Those storms came fast from the black-gray sky, the wind turned into chilled steel, and when the storm really hit the snow thickened until it almost smothered a man bucking the wind. Dewey knew the danger, but he changed saddles fast and struck out for Ashford's, and the norther caught him two miles away.

Snow came on the wind, smashing against his right cheek, pushing the pony off line, wiping out all landmarks in one swift come-down of night and clouds, of snow and wind. He held his course and ran into Ashford's fence and followed it into the yard. He turned the pony into the barn and fought his way to the house, unable to spot window light until he stumbled on the bottom porch step. Jim and Mary let him inside and helped broom off the snow and strip down to his pants and deerskin sweater. Then Jim gave him holy hell for chancing the ride so late in the day.

"Anyway," Jim said, "you couldn't make Johnson's tonight. You bunk here."

"Glad to," Dewey said. He felt lucky to get this far, and no matter if he slept on the floor. He smelled fresh doughnuts and coffee, and he got all that plus the good talk at the kitchen table. But half an hour later Jack Stinett pulled in, brushed off a bushel of snow, and declared it was a sure-enough blister of a storm and he'd have to impose on the Ashfords, too.

Two was company, three a crowd, and now the storm had added a joker. They sat at the table and listened to the wind and felt the house shake in the blast. Jim dealt some rummy but nobody cared about cards, and that gave Jack a chance to talk bronc riding and roping. Jack sat there in his fine clothes and fancy boots, making gestures in the proper way, telling Mary about broncs he'd rode and steers he'd roped in record time. Dewey drank coffee and kept his mouth shut until Jack finished up a hair-raising account concerning a Big S bronc and said, "Jones, ain't it so that you contest riders are no better than most any top hand out here?"

"If you mean range work," Dewey said, "that's true. A man stays away from the range and he gets rusty in a lot of things the regular hand keeps all polished up."

"That ain't what I mean," Jack said. "I mean you contest riders are not better on broncs than our top hands."

"In that case," Dewey said, "there's no doubt. The contest rider has the edge."

"Hell," Jack said. "I know how you saddle bums work your dodge. You ride them same old weary broncs all season long, rope the same stock. You get so you know every one like a brother. It ain't so easy goin' out and forking a real salty bronc."

"I don't get your point," Dewey said. "You tryin' to say you're a top hand?"

"I'll ride and rope with any man," Jack said. "I've seen you ride, Jones. I'll fork any horse you do."

Dewey kept a tight hold on his temper. Jack had deliberately veered the talk to bronc riding and roping, trying to show Dewey up in such a way that he came out bottom card in the deck. Dewey said, "Well, we can't prove you wrong tonight."

"Tonight?" Jack said. "I mean any time. You backin' water on me?"

"No," he said quietly. "Just no broncs handy.

He tried to be a gentleman and tonight he saw Jack for what he was—nothing but a blow-hard, a spoiled brat that never grew up, trying to impress Mary with his fancy talk. He didn't want to keep arguing, but it seemed like that was making Jack madder than ever.

"If that's all holding you back," Jack said, "I can sure arrange that little detail. You figure on finishing this job by Christmas?"

"Hope to," Dewey said.

"Well, that's just dandy," Jack said. "All the boys are goin' into Des Moines Christmas Day. I'll be there. Jerome's bringing in some real wild stock. How about a match ride, just you an' me?"

Mary was watching him, her eyes puzzled, as if she understood that he loved nothing better than a good matched bronc contest with a chance to bet his last dollar, his saddle and all, and stand a chance of walking away in his underwear. Mary seemed to be looking into his mind and reading the truth: that he was a gambler in that respect, he'd won and lost his share, and that was exactly why he'd never amount to anything. And, as usual, he got his dander up and snapped back.

"Sure, Stinett, but it's not fair."

"Why not?" Jack said. "Don't worry about me."

"All right," he said. "If I can make it, I'll try to oblige."

Jack made a big show of being tickled to death over the match. "Now we got that settled, Jones, I don't ride without a bet down."

"Name it," Dewey said.

"Oh—" Jack grinned—"I'll just cover whatever you got, Jones."

With his pay due for the circle job, he'd have over three hundred dollars. He said, "Two hundred and fifty all right, Stinett?"

"Covered," Jack said. "Too bad we can't make it worth real money."

Mary got awful busy with the coffeepot. Jim went to the south window and looked into the night and rolled a cigaret. Jack was showing Dewey Jones up for what he was in the eyes of the world: a saddle bum with only a few dollars to show for all those years. Dewey said gently, "It's real money to me, Stinett," and picked up his bedroll and left the house before anyone could say a word. He bucked across the yard to the barn and dug deep into the hay and stayed there all night, rather than sleep in the same house with Stinett. Next morning he overslept, being dog-tired from the long work drag, and didn't wake up until Jack saddled the palomino and left out for the Malpie post office. The wind had dropped, the storm was over, and he sat up in the hay, shivering, cussing himself for acting like a damn fool. Then he heard the door open again, and Mary called, "Dewey. Dewey, you all right?"

"Sure," he said. "Comin' down."

He tossed the bedroll and followed it down the ladder and tried to grin, but his face was too stiff and cold. Mary said, "Jack's gone, you can come inside now."

"Heard him," Dewey said.

"Nobody ordered you out last night," Mary said.

"Didn't want to cause no trouble," Dewey said.

"Wouldn't of been any," she said sharply. "Not in my house. Well, you goin' to make that ride against Jack?"

"Have to," he said. "We made the bet."

"What if you lose?" she asked.

Dewey knew he'd been wrong to take up that bet. He was one of the best any way, any time, and Jack was that prize sucker his kind curried happily whenever met. But he didn't like it, now he thought it over. He was doing just what Mike wanted him to stop.

"Somebody's got to lose," he said.

"Say you do—what then?"

"Nothin'," he said. "I'll get along."

"Sure," Mary said. "Doin' the same old thing."

"Damn it!" he said. "What's wrong with that?"

She looked at him, and then she began crying and ran from the barn. He said aloud, "Now what the hell?" and wondered what had got into her this morning. Probably crying because she was such a fine, pretty girl with a limited selection of lobos like himself to look at and think about. He saddled one of Jim's ponies and headed for Johnson's, swearing to himself that he'd never get caught overnight again and cause her trouble. Johnson got the whole story from him that morning and chuckled over the chance of skinning Jack Stinett for maybe the first time in the valley's history. Johnson harnessed up his team and took off for Des Moines, saying they needed supplies, but Dewey knew damn well Johnson just couldn't wait to spread the news about the bet. Well, a few friends present on Christmas Day wouldn't hurt none. Dewey sat lax beside the stove and thought of the job almost done and the answer he'd have to give Tully very soon.

Chapter Nine

DEWEY FINISHED out the job, got paid off, and rode into Des Moines the day before Christmas. All that last week, whenever he came by, Mary stayed to herself. Jim paid him at the barn on his last go-round and said, "We'll be there," and gave him a rough slap when he turned away. But he didn't see Mary, and evidently she didn't want to see him. He rode to Johnson's, packed up, and headed in.

Des Moines was twenty miles east of Johnson's, a little cowtown of about five hundred people, the trading center for the whole area. It was on the Fort Worth and Denver Railroad running down from Trinidad, the town located mostly on the south side of the tracks with the big stockpens at the upper, northwest side flanking the tracks. Dewey left his horse at the livery barn behind the general store and headed for the Ray Burnett's saloon. The stores had Christmas decorations in the windows and the kids were playing with their toys in the houses, and he'd had nothing last night or today, not even an old friend to drink a toast. He stepped into the saloon and there was Mike and old Tully and others from Raton, grabbing his hands and slapping his back, plainly getting ready for a big tomorrow.

"Been waitin' on you," Mike said. "Come over here and catch up."

Dewey said, "What you doin' down here, Mike?"

"Why—" Mike grinned—"we heard some green horn was goin' to ride a bronc. Figured we'd place bets and hold money."

"Sure," he said softly. "Mike, I'm glad to see you."

He knew full well that Mike and the others had come to see fair play done; and now, looking around the saloon, he realized that the entire country would be on hand tomorrow. Mike got him off to one side for the low-down and whistled protest when Dewey told that Jerome was furnishing the stock.

"Don't like that," Mike said. "But we can see that things are handled correct."

"Can you dig up judges?" Dewey asked.

"We was talkin' that over," Mike said. "Tully can get Bill Stevens and George Wattingburger. Course there won't be no association rules or nothin' like that. Got to ride in the main stockpen, there ain't no chutes, got to bring out a bronc and ear it down, saddle up, and just turn him loose. An' no gun either. Just ride till they say get down."

"That's fine with me," Dewey said.

"If everything is on the level," Mike said, "now let's drink up."

So it turned out a better Christmas even than most he'd spent in past years. He was talking with friends and feeling decent inside, not drinking himself blind in some lonely room or far out on a line camp. Old Tully sat with them and talked his share, but never mentioned the ranch. It seemed when the news came to Raton about the match ride, Tully heard it first and told everybody, declaring they had to come down to Des Moines and see fair play done. He tried to thank Tully for that, but Tully just shrugged it off and gave him a sharp look.

"You in good shape?" Tully asked.

"Never better," he said. "Except maybe last spring comin' off the Flying A."

Mike reached down and squeezed the bad ankle. "It healed good, eh?"

"No trouble," he said. "No ache."

"Then, by Gawd!" Tully grinned. "We'll just win some money on ye."

"We never come for no other reason," Mike said. "I hope them Jeromes and Stinetts are loaded for bear."

"They'll come loaded," Dewey said.

"An' go home with the empty sack," Mike said.

Old Tully went off to bed and the others drifted away to the poker game and bar. Alone with Mike at the back table, looking up at the green-and-red wreath above the cash register, Dewey drank his hot toddy and hoped tomorrow was a clear day.

"Well," Mike said. "Made up your mind?"

"About what?"

"Tully's," Mike said curtly. "You're finished on the job. You got to let him know tomorrow."

"Fort Worth's almost due," he said. "Be nice down there."

"No," Mike said. "Moreno Valley's better."

"All that damn snow up there," he said dully. "Wind and snow, an' nobody with a man."

"Since when did you start thinkin' that way?"

"Just thinkin'," he said.

"I guess you saw the Ashfords down here," Mike said.

"Sure," he said. "Rode out two ponies for 'em."

"How's Jim?"

"Busted his arm," Dewey said. "It healed up perfect. He's a good man."

"He is," Mike said. "Mary still single?"

"Yes," he said stiffly.

"Now there's a woman to work alongside a man," Mike said. "In snow and wind, anywhere. She'd like that Moreno Valley."

"With somebody like me?" Dewey said. "There's sure a limit to any woman's ideas about living."

"You sound funny as hell," Mike said. "I was just talkin' in general terms. Was you thinkin' that Tully's spread might look a lot better with somebody like her on it?"

"I'm tired," Dewey Jones said. "See you in the morning."

He went upstairs to the rooms above the saloon, sat on the bed, and toed off his boots; and then he looked at the bare wall with the paper peeling in the corner and knew Mike had triggered him off for keeps. The only thing that stopped him from going down to Tully's room and giving his promise was thinking of being alone in Moreno Valley. And now that he knew what had happened inside him, he had no chance ever of making that dream come true.

CHAPTER TEN

DEWEY SLEPT LATE the next morning, ate a good breakfast with Mike and Tully, and loafed around the saloon until one o'clock. They walked up to the stockpens then, and arrived behind the Jerome and Stinett outfits. Jerome's boys were hazing several head of wild stock into the small pens off the big cutting pen, half a dozen of the wildest looking broncs he'd ever seen.

"Rough string," Dewey said.

"Winter hair," Mike said. "No rougher'n you popped before."

Then everybody was showing up, crowding into the main pen, talking and laughing, kidding back and forth, making a few small bets that were always the preview to the serious business. Mike helped Dewey carry his gear into the main pen where the Jerome and Stinett crews were waiting. But old man Jerome wasn't there, and neither was old Stinett.

"That's damn funny," Mike said softly. "Nobody but the boys and the kid."

Dewey thought it had a strange look, too, and should have guessed neither of those tough old coots would associate with anything not on the square. But he didn't have time to figure it out. Jack Stinett turned from his bunch, money fanned out between his fingers.

"All right, Jones," Stinett said. "Get your money out."

Dewey handed his two hundred and fifty to Ray Burnett who was acting as stake holder. Jack covered that, laughed harshly, and said, "Sure that's all you got, Jones?"

Mike murmured, "Never no mind, Dewey," but it was too late. Dewey Jones fought his anger and lost, and heard himself betting his saddle and all his gear against another hundred dollars. Jack covered that bet and said, "Well, if that cleans you, let's draw."

Dewey said, "How many broncs you got?"

"We brought six," Jack said. "You saw 'em, Jones. No contest plugs, all real broncs."

"Get the hat," Dewey said.

One of Jack's men held out a hat with six slips of paper in the crown. Dewey reached in and drew a slip, opened it, and said, "Number two," and handed the slip to Mike.

Then Jack dropped his big hand into the hat and lifted out a number and read off, "Five," and handed the slip to Mike. And right then, it came to Dewey that he didn't know one of the broncs from the other, and neither did Mike, not rough string broncs from the back country. The Big S rider crumbled up the other slips and put his hat on, and that was the end of the draw. Jack tilted his hat back and said, "We drew a good pair, Jones. Two of the best. Who goes first?"

"We'll draw for that," Mike said very softly.

Jack Stinett gave Mike a cold stare. "Why, sure."

Mike pulled a deck of cards from his jacket pocket, shuffled them up, and held out the fanned deck. Mike said, "Cut your card, Stinett."

Dewey knew then that Jack had another hat draw in mind, but he couldn't protest. Jack turned red but he had no choice. Mike closed the deck and held it in his right palm, and Jack cut a ten-spot. Mike turned gravely to Dewey and said, "Cut, Dewey," and Dewey laid his hand over the remainder of the deck, felt the tiny stick-out edge, and cut the ace of hearts. Mike said, "Dewey rides last," and pocketed the deck and got down to business at hand.

"Who's judging?" Mike asked.

"Who cares," Jack Stinett said. "You can pick 'em."

By now they were surrounded by a hundred people. Looking around, Dewey saw Johnson and Rube Weston, all the folks from the circle job, Jim and Mary Ashford, other people he'd met in bygone years. Mike said, "We'll have Bill Stevens and George Wattingburger judge."

"Fine," Jack said. "They here?"

"Ready an' waitin'," Mike said curtly, waving at the two old-timers standing nearby. "We use association saddles. Me and Zootz here, an' two of your boys, we'll ear down and hold. Bill Stevens will give the signal, then you ride till the judges tell you to step down. Bueno?"

"Bueno," Jack said carelessly.

Then Mike smiled. "Now, in case somebody wants to cover me, I'd bet a few dollars on Dewey."

"Lay it down," Jack said loudly. "We'll cover you an' ten like you."

Dewey knew Mike didn't have big money, but just then he saw the horse and mule buyer from Capulin slipping up beside Mike, a man named Beanbelly Mellom who bought horses and mules for old John King of J Bar J. Beanbelly wrote checks on old John, and Dewey saw King then, standing back against the fence with a bunch of cowmen. Beanbelly stuck a check into Mike's left hand and said hoarsely, "Put that with the other, Mike," and gave Jack Stinett one of those cold, flat looks that spoke louder than a thousand words.

Mike dipped into his left jacket pocket and pulled out a big roll of bills. Even before Mike spoke, a sigh went around the crowd. So much money on a single bronc ride was unheard of down here; either everybody was drunk or something else was going on.

"Here's four thousand, Stinett," Mike said. "An' here's another thousand. Take all or any part."

Dewey turned away and walked blindly through the crowd and sat down on a snow-crusted hay bale in the fence shadow. He rolled a smoke, hearing the hum of talk from that crowded circle, as Jack Stinett backed water and learned how it felt to be faced down. Jack and his friends finally covered fifteen hundred dollars, which meant old Buck Stinett was not allowing Jack to write checks on the account today. Dewey's fingers shook over the brown paper and Durham. They were his friends, they believed in him, and now their faith had put him in a terrible spot. Finally, after all the years, the rides, the bets, he had it come home to him; and maybe Mike had done this on purpose, but no matter, he saw the foolishness today. He didn't hear Mary until she sat down beside him and blew on her cupped hands.

"Cold," she said.

"Is it?" Dewey Jones said. "So you come in."

"Had to," Mary said.

She was wearing the red dress under her winter coat. He saw the neckline and the hem down below above her heavy boots. The red dress was not made for winter wear, and that meant she was wearing it today as good luck charm. But who for?

"You come in to watch him?" Dewey asked.

She turned on the snow-crusted hay bale and looked at him and smiled. He knew better then. He had never doubted her honesty, her ability to judge people. They came from the same stock, from people who worked for a living and cared less for a dollar than they did for the satisfaction of living the right way. He'd been off the trail a long time, but that still held true. But he had to know how she felt, if she did have some feeling for him, and he could never find the right words. He said bluntly, "To watch him?"

"To watch you," Mary said. "To see if it's worth it."

"Worth what?" Dewey said.

"You," Mary said. "I got the red dress on, Dewey. For luck."

He forgot about the main pen jammed with people. He didn't hear the broncs behind the alley door, shuffling against the boards, scraping off winter hair as they waited for whatever came next. He didn't see the crowd split up, head for front row seats on the top board. He sat there on the frozen hay, his breath puffing out white against the lead-colored sky, and thought of the girl plowing in the red dress, and how he'd known deep inside that first day. Folks were turning now, watching him, but he put one hand over hers, and saw only her face, red in the bitter wind, the freckles standing out, the blond hair pulled tight under her stocking cap.

"Thanks," he said.

"You remember what we talked about once?" Mary asked.

"Sure," Dewey said.

"Changed your mind?" she said. "About goin' on this same way?"

"Listen," Dewey said. "Would it make any difference to you which way I went?"

"No," she said. "It don't matter. You know that now."

Then they didn't talk any more. They stood up, holding hands, his bare, callused fingers against her small hand, and he said quietly, "You climb up on the top board, Mary. I'll make you a ride."

The judges were waiting. Mike and Zootz were helping Jack's men lead out the number five bronc, ear it down, cinch up, watching each other close, suspicious of everything. Dewey walked over and stood beside Mike and watched Jack slip into the saddle, settle down tight and snug, and call, "Turn him loose!"

"Damn funny," Mike said.

"What?"

"That bronc," Mike said. "He's been rode plenty. Saddle scar on his back. Now look!"

They stopped talking, for Jack and the bronc were up, the bronc was twisting out from the ear-holders, heading into the middle of the big pen, gathering muscles for the first jump that came hard and high, then bucking around the pen in high and fancy style while Jack spurred and rode out a real fine ride until Bill Stevens bellowed, "Get down!" Jack ignored the pickup men, stepped off, and came walking back with a big, cocky grin on his face.

"A ringer," Mike said softly. "See how they worked it, Dewey."

"Sure," he said. "No matter."

For nothing mattered now but making a ride. Dewey knew what Jack Stinett had pulled. He and his friends had been working for two weeks, ever since Jack made the bet. Jack had been riding that number five bronc at the home ranch, riding him until Jack knew that bronc like a brother, could go out on him and make a good, top ride. And, while doing that, they had picked out the meanest bronc in the country for Dewey. Jack had palmed slip number five when he drew, and all the other slips in the hat were number two, so Dewey was certain to draw the bad horse. Nobody knew those broncs but the Jerome and Stinett crews, and now they were bringing number two from the side pen.

"Look at that," Mike said. "A real nice little pony."

Dewey watched that big blue roan bronc fighting as they eared him down, and saw certain likenesses between this bronc and the little blue of Minot Prince's. He could imagine the time spent finding this bronc, this rogue, a horse with killer wrote all over him, a hammer-headed blister of a horse that fought all the way to the ground and quivered with rage while saddle and hackamore went on.

"Yes," Dewey said. "A real nice pony."

"Come on," Mike said.

They moved in and Mike remembered something else and said, "I worked on your boots after you went to sleep."

"Noticed it," he said. "Thanks."

Mike had borrowed a rasp somewhere last night and filed his boots to the quick. He hadn't paid much attention to that on the circle job, and he'd need all the extra strangle hold he could get on those stirrups. Dewey went forward and slipped into the saddle, felt that kinky back knot under him, got his boots tight in those stirrups, and said, "Turn him to me!"

No grandstand yelling, no bunting, no judges on the platform and in the arena, no bronze statue on a bucking rein.

They jumped back and the big horse came up in high gear, off the frozen ground, bucking as he turned and leaped for the center of the pen. Dewey was spurring before the first jump, riding wide and handsome, getting with the bronc the only way a man could if he wanted a top ride, the very best, the kind that took first money anywhere on the big circuit. Dewey laid into that bronc with the knowledge learned the hard way through the bitter years, the savvy no man like Jack Stinett could ever learn or understand, the savvy that kept a top man on a top horse when nobody believed the ride could be made. You rode Pretty Dick and Done Gone, Midnight and Overall Bill, Preacher Dun, you rode them through the years and they came home when you needed them now.

He heard Mike shouting from somewhere near, heard the crowd shouting and banging boots against the fence boards. He saw the gray sky revolve above his head as the bronc headed for the opposite side of the pen, one of those untamed horses, all cimarron, that would rather die than submit to man. Dewey had his boots clamped over the stirrup bars iron-tight; then he had to kick his right boot loose and swing the leg up and over as the bronc hit that board fence like a runaway freight, hit it with a last sideways twist, bounced back, bucked and hit it again, turned cat-quick and headed back toward center pen, bucking and coming down stiff-legged, throwing the power as Dewey got his right boot back in the stirrup and again spurred high on the neck and began yelling then, not knowing it, just yelling as his kind had to do, riding that bronc into the final seconds of what should have been a regulation ride, riding him past the gun that would not fire here, riding him around the big pen until the blood clouded his eyes and the driving force of those stiff-legged bucks had him riding without knowledge, his head starting to bobble on his shoulders, but boots still tight and body clinging to the saddle with the grace a man acquired through the years. He rode the bronc almost to a standstill before Bill Stevens yelled, "Get down!" and then he rode the bronc over to the side-pen gate and slipped to the ground and laid one hand out blindly against the fence. Everybody was yelling their fool heads off, the bronc had given his last ounce of power and stood trembling and quiet until someone turned him into the side pen; and old Stevens rode up and looked coldly at Jack Stinett and said, "Dewey Jones, by about three miles. Stinett, you made a good ride—on a lady's horse!"

"Pay off," Mike was shouting. "Pay off, an' the winners buy!"

Somebody shoved money into Dewey's hands, Mike and Tully and Beanbelly Mellom were splitting up the winnings from a big pile of bills, everybody plain howling with joy. Dewey shoved the money into his pocket and walked unsteadily over to where Mary was standing beside that frozen hay bale. He took her arm and turned toward the main gate, and Mike called, "See you downtown, Dewey." Then Dewey Jones stopped, turned, and looked for Jack Stinett. He wanted to finish this off one more way, but she said, "He ain't worth it, Dewey."

"I guess not," Dewey said, and then he smiled. "You like it?"

"Like it?" she said softly. "Yes, I guess I can say you won hands down."

But her eyes told him how much she appreciated the thing he could really do: get up there and ride a bronc as good as any man in the world. They came to her buggy and stood there, holding hands, and Dewey said, "Look, I don't know how to say this."

"Let me," Mary said. "I can be ready in a week."

"Then I'll go see Tully right now," Dewey Jones said, "if you'll take my word for it sight unseen."

"I'll take your word," she said, and the shine in her eyes was enough to blind a man. "You want me to buy a new red dress, Dewey?"

"Don't never be without one," Dewey Jones said.

Frank O'Rourke (Oct. 16, 1916 – April 27, 1989) was a prolific, versatile, and popular writer of novels, westerns, mysteries, sports fiction, and short stories. He wrote more than 60 novels; his first, *E Company*, based on his life in the wartime Army, was published in 1945. He wrote so quickly, sometimes three books a year, that on the advice of agents he used such pseudonyms as Patrick O'Malley, Frank O'Malley, and Kevin Connor. Some of his works were made into movies and television plays, including *The Bravados*, starring Gregory Peck in 1958, and *A Mule for the Marquesa* (retitled "The Professionals"), starring Burt Lancaster in 1966.

Molly Gloss is a fourth-generation Oregonian who lives in Portland. She is the bestselling author of *The Jump-Off Creek*, *The Dazzle of Day*, *Wild Life*, *The Hearts of Horses*, and *Falling from Horses*. Her work has earned numerous awards, including an Oregon Book Award, a Pacific Northwest Booksellers Award, the PEN West Fiction Prize, the James Tiptree Jr. Award, and a Whiting Writers Award.

Printed in the United States
by Baker & Taylor Publisher Services